Gambling on the Duke's Daughter

By Diana Bold

This is a work of fiction. Names, characters, places, and incidents are products of the author's imagination or are used fictitiously and are not to be construed as real. Any resemblance to actual events, locales, organizations, or persons, living or dead, is entirely coincidental.

Gambling on the Duke's Daughter
By Diana Bold

Copyright September 2018

Cover Artist: Sweet 'N Spicy Designs

Dedication

To Emma and Briar, my little angels.

Chapter One

London, 1867

The Earl of Warren's London townhouse stood in fashionable Grosvenor Square. The Palladian monstrosity with its imposing white columns had been in the Blake family for generations. On this particular May evening, every window blazed with light, even though dawn would break in a matter of hours.

Dylan Blake, the earl's youngest son, paid the driver of the hired hack that had brought him and alighted from the vehicle with a jaunty step. His black velvet cloak whipped in the chill spring breeze, and the solid weight of his dress sword bumped against his thigh. He strode toward the red brick mansion, which had never felt like a home, with rebellion in his heart.

Half a dozen footmen in deep blue livery waited on the front steps, their faces impassive as they shivered in the cold. One of the young men bowed deeply and hurried to open the door, letting the festive sounds of laughter and music drift out into the night. Dylan grinned at the lad as he crossed the threshold.

The midnight supper had ended but plenty of guests remained for the dancing. His timing couldn't have been better.

The butler, Wadsworth, lifted a disapproving brow as Dylan entered, but the old man was too well-trained to chide his employee's son for his late arrival. "Shall I announce you, sir?"

Dylan nodded, his blood pounding with the thrill of having thwarted one of his father's plans. Childish, he knew, to continually provoke the man, but sometimes he just couldn't help himself.

Surrendering his cloak to one of the footmen, Dylan followed the aging butler up the grand staircase with its intricately carved banisters, then down the long hall that led to the ballroom. He was dressed for effect tonight in his scarlet military regalia, his medals and gold epaulets flashing in the candlelight. They passed several aristocratic guests along the way, but Dylan ignored their stares and whispers.

The heady scents of beeswax and roses assaulted his senses as he entered the ballroom. The laughter and buzz of conversation indicated the earl's privileged guests were having a good time.

Dylan scanned the crowd, his smile widening. He hadn't been to one of these affairs in more than a decade, but nothing had changed. Society girls in elaborate gowns still whirled around the parquet dance floor on the arms of suitable young gentlemen. Titled matrons still schemed and plotted from the corners as the older men congregated in small groups, looking bored.

When the last notes of the current waltz faded away, Wadsworth cleared his throat. "The Honorable Captain Dylan Blake."

For a moment, utter silence reigned. Scores of interested nobles craned their necks for a glimpse of the earl's prodigal son, home at last after twelve long years of dedicated service to the Crown.

Dylan met his father's furious gaze. He smiled, then turned his back and skirted the gleaming dance floor. *Let the old bastard come to me.* His days of seeking the old man's favor were long past.

After an awkward pause, the music started up again, as did the whispers.

Julian Tremaine, Lord Basingstoke, who was Dylan's only friend in this whole crowd, strode toward him. Dressed in austere black, as usual, the earl's eyes glinted with welcome. "Blake! Where the hell have you been?"

Dylan shrugged, amused by the knowledge that everyone else wanted to know the same thing. "I had a prior engagement."

Basingstoke stared at him for a moment, then chuckled in admiration. "You were with Cassandra, weren't you?" He shook his head in astonishment. "Has there ever been a woman you *couldn't* get, once you set your mind to it?"

"Never." Dylan grabbed a glass of champagne from a passing waiter and took a long, appreciative drink. "It's the uniform. Besides, I'm making up for lost time. I was in the Army for a bloody long time, you know."

Basingstoke laughed, then sobered and nodded in Warren's direction. "Well, I hope she was worth it.

Your father was furious when you didn't show up for dinner. Threw off the whole thing. Uneven number, and all that."

Exactly one hundred of London's most elite and fashionable attended Warren's annual ball. Because of its exclusivity, the *ton* considered an invitation to be the height of social accomplishment.

The earl had debated long and hard about allowing his younger son to attend. By selling out early in his career, Dylan had taken the place of some far more deserving social climber. The earl had lectured Dylan endlessly about the importance of the occasion and threatened vague, dire consequences should Dylan do anything beyond the pale.

For these reasons and a thousand more, Dylan had taken a sinful amount of pleasure in the fact that his late arrival had turned his father's One Hundred Ball into a dinner of ninety-nine.

There would be hell to pay for this latest transgression, but Dylan was enjoying the moment anyway.

"My father has been furious with me since the day I was born," he told Basingstoke with a shrug. "I figured I might as well give him a reason."

Out of the corner of his eye, Dylan saw his older brother, Michael, confer with the earl, then move through the crowd in Dylan's direction.

As blond and golden as Adonis, Michael had always been the earl's pride and joy. Viscount Sherbourne from birth, Michael would one day inherit the earldom and all the wealth and privilege that went with it. In return, Michael kept his reputation above reproach and obeyed their father's every command.

No doubt he was obeying one of those commands now.

"Let's go down to the billiard room." Dylan refused to stick around and be chastened in such a civilized manner. He'd much prefer it if his father made a scene and took him to task for his irresponsible behavior once and for all.

But that would never happen. The earl didn't care enough about his second son to expend such emotion.

* * *

"He's a disgrace! Honestly, can you believe the nerve! Making a scene and ruining a perfectly lovely ball!" Lady Amelia Lansdowne fluttered her filigreed fan with unusual vigor, an unbecoming flush on her pale cheeks.

"I wouldn't call this a scene, Amelia. He merely arrived a little late. I'm sure he had a good reason." Lady Natalia Sinclair sighed with impatience over her companion's melodrama, but her own fan fluttered a bit faster as she watched Captain Blake chat with Lord Basingstoke.

Captain Dylan Blake, recipient of the Victoria's Cross.

Natalia knew all about him. She'd read dozens of newspaper articles touting his courage, but she'd never actually met him.

"He's dreadfully good-looking," she mused, as she cast a subtle glance in the captain's direction.

In his scarlet dress uniform, with his confident military bearing and chest full of medals, he stood out in the crowd of somber, black-garbed lords. His thick black hair, caught at his nape with a piece of scarlet ribbon, contrasted sharply with his light blue eyes. His high, chiseled cheekbones, square jaw, and clear, sun-kissed skin stole her breath.

Amelia gave a delicate shudder. "How can you say such a thing? He hasn't a title nor farthing to his name. He's been in the military for years, serving with the very dregs of society, and probably doesn't know the first thing about how to act around civilized people."

"Surely, the fact that he fought to preserve our way of life gives him the right to a few eccentricities. He's a hero, Amelia." Natalia didn't bother to point out that a man's wealth had nothing to do with how attractive he was. It wouldn't do any good. In Amelia's eyes, money and power *did* determine a man's worth.

Unfortunately, Natalia's father shared Amelia's opinions, and he would choose her future husband.

Amelia turned up her nose with a condescending sniff. "Well, hero or not, you wouldn't catch *me* marrying such a man."

"No." Natalia fought to maintain a civil tone. "I don't suppose so." *Not that a hero like Captain Blake would want to marry a little cat like you anyway.*

To her relief, Amelia soon drifted away, obviously in search of someone more inclined to share her narrow-minded opinions. Natalia found herself alone for a few moments, free to daydream about Captain Blake.

She wanted to meet him, even though her father would never permit a man like Captain Blake to court her. It seemed so unfair. What good were wealth and a title, when so many of those who had them lacked even a hint of character?

Captain Blake had risked his life to save his men. He'd dashed back into the fray three times before he'd been wounded. The mere thought of his courageous actions sent a shiver down her spine.

Unfortunately, Captain Blake and Lord Basingstoke left the ballroom before she could work up the audacity to arrange an introduction. Disappointed, Natalia forced a smile as the next young man on her dance card claimed her for a mazurka.

Lord Roger Densby was the son of a duke. While undoubtedly her social equal, he was at least two stones overweight and stank of sweat and brandy.

He managed to step on her toes twice before he even got her out on the dance floor and didn't have a heroic bone in his entire well-fed body.

Densby, or someone like him, was her fate. Still, her entire soul rebelled at the thought of spending her life with a man who wasn't interested in anything but the next hunt or glittering party.

What she really wanted was someone like Captain Blake—a man with poetry in his face and courage in his heart.

Chapter Two

At least a dozen of London's most eligible bachelors occupied the Earl of Warren's posh, walnut-paneled billiard room. Some lounged on deep leather chairs, immersed in card games, while others stood around the billiard table, wagering on everything from who would sink the next shot to who would win the next Derby. Here they were free to drink, smoke, and gamble away from the censorious eyes of prospective mothers-in-law.

Dylan had spent a fair amount of time with this crowd, out of sheer boredom and disillusionment, but, save Basingstoke, he didn't like or respect any of them. They reminded him of a flock of squawking crows, circling restlessly as they waited to come into the wealth and position they hadn't earned and didn't deserve.

Unfortunately, his own days were just as meaningless.

He'd sold his commission in hopes his father would allow him to take over the management of one of the many estates entailed to the Blake family. He'd wanted the peace of England's lush green hills. Homesickness had consumed him during those last endless months in the Army.

But he should have known his father would never allow him to have what he wanted. The earl met his request with incredulous laughter, and nothing came of his subsequent attempts to find such work on his own. No one believed the son of an earl, even a second son with no money or prospects, actually wanted to get his hands dirty.

Was his need for peace and tranquility so hard to understand? All he wanted was a quiet place to lick a decade's worth of wounds.

"Well, well," Lord Jonathan Taylor drawled, as Dylan and Basingstoke took seats at a table in a secluded corner of the room. "Look who finally managed to put in an appearance."

Jonathan had been picking fights with Dylan since they were in short pants, and he was already well in his cups, his pale eyes glittering with animosity.

The little bugger is in fine form tonight. Dylan suppressed a weary sigh and accepted another drink from a nearby waiter. The thrill of thwarting his father had worn off. He'd need plenty of liquid fortification in order to get through the rest of the evening.

"I know where he's been." Viscount Harding, one of Dylan's old schoolmates, winked before he sank a ball in the far pocket. "I saw him with Cassandra Lockhart this afternoon."

Basingstoke chuckled and quaffed his drink. "He's a master, gentlemen. I've yet to see a woman who didn't succumb to his charms."

Jonathan gave a derisive laugh. "I'm not impressed. Miss Lockhart is an actress. What sport is there in that?"

Quite a lot, actually, since Cassandra was the actress in question. The fiery redhead had taken London's theater set by storm. Every man in this room had tried to seduce her, but she'd refused all suitors until Dylan had charmed his way into her bed earlier this evening.

Dylan gave Jonathan a measuring look. "Do you have a more challenging target in mind? Your sister, perhaps?" He knew he was being obnoxious, but Jonathan's last taunt had hit a nerve. The endless couplings with actresses and high-priced courtesans left him empty.

Jonathan's homely, sharp-featured face flushed with anger. His older sister resembled a horse and had been on the shelf for years, despite her distinguished family name. "Take it back, Blake, or I swear I *will* call you out this time."

Dylan shrugged. "Name your second."

"Now, gentlemen," Basingstoke interceded, ever the mediator. Jonathan had challenged Dylan to at least a dozen duels in the past. "We're all friends here. I don't think it needs to come to that."

Viscount Harding drifted near enough to hear the gist of the conversation and clapped his hand on Jonathan's thin shoulder. "Think about what you're saying, old chap. Blake is a bloody national hero.

He's killed dozens of men. Do you really want to be added to that number?"

With seething impatience, Dylan waited for Jonathan to make up his mind. He wouldn't kill the little fop. Harding was right—enough blood stained his hands.

At last, Jonathan seemed to realize the odds were against him. He glared at Dylan with unconcealed hatred. "Perhaps you'd like to make a wager, instead? Your somewhat dubious charms against a woman of my choosing?"

Dylan ignored the low rumble of excited whispers their little scene had provoked. He didn't understand why Jonathan took Dylan's every victory as a personal defeat. "I don't gamble on women. Besides, Cassandra and I have barely begun our liaison."

But he thought of the emptiness he'd felt even in Cassandra's most intimate embrace and knew he wouldn't bother to see her again.

"Afraid you'll lose?" Jonathan mocked. "Afraid no decent woman will have you?"

At this little bit of absurdity, Dylan laughed outright. "Why on earth would I want a respectable woman? If I go sniffing around one of them, I'll end up married to the chit."

Basingstoke raised a brow and gave Dylan a wry smile. "And what would be the harm in that? A big fat dowry is exactly what you need."

Unfortunately, Basingstoke knew the way of it. Nine months of high living had depleted the funds Dylan had received for selling his commission. Actresses might be easy, but they weren't cheap.

Soon, he'd be forced to ask his father for an increase of his pitiful quarterly stipend. Anything would be better than that, even marriage.

Perhaps this foolish bet could stave off that necessity for a little while longer.

"All right," Dylan murmured. "Who is it to be, then? I've always wanted to make a good girl go bad."

Jonathan stepped a little closer and lowered his voice, so only Dylan, Basingstoke, and Harding could hear. "How about Lady Natalia Sinclair?"

"Out of the question!" Basingstoke shook his head and flashed Dylan a warning glance. "Don't even think about it, Blake."

Unnecessary advice. Even Dylan had heard of the fair Lady Natalia.

The Duke of Clayton's daughter had an enormous dowry, perhaps half a million pounds. But she'd cut through the men who tried to court her like a knife through butter.

Given Jonathan's simmering anger, Dylan guessed he'd felt the sting of her rejection. The bet suddenly made sense. Jonathan wanted to see Dylan fail.

Although Lady Natalia might be a worthy adversary, Dylan wasn't foolish enough to trifle with the duke's daughter. Clayton was one of the most powerful men in Britain and would never allow his daughter anywhere near a penniless younger son.

"Have you seen her?" Jonathan persisted.

Dylan shook his head. He'd tried to steer clear of this kind of social event since his return. Besides, he had no interest in the marriage-minded young women who populated London's exclusive drawing rooms.

Not that a woman like Lady Natalia Sinclair would have been within reach, even if he had been looking.

"Give it a try," Jonathan urged. "I'll make it easy on you. All you need to do is get her to agree to a second dance, a boon she has yet to grant anyone. One hundred pounds if you succeed."

One hundred pounds. It was a small fortune, and Dylan badly needed the funds.

He'd much rather dance with some silly young girl than beg his father for an advance. Especially given his behavior tonight.

"All right," Dylan agreed. "You're on."

* * *

Natalia spent the next hour sending covert glances toward the ballroom entrance, hoping for another tantalizing glimpse of Captain Blake. She refused to believe he'd already left. Who knew if she'd ever cross paths with him again?

Just when she'd nearly given up hope, she caught sight of his brilliant scarlet uniform. Her heart gave a little thrill of delight. Perhaps she'd have a chance to meet him, after all.

Unfortunately, Captain Blake accompanied Lord Jonathan Taylor, one of her most annoying and persistent suitors. Usually, she dissuaded unwanted attention with a condescending stare, but Lord Jonathan had not yet taken the hint.

She wondered what the little weasel had in common with a hero like Captain Blake. Surely, they weren't friends?

The two men spoke intently for a few moments, but to her relief, Lord Jonathan soon drifted away, leaving Captain Blake alone. Perfect. She was breathless with excitement at this unexpected stroke of luck.

The next man on her dance card arrived, and Natalia sent him off to fetch a glass of champagne. Having bought herself another moment or two of solitude, she plotted her next move. How could she arrange an introduction to the captain without damaging her reputation?

The captain remained at the edge of the crowd, leaning against one of the marble pillars as he cast his brooding gaze over the assembled guests. His thick, inky black hair made a stark contrast to the white stone, and his broad shoulders spanned the entire width of the column.

To her everlasting embarrassment, he caught her staring. One corner of his mouth lifted in a questioning smile, and his disturbing blue gaze met hers with shocking familiarity. A strange little quiver raced up and down her spine.

He'd been the main topic of conversation during the past hour, and everything she'd heard only intrigued her more. Dylan Blake was one of her peers, yet he'd chosen to break free of the stifling restraints aristocratic society placed on its members.

Ever since he'd sold his commission and returned to London, he'd refused to conform to his father's wishes. Rumor had it that his father had been furious with him for selling out and had refused his request to give him an estate of his own to manage.

Undaunted, Captain Blake had begun searching for work as an estate manager somewhere else, a quest nobody could understand. A gentleman did *not* work. It simply wasn't done.

In response to his scandalous actions, the *ton* had closed ranks against him. None of them would allow him to manage so much as a haystack.

But Natalia approved of his need to do something worthwhile. How could anyone expect a man who had done such great things, who was used to being in command, to come back to England and rest on his laurels?

The other rumors concerned her a little more, given her intense attraction to the man. Apparently, he was a rake and a womanizer, but Natalia decided those were small things, easily forgiven in light of the fact that he'd spent the last twelve years fighting for his country.

Perhaps all he needed was the right woman. Someone who would love him enough to calm his restless spirit. She desperately wanted to talk to him. She needed to prove to herself that the man she'd idolized for so long was worthy of her affections. Something good and fine lurked behind that too-handsome face and mocking smile; she just knew it.

Unfortunately, she still hadn't figured out how to initiate a conversation with him.

For the Duke of Clayton's daughter, the world was a narrow and confining place. Soon, her father would decide on a suitable husband and, after her marriage, she'd be sent away to some country pile to produce the requisite heir and spare. Her own wants and wishes didn't matter.

Still, she couldn't resist glancing at Dylan Blake again and again. Why did he keep looking at her? From everything she'd heard, she didn't think he cared about marriage.

Surely, he realized her father would never consider him?

Her gaze met his once more and a ripple of awareness sent shockwaves through her very heart. The duke might not consider Dylan Blake suitable, but she found him absolutely perfect. More than handsome, he embodied all her dangerous dreams.

As though he'd read her mind and knew how much she wanted to meet him, he smiled and moved toward her through the crowd. She watched, torn between terror and heady excitement as he paused to speak to her cousin, Nigel Sinclair. Nigel frowned a bit, then nodded, and the two men headed her way.

As they approached, Nigel gave her an apologetic little smile, as though on a distasteful but necessary mission. She clenched her fists, and her nails bit into her palms as she struggled to keep her emotions in check. She shouldn't want this introduction so badly and must never allow her true feelings to show.

"Lady Natalia Sinclair, allow me to introduce Captain Dylan Blake." Nigel smiled at her again, as though the two of them shared a private joke at the expense of the earl's prodigal son.

Captain Blake smiled as well, drawing her gaze to the lush, full curve of his lips, so at odds with the harsh, uncompromising line of his jaw. His dark lashes, too, seemed out of place. The thick fringe framed his eyes in a sensuous tangle.

And the impact of that stare up close took her breath away. His eyes weren't really blue, she discovered. They were gray, the color of smoke and stormy skies.

He bowed with effortless grace and then brought her gloved hand to his lips. The heat of his mouth warmed her skin through the thin layer of silk. "Lady Natalia." His voice was smooth and cultured, as beautiful as the rest of him. "It's a pleasure to make your acquaintance."

Unsettled and strangely breathless, she forced herself to hide her unusual attack of nerves. "Good evening, Captain Blake."

Ever since her debut, men had thronged to her side in hopes of winning her dowry. She'd learned early to protect herself, to be cool and cutting and utterly unimpressed with the many insincere words her suitors lavished upon her. As a result, London's young rakes thought her cold and haughty.

She took a certain amount of pleasure in that.

It wouldn't do to let Dylan Blake know he'd melted all her defenses with one burning glance in her direction.

"Would you do me the honor of the next dance?" His smile dazzled her, even though it was practiced and didn't quite reach those spectacular eyes.

But something in his tone, in the falseness of that wicked grin, gave her pause. She looked deep into those silver-gray eyes and found... nothing. No answering spark of attraction, no emotion whatsoever. For such a young man, his eyes were incredibly old. Dead.

In fact, she had the feeling he didn't really see her at all.

Disappointment lanced through her. She'd thought him a hero, but he was no different than the rest. She was a dowry, a prize to be won, nothing more. Certainly not a real person, with hopes and dreams of her own.

When he looked at her, all he saw was a way of financing an estate of his own.

She hated him suddenly, hated him for making her want him when he felt nothing in return.

"I'm sorry, Captain Blake, but my dance card is full." She gave him her most wintry stare, the one intended to put him in his place.

His look of astonishment was almost comical. Apparently—and not surprisingly—he'd had little experience with feminine rejection.

"Of course. My mistake." Giving her another graceful bow, he pivoted and strode off through the crowd.

"What an insufferable boor." Nigel tossed her a superior grin. "Well done, Nat. You certainly let him know the way of things."

Natalia ignored her cousin's inane chatter. As she watched Captain Blake walk away, she wished with all her heart that he'd stayed on the other side of the ballroom. Far better for him to have remained a beautiful fantasy than to have learned the truth.

Dylan Blake was not the answer to her prayers.

He was just another fortune hunter—one who hadn't even pretended to like her for something other than her dowry.

Chapter Three

"I need two more weeks," Dylan told Jonathan as they exited the ballroom. "You can't expect me to win her over in two minutes."

Jonathan laughed, the sour sound tinged with satisfaction. "It wouldn't matter if I gave you a year. Lady Natalia will never want what little you have to offer."

Dylan said nothing. Lady Natalia's dismissal had left him reeling.

When Jonathan first pointed her out, Dylan thought the whole thing would be ridiculously easy. She'd seemed transfixed by him, breathless with yearning.

But when he'd asked her to dance, the light had gone out of her lovely green eyes. She'd become every bit as cold and condescending as he'd heard.

Needless to say, the challenge she presented made her infinitely more appealing. Besides, he couldn't afford to lose this bet with Jonathan. He didn't have one hundred pounds to give the bastard.

"Two more weeks," he bargained. "And we'll double the wager. Two hundred pounds if I lose."

Jonathan thought it over for half a second and then nodded. "All right. Two hundred pounds. But you'd better be good for it."

"I'm good for it," Dylan lied.

"Excellent. Then it's settled." Jonathan's wide smile seemed out of place on his pinched little face. "Shall we have another drink?"

Dylan shook his head and glanced toward the stairs that led to the family's private rooms. He had no desire to return to the party. "No, you go ahead. I'm off to bed."

Turning his back on Jonathan, Dylan made his way through the deserted upper floors of his father's house to the suite of rooms he seldom used.

Lady Natalia presented an intriguing puzzle.

She was nothing he'd expected her to be. Young, yes. But not silly or simpering. Her looks were far too striking to be fashionable, but he'd never cared much for the pale, willowy blondes who were all the rage.

The top of the tiny brunette's head didn't even reach his chin, and her demure white gown did nothing to hide her voluptuous curves. Her mother, the duke's first wife, had been a Russian princess. Perhaps that accounted for the exotic tilt of those wide, emerald eyes, and the full lush mouth he'd instantly imagined kissing.

He let himself into his old room and sank down on the huge pedestal bed. Loosening his cravat, he stared into the empty grate, still trying to make sense of what had gone wrong.

He'd thought her pretty at first sight, exquisite up close. But when she'd stared deep into his eyes—and he'd noticed the passion and light fade from hers—

she'd become more than just a quick way to make a hundred pounds.

Since his return to London, no one else had made an effort to see behind the careful façade he'd erected to keep the world at bay. Unfortunately, he had the distinct impression that what she'd seen had disappointed her in some soul-deep way.

If she'd caught even a glimpse of the things he kept hidden, it was no wonder. Ugliness seethed within him. It seemed a farce that God had gifted him with such a pleasing form and face. Then again, Lucifer had been the most beautiful of all the angels.

"What did you see, Natalia?" he whispered into the stillness of the room. And he wondered why he cared.

* * *

The Earl of Warren's ball seemed to last forever. Natalia went through the motions. She smiled and danced as though having the time of her life, but in truth, her feet were killing her, and she was desperate for the evening to end.

As she fended off Lord Jonathan Taylor's advances for the dozenth time—and earned a fulminating glare from the gentleman in question— she wished for the peace and quiet of her father's country estate. Now that she saw the reality of Town life, she couldn't imagine why she'd been so excited to make her debut.

The Season was only a few weeks old, but she'd already grown tired of the constant social whirl. The endless balls, teas, concerts, and soirees exhausted her.

It might have been different if she'd been allowed her to choose her own husband, but she knew she wouldn't have any say in the matter. Her father would choose for her, and there wasn't a single thing she could do about it.

Why take the time to get to know any of the young men who flocked to her side? If she foolishly fell in love, she'd only wind up with a broken heart.

She felt like a fraud, a carrot her father dangled in front of London's most eligible bachelors for the contrary satisfaction of snatching her away. It was a game to him.

She suspected he'd already struck a deal with one of her mother's Russian cousins. No ordinary earl or marquess would do. No. The duke's daughter would marry a prince.

As a matter of fact, when the Season ended, the duke intended to take Natalia to St. Petersburg for a prolonged visit with Prince Nikolai Ivanovich.

The duke assured Natalia nothing was definite. He claimed she'd have the chance to get to know Prince Nikolai before he agreed to the marriage. But she'd already met the prince, long ago, and had no desire to further their acquaintance.

Nikolai was handsome, but calculated cruelty lay in the depths of his ice-blue eyes. The mere thought of becoming his wife made her uneasy.

Her father refused to listen to her fears. She'd been a child the last time she and Nikolai met, he reminded her. She needed to give the prince a chance, see him with the eyes of a woman.

In response, she'd tried to make herself unapproachable, going so far as to deny any man the privilege of more than one dance a night. She didn't want to encourage anyone unduly, didn't want to make any of these young men think they had a chance at winning her hand and, more importantly, the fortune that came with it.

"I believe this last dance is mine."

The gentleman who'd spoken approached when Natalia's former partner—an elderly German count, who'd trampled on her toes—led her off the dance floor. The handsome newcomer, with his golden hair and deep blue eyes, looked familiar.

Natalia smiled with more enthusiasm than she'd shown all evening. The last dance. *Finally.*

She glanced down at her dance card, and then back at her new partner with renewed interest. "Lord Sherbourne?" Michael Blake, the Earl of Warren's heir—and Captain Blake's older brother.

Sherbourne nodded. Genuine warmth sparkled in his eyes. "I've been looking forward to this dance all evening, Lady Natalia."

"You flatter me, Lord Sherbourne." The practiced words slipped easily off her tongue. For once, she allowed herself to relax and be a little flirtatious. It was late, and she grew tired of guarding her heart.

The string quartet began yet another waltz. To her delight, Sherbourne danced divinely. As they whirled across the thinning dance floor, she took the opportunity to study him and marveled at his lack of resemblance to the captain. She would never have known they were related, if not for their names.

Unfortunately, Sherbourne came up lacking.

Sherbourne was a bit shorter and thinner than his younger brother, and his warm blue eyes weren't as intense. Nothing mysterious or rebellious about this man. In fact, she'd bet a million pounds he'd done exactly what was expected of him his entire life.

He was titled, wealthy, and handsome—everything Society found attractive in a man. So, why didn't he have the same effect on her that his brother did? In Sherbourne's arms, she felt none of the rioting emotions Captain Blake elicited with one casual glance.

"It's been a wonderful party." Afraid Sherbourne might somehow read her wayward thoughts, she kept up a steady stream of small talk. "Your father is a magnificent host."

Sherbourne gave a short laugh. "I'm just glad it's over. If I never see another guest list in my life, it will be too soon." His candor surprised her. Perhaps she'd been wrong, and there was a bit of rebelliousness behind his blandly perfect features. She wanted to commiserate, tell him of her own impatience with the endless rounds of invitations, but years of training kept the words locked in her throat.

Before she could think of anything else to say, the music died away. Sherbourne released her with obvious reluctance. "The dance was much too short. Perhaps you would allow me to call on you tomorrow?"

Such a simple request, but she'd yet to grant such favor to any of her suitors. Her first impulse was to refuse him, as she'd done all the others. But thoughts of the foolish way she'd behaved over his sinfully attractive brother stayed her tongue.

Perhaps, she'd refused the others because she'd secretly been searching for a hero, *someone to love* all along. Somehow, she'd turned Captain Blake into such a paragon of virtue in her mind that no one, not even the captain himself, could live up to her imaginings.

If so, she truly was a fool. Far better to play the game and continue to guard her heart.

"I'd like that," she told Sherbourne. "I'd like that very much."

* * *

By the time Dylan entered the dining room the next morning, every trace of the party had been swept away. A sideboard of delicacies gave off assorted tantalizing smells, and his stomach growled noisily.

He'd missed dinner, after all.

Michael entered the room while Dylan filled his plate. They eyed each other warily. The easy friendship they'd enjoyed as children had disappeared long ago.

"Good morning," Dylan said, hoping to set a light tone. He wasn't in the mood to argue or to be lectured. He wanted to eat and then make his exit before his father showed up.

"Hello." Michael sounded surprised by his pleasant greeting. "I didn't know you'd spent the night."

It was a good beginning. Dylan couldn't even remember the last time he and his brother had managed to carry on a conversation not marred by anger, jealousy, or defensiveness.

"I stayed for breakfast." Dylan sat down at one end of the huge walnut table and dug into his kippers with relish. "You can't get fare like this down at Mrs. Tweed's."

Michael filled his own plate and then took the place across from Dylan, frowning. "You don't have to live in that deuced boarding house, you know. You're welcome to come home anytime you wish."

"But I like that deuced boarding house. I can come and go as I please without having to listen to Father's various complaints about my behavior."

"He's not so bad. and he wouldn't be so angry with you all the time if you behaved with a little more discretion. How do you expect him to react when you taunt him the way you did last night? That blasted party means a great deal to him."

For once, Dylan decided against a flippant reply. He met Michael's chiding glance head on, as he tried to find an answer to the question that had haunted him all his life. "You know how hard I've tried to win his favor. I was awarded the bloody VC, for Christ's sake, and he didn't even come to the ceremony!" His voice rose, and he made an effort to regain control. "He hates me no matter what I do."

Michael looked away. To his credit, he didn't try to deny it.

Watching the play of emotion on his brother's face, Dylan felt a twinge of guilt. He knew Michael didn't enjoy the responsibilities that came with being the heir. And Michael didn't understand any better than Dylan why their father chose to draw a line so sharply between them.

As children, Michael had often tried to take the blame for Dylan's many real and imagined transgressions, wanting to spare his little brother at least some of the constant beatings. But the earl never allowed it.

In their father's eyes, Michael could do no wrong, and Dylan could do no right. "Ah, hell. Let's just change the subject, shall we?" The last thing Dylan wanted to do was dredge up the hurt and pain of the past.

Seeming relieved, Michael cleared his throat and picked at his breakfast. "The old man's been after me to marry. I've begun courting the Duke of Clayton's daughter."

"Lady Natalia?" Dylan pushed away his plate, a sinking feeling in his gut. This was one complication he hadn't counted on.

"I danced with her last night, and she gave me permission to call upon her this morning. She's a strange little thing, a bit too foreign looking for my tastes. Not much for conversation either, but her dowry is enormous."

"I think she's lovely." Dylan schooled his face into a smile and hoped his anger and dismay didn't show. Everything came so easily to Michael. It seemed Lady Natalia was no exception. Michael had been given permission to call, while Dylan hadn't even been able to win a dance.

Michael raised a brow. "I thought redheaded actresses were more your type."

"So, you've heard about Cassandra." Dylan continued to smile, but he knew what Michael thought. Like Jonathan, Michael assumed no respectable woman would ever look twice at a penniless younger son.

They were probably right.

"I believe everyone has heard about Cassandra." For once, a hint of admiration laced Michael's voice. He leaned forward, rampant curiosity in his warm blue eyes. "What's she like?"

Dylan shrugged. "Beautiful. Sensual. Wildly imaginative."

Michael sighed and leaned back in his chair. "I envy you. It must be nice to have a woman you can relax and be yourself around. Perhaps I'll take a mistress as well, after I'm wed."

A woman you can be yourself around. What a fascinating concept. Dylan decided not to inform his brother he'd never found any such thing. The women he met expected him to be the hero they read about in the papers. He'd never had the courage to disappoint them.

"Why wait until after the wedding?" Dylan asked, truly curious. "Why not take a mistress now?"

"I can't afford even the hint of a scandal," Michael explained, an odd note in his voice. "Not if I'm to win the duke's daughter."

Dylan kept his opinions of his brother's hypocrisy to himself. He finished his breakfast, and then bid Michael farewell. As he hurried from the house, he cursed beneath his breath. Of all the girls in London, why did this bet have to center around the one *Michael* wanted?

He wondered if Jonathan knew about Michael's interest in Lady Natalia. Had the fop put Dylan at odds with his brother on purpose?

The wisest thing to do, given this new information, would be to bow out gracefully and let Jonathan win the infernal wager. He'd come up with the money somehow, even if it meant going to his father.

But as soon as the thought occurred, he dismissed it. He'd never been one to simply give up, and he'd be damned if he'd start now.

Besides, the girl intrigued him, and he was tired of stepping aside for his brother. Perhaps he needed to prove to himself that he could be first in *someone's* heart.

Chapter Four

Dylan spent the rest of the morning and early afternoon at his club. He drank, played cards with Basingstoke, and tried to pretend nothing was wrong. He laughed off questions about the wager with a confidence he didn't feel.

In truth, the thought of competing with Michael terrified him. After all, he'd been compared to his perfect brother all his life. And all his life, he'd come up lacking.

As he left the club, he railed inwardly against his father for promoting such a strong rivalry between his sons. Dylan had always hated himself for his driving need to beat Michael, especially since Michael seemed beyond such petty behavior.

Then again, Michael didn't need to compete, since he always won without effort.

Sighing, Dylan hailed the nearest hack, gave the driver his address, and then settled back in the stained seat for the long ride home. Fleet Street was a long way from Pall Mall,

Evening had already descended by the time he reached the rundown yet painfully clean boarding house where he'd taken a room. Well into his cups, he decided to take the back stairs in order to avoid his landlady, Mrs. Loretta Tweed.

He was late with his rent again and had no idea how he would pay if he didn't win this bet. He wasn't due to receive his quarterly allowance from his father for another month.

Unfortunately, Loretta lay in wait for him. By the time he got to his room on the second floor, she was marching up the front stairs.

"Captain Blake!" she called, giving him no chance to pretend he didn't see her. "Might I have a quick word with you, sir?"

Dylan sighed and pressed his forehead to the scarred wooden door for a moment, trying to summon the charm that had worked so well for him in the past. Turning, he pasted on a smile. "Loretta. How nice to see your lovely face."

Grossly overweight and near fifty, Loretta had never been lovely. Still, his compliments usually managed to buy him some time.

"Don't you try to charm me, you naughty boy." She mounted the last few stairs and bustled toward him, her breath hitching from her exertion. "You know you're over two weeks late with the rent."

Dylan smiled wider, his mouth aching with the effort. "Am I? So sorry, my love. A mere oversight. I'll have the funds for you in the morning."

"That's what you said last week." She gave him a weary shake of her head. "I can't keep letting you slide, even if you are gorgeous as sin. I've got bills of my own to pay."

Too tired to keep up the pretense, Dylan let the smile slip from his lips. "I know, Loretta. I'm truly sorry. I'll get the money somehow. I swear I will."

She stared at him for a long moment, then nodded and gave him a wan smile of her own. "Just try and have the money for me by the end of the month. Otherwise, I'll have to evict you."

He watched her trudge back toward the stairs. She'd given him more of a reprieve than he deserved. He felt guilty for taking advantage of her generous nature.

Letting himself into his room, he lit the closest lamp and cursed as he burned his fingertips. He waited impatiently as the flame sputtered and flickered before catching hold.

The light illuminated a small suite of shabby rooms. It wasn't Grosvenor Square, but it was neat and clean, a veritable palace after the tiny crowded spaces he'd occupied during his years in the Army. At least the flat was warm and dry, two things he'd have sold his sour for in the Crimea.

It was also lonely.

Sometimes, the loneliness ate at his very soul, and he wished he'd never sold his commission. He didn't miss much about his former life. Not the boredom that gave way to bloody frenzy, nor the endless rules and regulations. But he did miss the companionship, the swapping of stories, and the friends who had become like family to him.

Blinking back the memories, he crossed the room and poured himself a shot of gin. He drank deeply, letting the familiar burn of alcohol drown his sudden sense of unease. Pouring himself a second drink, he settled on the sofa to read the *Times*, only to be interrupted by a knock at the door.

He frowned at the sound. Who on earth could it be? Too loud to be Mrs. Tweed, too impatient to be Michael, and Basingstoke made it a matter of principle never to be seen in Dylan's neighborhood. Muttering under his breath, Dylan tossed the paper aside and went to answer the summons.

When he saw who'd come to call, his heart sank, and his gut knotted. *My father.*

Though impeccably dressed, the earl's usually impassive face was flushed with anger. Dylan had never seen the man in such a state.

Alarmed, Dylan took an unconscious step back. A decade had passed since the earl had last beaten him, but he supposed a shadow of the terrified child he'd once been lurked somewhere deep inside him.

"Father," he muttered, steeling himself against any further signs of weakness. "This is an unexpected surprise."

Unexpected and *unwelcome*. Shutting the door on a few curious neighbors who stood in the hall, the earl moved to stand in the middle of the small parlor. He cast a disparaging glance around the humble surroundings and then allowed his wintry gaze to settle upon Dylan once more. "You needn't act as though you're pleased to see me. This isn't a social call, I assure you."

"I didn't think it was. You've certainly never bothered to visit before." Dylan sank into the nearest chair and stared at his father in brooding silence.

What the hell is he doing here?

As if in answer, the earl tossed him some official-looking documents. Dylan's foreboding intensified as he unfolded the crisp sheets of paper.

When he'd read enough to realize what they were, his blood ran cold.

"You've written me off." He schooled his face into a controlled mask, determined not to let his true emotions show. All he had left was his pride, and he wasn't about to let the old bastard know how much this final repudiation hurt.

The earl stepped forward, seized Dylan's chin, and forced him to meet his furious gaze. "You embarrassed me, you ungrateful little bastard. All your life, I've given you more than you deserved, and this is how you repay me?"

Dylan jerked away. "You've given me nothing! No love, no respect, certainly no mercy. My mother was barely cold in her grave before you shipped me off to boarding school."

"Don't speak to me of her!" The veins in the earl's forehead pulsed with anger. They stared into each other's eyes for one long, endless moment. Then the earl spun away and paced the length of the small room like a caged tiger. "You never should have left the Army. That's where you belong. There's no place for you here."

Each word hit him like a slap. Dylan knew his father bore him no great love, but this was the first time the earl had allowed him to see this seething hatred.

"You shan't get another farthing from me," the earl continued. "Not ever."

"I believe you've explained all that quite clearly." Dylan flung himself out of the chair and stalked to the window. "So, if you haven't anything further to add, why don't you get the hell out of here?"

Lengthy silence greeted Dylan's words. He turned and found his father less than a yard away, face contorted with rage.

"I have rued your existence since the day you were born. You are no son of mine."

Dylan gave a cynical laugh. "God. As though I hadn't ever heard that before."

The earl spun on his heels and slammed the door behind him. The sound reverberated in Dylan's skull, freezing him into immobility for a long, long moment. The last little part of his heart that had believed in his father's love withered and died.

Written off.

Despite everything, he'd never thought his father would go this far. Trembling in delayed reaction, he sank gracelessly down the wall. His limbs failed him as he contemplated his dwindling options.

Though he and his father had never gotten along, he'd never dreamed there would come a day when the old man would cut him off completely. A terrible predicament, to be sure. Made even worse by the fact that he had nothing to fall back on.

He'd already failed to find employment as an estate manager. The only jobs to be had in the city were menial in nature and wouldn't even pay his rent at Mrs. Tweed's. English Society wasn't set up to provide for gentlemen who were down on their luck.

Still, he wasn't without talents or resources. An old friend from India had already offered him a partnership in a lucrative trading venture. And opportunity abounded in American, now that the States had finished their bloody civil war.

All he need was an entrepreneurial spirit and a small stake to get started.

At the moment, however, he didn't have the funds for a coach ride to the country, let alone fare for a passage to India or America. Besides, he'd spent the last twelve years aching to return home to England. He couldn't bear the thought of leaving so soon.

Marriage. There seemed to be no way around it. *A marriage for money.*

Restless, he stood and poured himself another drink. Basingstoke was right. He needed an immense dowry. He needed to find a woman so impressed by his war record and impeccable breeding she wouldn't notice his complete lack of funds.

Though he hated the thought of spending the rest of his life with a woman he did not love, it seemed better than the alternative. He comforted himself with the thought that he could surely find a girl who was both rich and attractive, someone he might come to care for.

Once again, he was brought up short by the reminder that a courtship of that nature would take months to pull off. Months he didn't have. At the moment, his largest concern was keeping a roof over his head.

He drained his glass, feeling the need to be far drunker that he was. Lost in thought, he poured another drink and carried it to the sofa as he pondered the humiliation of asking Michael or Basingstoke for a loan. Either one would give him the money he needed without question, but his entire soul rebelled at the thought.

Then, suddenly, the answer became clear.

The wager.

Of course. He needed to win the bet he'd made with Jonathan. Two hundred pounds would easily finance a lengthy search for a suitable bride.

What had begun as a mere challenge had become his only chance to save himself.

His conscience balked a bit at the thought of using the girl in such a manner, but he quieted the little voice. He didn't plan to ruin her. It was just a couple of dances, which would do nothing but raise an eyebrow or two.

He needed to charm Lady Natalia Sinclair. Not an easy task but one he had yet to pursue wholeheartedly. He smiled, thinking of all the unused weapons in his arsenal.

He would put her icy reserve under siege. He would assault it from every side until he wore down her defenses.

She didn't have a snowball's chance in hell of resisting him.

Chapter Five

"Just one dance. That's all I'm asking."

Natalia sighed as she stared into Dylan Blake's persuasive gray eyes. A little more than a week had passed since she'd first met him, and he had made her the target of a very heated campaign. Everywhere she went, he was there, charming and cajoling her into granting him a dance.

Tonight, they'd both attended a costume ball in prestigious St. James Square. She'd come garbed as Diana, the Huntress, but he'd had no trouble seeing beyond her disguise.

Of course, she'd also recognized *him*. Dressed as a desert sheik in flowing white robes, he wore a turban and a gold demi-mask.

Even disguised, he was the most handsome man in the room. She thought his appeal must lie in the confidence of his walk. Or perhaps his height and the ungentlemanly breadth of his shoulders made him stand out,

More likely, the sensual curve of his lips drew her. What woman could ever look at that mouth and think of anything but the way it would feel to have it pressed against hers?

She'd hoped her attraction to him would fade, but instead, it had intensified. So far, she'd managed to keep him at arm's length, but that hadn't been easy. Denying him the requested dances took every bit of willpower she possessed. The righteous anger he'd elicited upon their first meeting faded a little with each new encounter, and this dangerous need to deepen their relationship grew.

Heartbreak seemed as inevitable as the tide, yet for the first time in her life, she considered taking the risk.

Mustering the last of her self-will, she shook her head and gave him a rueful smile. "Why do you continue to plague me, Captain Blake? Hasn't any woman ever told you no before?"

He made her feel reckless, able to speak her mind and flirt shamelessly, safe in the anonymity of her mask and the knowledge that their nearest observers were several yards away.

He laughed, a surprised, openly amused sound that sent heads turning in their direction. He flashed a charming grin, revealing a deep dimple in each lean cheek. "Never. I'm afraid I'm rather spoiled where women are concerned."

"Then let me be the first." Natalia delighted in the verbal sparring. "I will not dance with you. Not tonight. Not next week. Not a month from now. You might as well give up and quit asking."

"Are you afraid of me?" he asked, changing tactics. "Do you fear even a moment in my arms will prove to be too much temptation?"

Natalia caught her breath, unwilling to admit, even to herself, how close he was to the truth. "Honestly, Captain! You think far too highly of yourself, I assure you!"

He clutched his chest dramatically. "You wound me, milady. Do you really think me such a cad?"

A cad? She looked into those sparkling gray eyes, no longer empty but filled with youth and vitality. He seemed different tonight, so much the man of her dreams. She wondered if her first impression had been wrong.

"I don't think you're a cad. Not in the least." The words spilled out as she lost the battle to remain aloof. She stepped closer and lowered her voice so no one else would hear her pour her heart out to him. "In fact, I've never known such a hero. I'd be honored if you'd share some of your experiences during the war."

His slate-gray eyes reflected sudden cynicism and the shadow she'd seen before returned full force. "Ah. You're one of *those*."

"One of whom?" He didn't seem to care for the type of person he assumed her to be, and she wanted to redeem herself.

"You want to hear stories of bravery and courage. You think it's all so romantic." Palpable anger and disdain filled his voice, quite out of proportion to the innocent request.

"Is that so wrong?" She'd obviously made a terrible blunder. "I didn't intend to offend you, Captain Blake."

He sighed and looked away. When his gaze met hers again, his anger had vanished, replaced by weariness. "There's nothing wrong with curiosity. But war isn't at all what you think. There's nothing romantic about young men dying of measles and dysentery. There's nothing romantic about watching your friends cut down and bleeding all around you."

Stark and full of pain, his words illuminated the brutal realities of war in a way she'd never considered. This glimpse of what the war had cost him made her feel shallow and very naïve. "Did you lose many friends?"

For a long moment, she didn't think he would answer but then he nodded. "There was one... he was like a father to me. I miss him every day." He gave a short huff of laughter. "Do you know you're the first person who's ever asked me that? They ask me about everything else, but they never want to hear about all those who died."

She desperately wanted to reach over and squeeze his hand. She wanted to hug him, give him comfort in some small way. Unfortunately, the circumstances and the crowd made such a thing impossible.

"You can find me riding in the park at ten each Tuesday morning if you'd like someone to talk to," she offered impulsively.

Dylan stared at her, surprise chasing away the shadows in his eyes. "I might take you up on that. But if you're willing to make such an improper offer, surely you can dance with me tonight? Come on, my love. It's just a dance. What harm can there be in that? You've danced with nearly everyone else who's asked you."

"I don't know..."

My love. How was a girl supposed to stand firm in the wake of such an inappropriate endearment?

He was simply too potent, too male. And tonight, he'd let down his defenses. He'd given her a small glimpse of the complex, emotional man beneath the charming scoundrel.

"Who's next on your dance card?" he asked, obviously sensing he was close to victory. "Tell me, and I'll go arrange to take his place."

She lifted the small square, which was attached to her wrist by a dainty ribbon, and scanned it. Her heart sank when she saw the next name on the list.

"It's Neptune, I'm afraid." Lord Sherbourne's golden perfection had also been impossible to hide.

"Michael." Dylan's smile faded. "You never seem to think twice before agreeing to dance with *him*."

Natalia stared into Dylan's turbulent gray eyes and saw yet another glimpse of what drove him. Here was a man who had been passed over for his brother far too often.

"Lord Sherbourne is a far more... appropriate partner," she told him, wishing things could be different.

"For once in your life, don't worry about what everyone will think." The fierce intensity in his voice sent a shiver down his spine. "Look at me. Don't shut me out the way you do all the others. You don't have to protect yourself. I'm not after your dowry."

She was stunned by his correct interpretation of her emotions. He seemed to understand her so well.

"Then what *do* you want from me?" She'd wanted to know the answer to that question since the moment they'd met. She held her breath and hoped his answer would be the one she longed to hear, terrified he'd disappoint her.

He smiled and brushed her cheek with his fingertips. "All I want is to make you laugh. I want to dance with you. Maybe even steal a kiss or two."

His voice dropped, so low and intimate she strained to hear it over the music and laughter surrounding them. "I could show you what it's like to feel passion before your father sells you off to some cold stiff like my brother."

If he'd been anyone else, she would have slapped him for daring to suggest such a thing. Instead, his honesty both thrilled and frightened her. Dear Lord, she wanted nothing more than to share an illicit kiss with this beautiful man.

But before she could answer, he stiffened and stepped away. "I'll see you again in a few days. Promise me you'll think about what I've said."

Then he turned and disappeared through the crowd.

She stared after him in dismay. How could he simply walk away after saying such a thing? And how could she survive the next few days with the images his words had conjured up running amok through her brain?

Irrationally, she considered chasing after him. What did her pride or reputation matter, when she'd been denied her heart's desire?

But then she saw the reason for his hasty retreat. Neptune approached, ready to claim his dance.

* * *

Dylan watched from the gallery above the dance floor as Michael offered Natalia his arm. She smiled and accepted, but she seemed distracted.

Despite Michael's untimely interruption, Dylan knew he'd gained a remarkable amount of ground. She'd invited him to meet her in the park, where she'd be chaperoned by nothing more than a groom.

Foolish girl.

He felt a momentary twinge of guilt about the white lies he'd told to earn her trust. He *did* want her dowry. Dear Lord, who wouldn't? But he felt safe pretending disinterest, because they both knew he could never have it.

She hated the fact that every suitable young man in England chased after her because she was a great heiress. She wanted to be wanted for herself— something he found far too easy to understand.

Unfortunately, the rest of what he'd told her was true. He did want to kiss her. He also wanted to dance with her; not because of the bet, but because he wanted to know how she'd feel in his arms.

He shifted, confused by his own emotions. She drew him for reasons he didn't understand. With each encounter, he found himself even more infatuated.

His previous conquests lacked Natalia's innate sweetness and tender, caring nature. Gentle and soft-spoken, she reminded him of his mother. A true lady.

But she also possessed a hidden core of fire, and he was dying to ignite the flames.

An uneasy frown pulled at the corners of his mouth as he watched the object of his pursuit twirl across the dance floor in his brother's arms. Jealousy clawed in his gut as he realized how very much he envied his brother the ability to court Lady Natalia Sinclair in truth.

"You don't seem to be having much luck, Blake."

Dylan whirled around at the sound of Jonathan's smug voice, instantly on the defensive. "I still have a week," he reminded his nemesis. "And I'm making progress."

Jonathan laughed. "Is that why you're up here and your brother is dancing with the lady in question?"

Dylan leaned against the rail and strove to maintain a casual pose. "Michael wants to marry the girl. I simply want to dance with her. We have two entirely different agendas."

Jonathan nodded. "Oh, I see. You have absolutely no desire to get your hands on Lady Natalia's dowry."

"Why are you trying so hard to provoke me?" Dylan asked, irritated. "Are you still angry I took your spot on the polo team all those years ago?"

Jonathan flushed and looked away. "Of course not."

"Then what's this about? Are you trying to stir up trouble for Lady Natalia? Perhaps because you've had even less luck with her than I?"

"Don't be absurd." Jonathan glared at Dylan, his anger so far out of proportion to the question that Dylan felt certain his barb had been correct. "Quit trying to change the subject, Blake. You only have a week left. I suggest you make the most of it."

"Oh, I will," Dylan called, as Jonathan walked away. "You can count on it."

Chapter Six

"I think you're very wise to set your cap for Viscount Sherbourne."

Startled, Natalia glanced up at her stepmother, Clarice. "Sherbourne? Whatever makes you think I'm interested in him?"

They sat in the duchess's lovely little morning room, which she'd decorated soon after her marriage to Natalia's father two years ago. Clarice's pale skin and white-blond hair were a lovely contrast to the ice blue and gold color scheme, as she'd no doubt known they would be.

Clarice laughed. "Well, you allowed him to call on you, which was certainly a first. And I saw your face when you talked to him at the masque. You positively glowed."

Only five years older than Natalia, Clarice didn't fit the picture of the wicked stepmother so often portrayed in fairy tales. Clarice had never tried to take

Anastasia Sinclair's place in Natalia's heart. Instead, she opted to fill the role of nosy big sister. They were the best of friends, and Natalia knew she must tread very carefully, lest Clarice guess the truth.

"Was I?" If she'd been glowing when she'd spoken to Sherbourne, it was because of the fire Captain Blake sparked within her, not anything Sherbourne had said or done.

"I don't blame you," Clarice continued. "He was my first choice, back when I had my Season. I would have married him in an instant, if he'd asked."

Natalia paused in the process of pouring the tea, surprised by her stepmother's candor. While Clarice thought nothing of giving Natalia advice and prying into her private affairs, she rarely spoke about herself.

Laughing, Clarice took the teapot and finished serving. "Don't look so shocked. Did you think it was my choice to marry a man thirty years my senior, who was interested in nothing except getting a male heir?"

"Has it been so terrible? Being married to my father?"

Clarice sighed and shook her head. "He doesn't mistreat me, if that's what you mean. I've learned to handle him quite nicely. But our marriage is hardly the romance I'd imagined for myself."

Natalia reached across the table and patted Clarice's hand. "I'm so sorry."

Clarice shrugged, obviously embarrassed. "Don't mind me, darling. I'm just a little melancholy today." She squeezed Natalia's hand as though it gave her strength and then released it. "My monthlies have started, and I dread telling the duke I've failed to conceive once again."

"Oh, Clarice." Natalia didn't know what else to say. She knew how much the duchess wanted a child of her own. The duke was a hard man, very verbal about the fact that Clarice's only worth lay in her ability to provide a male heir.

Clarice took a long, bracing sip of her tea, then pasted on a bright smile. "I'd much rather talk about that stunning young viscount. Do tell me you're considering him."

"I have no say in the matter," Natalia reminded her. "You know Father will never allow me to choose a mere viscount over Prince Nikolai."

"But Sherbourne will be an earl someday. I'm certain we can convince your father to consider him." Clarice clapped her hands together, her excitement obviously growing as she thought her scheme through. "All you have to do is bring him to heel. He needs to propose soon, before the end of the Season. Then there will be no need for our trip to Russia."

Natalia looked away, shamed by her stepmother's enthusiasm. "I like Sherbourne well enough," she admitted. "He'd make a much better husband than Prince Nikolai."

"But…?" Clarice stared at Natalia, a knowing look her eyes. "There's someone else?"

Natalia decided it might help to talk about this with somebody. "Oh, Clarice! He's so dreadfully wrong for me. I know I can never have him, but he's all I can think about. All I dream about."

"Do you love this young man?" Clarice's voice dropped to a mere whisper. "Have you let him compromise you?"

"No. Of course not," Natalia said quickly. Too quickly.

Clarice leaned forward, her forehead puckered with concern. "Which part are you denying?"

"I hardly even know him, so I can't be in love." Natalia closed her eyes against the thought, but that didn't help. Dylan Blake's darkly handsome image was seared beneath her lids.

She couldn't wait to see him again, but this was only Sunday. Tuesday seemed an eternity away. Would he take her up on her impulsive offer to meet her in the park?

With a shiver, she tried to pull her mind back to the matter at hand. "As for the other part… I haven't so much as let him touch my hand. Yet."

"Yet?" Clarice shook her head in dismay. "You can't honestly be thinking about allowing this man to take liberties?"

Natalia gave an uneasy laugh. "I just told you that I can't think of anything else."

Clarice moved to sit beside her on the small sofa, her gaze searching and intense. "Natalia, no good can come of this. You have to forget these wild ideas."

Natalia closed her eyes and took a deep breath. "You're right. I know you are."

"Then promise me you'll consider Sherbourne. You could be so very happy with him, darling. And I'll speak to your father, if you want me to. Smooth the way. I know he doesn't really like the idea of marrying you off to that Russian. We'll probably never see you again if Prince Nikolai manages to win your hand."

Natalia hugged Clarice, overwhelmed by her stepmother's generosity. "You don't have to do that, but thank you for offering."

Clarice wouldn't be dissuaded. "I know this other young man seems very appealing, but wouldn't you rather know for certain that you're going to marry someone like Sherbourne? Someone handsome, kind, and virile? You've told me how much Prince Nikolai frightens you."

Clarice seemed quite taken with the idea of having Michael Blake as a son-in-law.

Natalia shrugged. "You're right. If it came to a decision between Nikolai and Sherbourne, the viscount would be the best choice."

"Then you have to let your father know you're interested. Right now, he believes you *want* to marry Prince Nikolai."

"Why on earth would he think such a thing? I've told him I abhor the idea more times than I can count."

Clarice shook her head. "To men, actions speak louder than words. He hasn't paid much attention to what you've said, but he watches you far more closely than you think. You've been so aloof, so uninterested in London's most eligible bachelors. He thinks you're holding out to be a princess."

Natalia choked back a laugh. "If that's the case, then he doesn't know me at all."

"What man ever truly knows any woman?" Clarice patted Natalia's knee. "Just think about what I've said. You've got some important decisions to make, and you're running out of time."

* * *

Tuesday morning dawned warm and bright, full of possibilities. Natalia hurried through breakfast then rushed down to the stables for her weekly ride.

The young groom, Alec, was still sweeping out the stalls when she arrived. The smell of manure and fresh hay reminded her of her father's country estate, where she'd spent much of her childhood. Although early, she chafed with impatience as she waited for Alec to saddle her small bay mare, Betsy.

Finally, they were off. Alec trailed respectfully behind her as they headed into the park.

Natalia took a deep breath of the crisp morning air and tried to calm her rioting emotions. She must consider the possibility Captain Blake wouldn't even show. But in her heart, she knew he'd been looking forward to this encounter as much as she had.

The park was nearly deserted at this time of morning, so the risk of being caught was minimal. And besides, she wasn't doing anything wrong. Just a chance meeting between two acquaintances. Alec would be within sight the entire time. It wasn't as though the captain could actually kiss her…

Shaking her head against such foolishness, Natalia rose up in her saddle and scanned the trees. With a sigh of disappointment, she sank back down and urged her mare toward the secluded back edge of the park. Maybe he didn't want to show himself until he knew they wouldn't be seen.

Just when she'd nearly given up hope, she caught sight of him. He skirted a stand of oaks, riding a magnificent gray gelding, his dark hair gleaming in the sunlight. She drew in a deep breath, dazzled as ever.

Smiling in delight, she lifted a hand and waved in a very unladylike manner.

He returned her wave with equal enthusiasm and guided his horse toward hers at a spirited canter. He rode with the grace of a born horseman. He must have been awe-inspiring in full dress uniform as he led the Calvary into battle.

"Good morning, Lady Natalia," he called, his voice filled with good humor. "What a surprise, running into you here."

Alec rode forward, ready to protect her, but she motioned him back, signaling that Captain Blake was a friend. The young man fell back to give them some privacy, yet remained close enough to provide proper chaperonage if anyone else should happen by.

"Hello, Captain Blake." Natalia gazed at him as he fell in beside her, noticing how fine his muscular thighs looked in his buff trousers. He wore high black boots and an emerald riding jacket, his handsome face flushed with healthy color.

He grinned at her intense perusal and returned her interest tenfold. His smoky gaze settled overlong on her bosom, even though her smart blue riding habit was quite modest. Blushing, she looked away.

"I didn't really expect to see you here this morning. I thought you'd come to your senses and change your mind," he said, energy and excitement in his voice.

She gave a breathless laugh, feeling a sense of freedom she'd never known before. "Well, apparently, I'm not a very sensible girl."

"Perhaps not," he agreed, though he seemed to appreciate her spunk. "But if you have to be foolish over something, I'm glad you've chosen to be foolish over me." He cocked his dark head toward Alec. "Are you certain he won't run and tell tales to your father?"

"He won't say anything," Natalia assured him. She and Alec were great friends, and she could count on the young groom to keep his mouth shut. *This time.* She was safe as long as she and Captain Blake didn't make this a habit.

For a moment, they rode in silence, while Natalia cast about for something to say. She'd invited him on the pretext of discussing the war, but she didn't think he wanted to talk about his painful experiences.

Reaching over, she patted his gelding's neck. "What a fine animal. Did he travel to the Crimea with you?" There. She'd given him an opening. Now it was up to him.

Regret flickered in his eyes. "This spirited young thing belongs to my friend, the Earl of Basingstoke. I had to sell mine. Couldn't afford the upkeep."

He'd given up the horse that carried him through battle? She wanted to ask why he hadn't stabled the animal with his father but feared making another blunder. Everyone knew he and his father weren't on the best of terms.

Another silence fell between them, and Natalia cursed her lack of conversational skill. He must think her a complete lackwit.

"You still haven't danced with me," he said at last, sparing her the need to think of something else to say. "Do you plan to remedy that in the near future?"

She gave him a sidelong look. Why was he so fixated on dancing with her? Not that a dance wouldn't be nice, but she was far more interested in the other things he'd mentioned. Passion… kisses…

"Of course, I'll dance with you. I'll dance with you the very next time I have the opportunity."

"Dance with me twice." He stared at her with breathtaking intensity, pushing her to break her own self-imposed rule, obviously wanting her to publicly state her preference for him in the only way that she could.

"All right. Twice." There would be gossip, but she didn't care. Let her father think on *that* for a while. Perhaps he'd realize character meant far more to her than any title.

Her answer seemed to release some of Captain Blake's earlier tension, but his gaze dropped a bit wistfully to her mouth. "I suppose I'll have to be content with my dances. But it's going to be more difficult than I ever imagined, to see you on my brother's arm and pretend I never wanted you for my own."

His words made her want to weep with the injustice of it all. Life was so unfair! She didn't want to marry a prince, nor the heir to some foolish title. She wanted *this* man, with his heroic heart, wounded soul, and beautiful mouth.

Perhaps, if she told her father what she really wanted—how much she cared for Captain Blake... It would be a risk, but what could it hurt to try?

Of course, even if the captain had her father's blessing, he might not want to marry her. He might be charming her just to see if he could.

The thought made her frown and tighten her fist on the reins. She wouldn't believe that, not until he gave her some reason to doubt him.

"You needn't worry. My father already has plans for me, and they don't include your brother."

He reached over and touched her gloved hand with his own, coaxing her to look at him. "What do you mean?"

She sighed and glanced back at Alec, knowing she didn't have much time. In just a few more minutes, she'd have to say goodbye and she still hadn't managed to learn anything new about her fascinating companion.

"I'm going to wed one of my mother's Russian cousins. My father has the mistaken idea I want to be a princess."

They'd reached the edge of the trees. He drew up his horse and stared at her with those intense gray eyes. "What *do* you want, Natalia? What would it take to make you happy?"

I want to be a captain's wife. I want a quiet life in the country with a man who loves me. I want to leave Society and all its rules behind.

But she wasn't brave enough to admit such things. Not when she still didn't know if he felt the same. Not until she'd spoken with her father and tried to make her foolish fantasy into something besides an impossible dream.

"I'll probably never have what I want." She smiled wistfully and glanced back at Alec, who looked more than a little nervous at the length of their chat. "And I fear it's time for me to go."

"I wouldn't want to get you in trouble." With hidden movements of his strong thighs, he coaxed his horse to make an elegant bow.

She laughed, enchanted. His equestrian skills went beyond riding into battle.

"Until we meet again then," he told her, his voice an intimate caress. "And don't forget about the dances."

"I won't." She let her gaze drop to his mouth and wished with all her heart for just five minutes alone with him.

"Goodbye. I'll see you soon." He reached out and squeezed her hand once more, then whirled his horse and disappeared through the trees.

Chapter Seven

Natalia wasn't surprised to find herself paired with Viscount Sherbourne at the elegant dinner party her father gave at his London townhouse on Wednesday night. She and the viscount were of roughly the same rank, after all, and Clarice had been in charge of the seating arrangements.

Her father gave her an approving smile as she entered the dining room on Michael Blake's arm. Natalia had rarely been the focus of the duke's approval, so she had no idea how to react. Apparently, Clarice's plan to marry her off to Sherbourne had a chance of success, a fact that only made things more complicated.

The huge, vaulted dining room boasted a table that would seat thirty. Crystal chandeliers bathed the elaborate dinner service in a warm glow, and her companion looked particularly handsome tonight as he pulled out her chair. As far as respective husbands went, Viscount Sherbourne truly was the pick of the litter. He was like her in so many ways, and they got along very well. She imagined kissing him would be pleasant, and she could easily imagine sharing her life with him.

There was only one little problem… *Captain Blake.*

His presence here tonight *was* a surprise. She couldn't imagine how he'd finagled an invitation, unless he'd managed to charm the duchess. Or perhaps Clarice thought it would please Sherbourne to have his brother present.

She would be horrified to know he was the very man she'd warned Natalia about.

In any event, Captain Blake was here, and it was impossible for Natalia to think about anything else. She had not expected to see him so soon after their meeting in the park.

Anticipation hummed through her veins. She couldn't wait until dinner ended and the dancing began. Even now, she could feel the captain's burning gaze on the back of her neck. It was all she could do to keep from turning around.

Diners of lower rank continued to file into the room, and Sherbourne tensed beside her. She raised an inquisitive brow, and he nodded over her shoulder toward the open doorway.

"I didn't know my brother had been invited." He sounded surprised and a little dismayed. "There he is, behind you, escorting Miss Marks."

She followed Sherbourne's gaze and attempted to appear as if she hadn't noticed the captain's presence. He'd abandoned his military dress and looked stunning in austere black evening wear. The somber color made him even more handsome and mysterious than usual.

The gorgeous American heiress on his arm had somehow managed to gain the support of the young Prince of Wales. Her dazzling emerald gown was inappropriate for an unmarried girl but complemented her black hair and dark eyes perfectly. Natalia's pale peach gown seemed downright dowdy in comparison.

Jealousy and doubt seared through Natalia as she stared at the handsome couple. Did Captain Blake also whisper sweet endearments to Emma Marks? Had he kissed her?

Given the frustrated look on Miss Marks's lovely face, the answer seemed to be no. The captain wasn't paying any attention to his attractive dinner companion. Instead, his concentration focused wholly on Natalia.

This evidence of his continued interest caused a familiar warmth low in the pit of her stomach. She hoped she wasn't blushing as deeply as she feared. "Dylan and I have met." His given name flowed off her tongue before she could stop it.

Captain Blake, she reminded herself harshly, but it was too late.

"Dylan?" Sherbourne frowned and glanced back and forth between them, obviously trying to figure out how they knew each other.

Dylan grinned. He met his brother's gaze for a long, tension-filled moment, and then glanced back toward Natalia. *"Dance with me."* He mouthed the words, but Natalia could understand them all too clearly.

"What did he say?" For the first time since she'd met him, Sherbourne's bland mask fell away, and fierce emotion filled his blue eyes. "What is going on between the two of you?"

She sensed his disapproval and knew he saw beyond her façade of dutiful obedience and respectability. "There's nothing between us. He's asked me to dance a few times, but I've always turned him down."

"I'll speak to him about it," Sherbourne said. "He won't bother you again."

A footman stepped between them to fill their wine glasses, and Natalia took that moment to compose herself. By the time the footman moved away, she'd managed to paste a smile on her face. "You needn't bother, Lord Sherbourne. I'm sure your brother's perfectly harmless."

She risked a quick look down the table and was pleased to see her cousin, Nigel, on Miss Marks's other side. Nigel might be without a title at the moment, but if the duke and Clarice were unable to produce an heir, Nigel would be next in line to inherit her father's. Nigel always looked out for his own interests, and marriage to someone like Miss Marks would be quite a boon. That way, he could maintain his accustomed lifestyle even if Clarice did manage to conceive a son.

Come on, Nigel. Be your usual arrogant self. Monopolize the conversation. She didn't want Captain Blake to fall under the spell of Miss Marks's many charms.

As dinner progressed, the conversation drifted on to other, safer topics, but Natalia could tell Sherbourne was still perplexed about what had transpired between her and the captain. Every few minutes, he sent a penetrating glance in his brother's direction, and Natalia knew he wouldn't leave the matter alone.

Apparently, he thought his brother had trespassed. Natalia felt a surge of guilt when she realized her own reckless actions had given Sherbourne the idea she cared more for him than she truly did.

She should never have allowed him to call on her.

But the damage was already done. All she could do now was try to let him know, in the kindest way possible, that her cap was set for his younger brother.

Society's rules exhausted her. For too long, she'd hidden her true thoughts and emotions and let her father's will carry her helplessly along.

Well, no more.

Tonight, she was going to dance with Dylan Blake. In fact, she was going to dance with him twice. Two *waltzes.*

She'd deal with the consequences tomorrow.

* * *

Dylan brooded over his dinner. He ignored the inane chatter of his companion, Miss Emma Marks, while cursing the fate that destined her to be his dinner partner.

"So, your father is an earl." Emma gazed at him in rapt delight. "Does that mean you'll be one, too, someday?"

The American was striking, but her drawling accent grated on his nerves, as did her admiration of the class system that was the bane of his existence. Apparently, the foolish chit planned to sell herself into marriage to get a title of her very own.

"Only if his older brother dies young," Nigel Sinclair interrupted caustically. Seated on Miss Marks's other side, Natalia's cousin had been making snide comments about Dylan ever since they'd sat down. Usually, Dylan would have been furious, but under the circumstances, he didn't mind. His thoughts centered on Natalia.

Still, he wondered a bit of his own disinterest. After all, Miss Marks's dowry was rumored to be even larger than Natalia's. And he would have to find a wife of his own, once he'd won the bet with Jonathan and secured the funds he needed for a courtship.

It would be so easy to dupe the lovely little American into believing his social status was higher than it actually was. He could play up the V.C, imply a knighthood might be forthcoming.

He stole a quick glance in Miss Marks's direction and knew he could do much worse. She was breathtaking.

Unfortunately, she wasn't Natalia Sinclair.

That thought brought him up short. And he realized with dazzling clarity that he'd let himself get far too involved with the duke's daughter.

"I'm sorry. I didn't realize." Miss Marks gave him an apologetic little smile. Despite her apparent polish, she didn't seem comfortable in Society.

He felt sorry for her and wondered whether she title hunted of her own accord or if her parents pressured her. He'd heard stories about her ruthless and vicious father. Had Black Jack Marks sent his daughter here to obtain the social cache all his gold mines and railroads couldn't buy him back in New York City?

Did they realize when she succeeded her millions would be spent to replace the roof of some moldering family pile instead of on expensive gowns and jewels? Far better to keep her money in America, where one's potential wasn't based upon the order of his birth.

At last, Emma allowed herself to be drawn into conversation with Sinclair, and Dylan concentrated his attention on the head of the table. His brother and Lady Natalia sat near the duke and duchess. Dylan had been relegated toward the very bottom with others of no particular social significance.

He supposed he should have felt privileged to have received an invitation at all. Luckily, the Duchess of Clayton was almost as easy to charm as his landlady.

Natalia and Michael seemed to be getting along quite well, although from time to time, Michael sent Dylan a calculating glance. Clearly, Michael understood he wasn't the only Blake interested in the fair Natalia.

With a moody sigh, Dylan quit watching them. He couldn't thwart Michael's success from this end of the table. Unfortunately, his gaze rested upon Jonathan Taylor, who held up two fingers and gave him an arrogant smirk.

Two more days.

If Dylan didn't get Natalia to agree to dance with him tonight, he'd lose the bet; he wouldn't attend another social event with her until after Jonathan's deadline passed. Dylan gave his old schoolmate a simmering glare, and Jonathan had the good sense to look away. Dylan glanced back at Natalia, feeling guilty for his deception but more resolved than ever.

The dancing couldn't possibly start soon enough.

Chapter Eight

After dinner, the small party adjourned to the ballroom, where a string quartet was tuning up behind a screen of potted palms. Dylan headed toward Natalia with single-minded determination, but Michael intercepted him.

"I need to talk to you." With a frown, Michael steered Dylan back the way he had come.

"What is it this time? Has Father sent you?" Dylan feigned ignorance, wanting to postpone the imminent lecture for as long as possible.

Michael shook his head and led Dylan down a long hallway. He stopped at the first open door, peered inside, and then beckoned Dylan to follow.

Dylan found himself in a small feminine sitting room, dimly lit by one small gas light in the corner. A dainty piece of embroidery laid over the arm of an upholstered chair. He traced the delicate leaves and vines with his fingertip, wondering if Natalia had been the one to leave it there.

"I never should have told you I was pursuing Lady Natalia." Closing the door, Michael leaned against the wall and fixed Dylan with a glare. "Do you find this amusing? Scheming to steal away her affection? Risking her reputation by whispering lewd suggestions across a crowded room?"

"I asked her to dance. I'd hardly call that a lewd suggestion."

Michael speared one hand through his perfectly arranged hair. Dylan had never seen him so agitated. "Why are you doing this? Does everything between us have to be a competition?"

Michael's barb stung, as he'd no doubt known it would. Dylan wondered if his brother regarded him the way he had Jonathan all these years. A pathetic little sod, always nipping unsuccessfully at his heels.

He hated the image but realized it was probably accurate. Still, he wasn't about to give up. Not now, not while there was still a chance he might win the wager. "Our father has been pitting us against each other since the day I was born. It is a miracle we haven't gone after the same girl before."

Michael shook his head in apparent disbelief. "Listen to yourself. Surely, you don't think you stand a chance at winning her hand? She's the Duke of Clayton's daughter, for Christ's sake!"

"Don't you think I know that?" Dylan glared at his brother, hating Michael's smug assurance. "I know the limitations of my position better than anyone. How could a penniless younger son possibly win against you, the future earl?"

"Is that what this is all about?" Michael lowered his voice, obviously ashamed of his earlier outburst. This rigid adherence to Society's rules, even in private, was what Dylan disliked the most about his brother. "I can't help being what I am any more than you can."

Dylan decided to bluff his way through this with single-minded bullheadedness. "I want this girl. I'm not going to give her up, just because you want her, too. She and I have gotten to know each other quite well during the last few weeks. I'm sure she'd choose me if she had any choice in the matter."

"Well, she doesn't have a choice." Tension laced Michael's voice. "Some of us don't have the luxury of choices. I have to marry whoever Father chooses, and so does Lady Natalia. You can't interfere. We need her dowry too badly."

"What are you talking about?" Dylan had always assumed the earl's fortune was limitless.

Michael sighed in frustration. "Must I give you a lesson in economics on top of everything else? Yes, we need her money. The country estates cost more than they bring in, and Father's gambling is out of control. We're in dire straits. If I don't marry Lady Natalia, I'll be forced to offer for that dreadful American heiress you dined with tonight."

"So, you want me to step aside? Let you save the old bastard from financial ruin, even if it means sacrificing your own happiness?" Dylan shook his head, all too aware of his own dire situation. "Why should I care if the earl needs money? It isn't as though I'll ever see a penny of it. He's cut me off for good, you know."

Michael's expression softened. "No. I didn't know that."

Dylan shrugged off the pity in his brother's voice. "It doesn't matter. Bound to happen sooner or later."

"How much do you need?" Michael's earlier tension vanished. "I have enough funds at the moment to offer some assistance."

"I don't want your money." The last thing Dylan needed was his brother's charity. He paced the room, trying to work things through in his mind, trying to orchestrate a scenario in which he might actually emerge from this little skirmish as the victor.

Finally, he sighed in angry frustration, conceding the futility. At least he had the satisfaction of knowing that Michael would fail, too. If the duke intended his daughter to wed a prince, the heir to an earldom would never do.

Petty of him, he knew. But he had no intention of letting Michael know he'd never win Natalia's hand. Not yet. Michael needed to know how it felt to aim too high.

"Just allow me to dance with Natalia tonight," Dylan muttered in resignation. "Then I'll give you a clear field and never bother either of you again."

"Why do you want to dance with her?" Michael eyed him with suspicion.

"Jonathan Taylor and I have a bet. If I can get Lady Natalia to dance with me twice in the same evening, I'll win two hundred pounds."

"A bet? You're willing to ruin this girl's reputation over a stupid bet?" Michael shook his head in disgust. "Christ, Dylan. Aren't you ever going to grow up?"

"I grew up the first time I had to send a man into battle and watch him die, so don't treat me like a child." Dylan managed to hold his anger in check, despite the overwhelming temptation to give in to it. Couldn't the bastard give him even this? "No matter what Father thinks, I'm not the devil. I won't ruin Lady Natalia's reputation with a few dances."

Michael turned away. He moved to one of the windows, his shoulders stiff with obvious anger of his own. Silence stretched between them for a long moment, but at last, Michael said, "All right. Go ahead and try to win your infernal dances."

Dylan breathed a sigh of relief. Perhaps he wouldn't be evicted, after all. And he could find another wealthy bride, perhaps a prosperous merchant's daughter.

Hell, maybe he should rethink his dinner companion, Miss Marks.

Unfortunately, at the moment, the thought gave him little pleasure. He still wanted Natalia. He couldn't imagine settling for anyone else.

"If you succeed, you'll have your 200 pounds," Michael continued. "If you don't, I'll pay off your debt to Jonathan. But either way, I want your word that you'll leave town tomorrow and stay gone until Lady Natalia and I are wed."

"Where the hell do you expect me to go?" Dylan asked in exasperation. Unlike his brother, he didn't receive a dozen house party invitations each week.

Michael turned around and gave Dylan a searching look. "I've never understood why you insisted on pissing your life away in the army, when you hated military life so much. Not when you could have lived at Aldabaran."

Aldabaran. Dylan closed his eyes and fought a wave of despair at the mere thought of his mother's family's Scottish estate.

Fiona Cameron Blake had taken her life when Michael was ten and Dylan a mere lad of seven. But until then, she and Dylan had journeyed to Aldabaran for three glorious months every summer. At Aldabaran, they'd ridden their horses through the heather, played games, and laughed with abandon, free of the earl's anger and Michael's shadow.

It was the only place on earth where Dylan had ever been happy.

"Don't make such an offer if you're not serious," Dylan told Michael, his voice unsteady. "You know how much I love Aldabaran. It's the only thing you own I covet."

It would kill him to live there and know it could never be his, but he'd gladly do so if Michael would let him.

Michael frowned. "What are you talking about? You know Aldabaran isn't mine. It's yours. And even if it were mine, I'd never keep you from going there."

"This isn't funny." Dylan's voice rose with hurt and anger. How could Michael jest about such a thing? "I have nothing of my own, Michael. Nothing. If Aldabaran truly belonged to me..." He shook his head and turned away, overwhelmed by the very thought. "Bloody hell. It would be a dream come true."

Michael squeezed Dylan's shoulder. "Christ. Didn't the old man ever tell you that grandfather left it to you?"

Dylan shuddered, afraid to believe Michael's words. "Do you think I'd have joined the army if I'd known? Do you think I'd beg Father for a stipend every month if I had anything of my own?"

"He told me you spent all the money." Michael's voice trembled with dawning understanding. "He said you had gambling debts and were too much of a wastrel to want the responsibility of running an estate of your own."

"That bastard." Dylan faced Michael again, not bothering to hide his anguish. "Why didn't you ever tell me this before?"

"I thought you knew." Michael looked sick about the whole matter.

"He's kept this from me ever since grandfather died? He's purposely made me dependent on him?" Dylan's fury mounted, but with it came an overwhelming sense of excitement.

Aldabaran is mine.

"I'm sorry. I've always hated the mere thought of the place... Because of Mother. I figured you felt the same way."

"Mother loved it there," Dylan whispered. "That's why she went there to die."

Michael swallowed hard and looked away. "You should go to Edinburgh. Speak to the solicitor, Mr. Byrnes. I believe he is in charge of your trust."

"I will. But first, I'm going to confront Father." The old bastard had a lot to answer for.

"Go to Scotland first," Michael advised, his face grim. "Secure your assets, think things through. Then come back and speak to Father."

When Dylan started to protest, Michael silenced him with a swift hard hug. "I'm sorry. I don't know why he treats you this way."

Michael's unexpected generosity made Dylan feel like the worst kind of an ass. Once again, Michael had proven himself to be the better man.

"If you pay off my debt to Jonathan, I won't dance with Natalia. But I must warn you, she's already promised to a Russian prince." Dylan hoped to make amends by telling his brother the truth, guilty for not having done so in the beginning.

Michael laughed and squeezed Dylan once more before he let him go. "Thanks for the warning, little brother. But I'm not worried. You're far more competition than any prince could ever be."

Chapter Nine

Natalia's heart pounded with nervous anticipation when the Blake brothers returned to the ballroom. They'd left half an hour ago, and she had been on pins and needles ever since. She liked both men and didn't want to be the cause of any further strain in their relationship.

Sherbourne scanned the room. When his gaze lit upon Natalia, he gave her a bright smile. Whenever he and the captain had discussed, he was obviously pleased with the result.

Captain Blake, however, refused to meet her gaze.

Oh, this was so unfair! Apparently, they'd decided Sherbourne was to have her.

Why had the captain bowed to his brother's demands? How could he? She didn't want him to give up on her now. Not when she was finally ready to take a chance and discover whether the reality of being in his arms lived up to the promise in his burning gray eyes.

Viscount Sherbourne had claimed her as his prize, but he had no right. His Greek God looks, title, and bland good manners didn't interest her. She liked her angels fallen. For the first time in her life, she wanted something enough to fight for it.

So few things were within her control, but in this one matter, she had the power to bend circumstances to her will. She wanted to dance with Dylan Blake tonight. Perhaps she'd even sneak away with him for that promised kiss. And she wasn't going to let Lord Sherbourne or even her father stand in her way.

She made her way through the crowd to stand by their side. "Hello," she said breathlessly, breaking every rule of etiquette she could think of.

A lady should never approach a gentleman. She should never initiate a conversation. And never, under any condition, should she scheme to find herself alone with one so he could kiss her.

Sherbourne raised a disapproving brow at her unladylike behavior, but the captain continued to ignore her. It was unnerving—she'd grown accustomed to being the center of his attention. He stared at the hem of her gown, a muscle ticking in his lean jaw, as he obviously tried to pretend she didn't exist.

"Lady Natalia," Sherbourne said, recovering from his shock. "I was just telling my brother what a delightful dinner companion you were."

At that, the captain laughed, the sound tinged with a touch of bitterness. He still didn't look at her. "Oh, indeed."

Sherbourne scowled at his brother, then returned his gaze to Natalia. "Will you do me the honor of the first waltz, Lady Natalia?"

She shook her head, enjoying the moment. Sherbourne was a nice enough fellow, but he needed to be taken down a peg or two. "I'm sorry, Lord Sherbourne. I'm afraid I'll have to decline."

She shifted her gaze to the captain, feeling as though she were about to jump off a very steep precipice with nothing beneath her to break the fall. "You see, I've already promised the first dance to your brother."

* * *

She chose me.

Dylan lifted his gaze, feeling off-kilter, as though he'd had the wind knocked out of him. He didn't know how to react to Natalia's unexpected pronouncement.

After weeks of obsessive pursuit, she was finally giving in. Now. When it was too late.

He shared a quick glance with Michael, who looked even more stunned than he was. Neither of them had anticipated this. But what the hell did Michael expect? Was he supposed to refuse her? *Not bloody likely.*

Giving his brother an apologetic shrug, Dylan turned the full force of his delighted smile on Natalia, enchanted by the look of tentative happiness in her beautiful emerald eyes. "Of course. Our dance. I'd almost forgotten."

Ignoring Michael's low mutter of dismay, Dylan took Natalia's small gloved hand and led her onto the dance floor. It was only a dance, he told himself, pushing away a twinge of guilt. Just one dance, and it had nothing to do with that infernal bet.

He just wanted to hold this lovely unattainable girl in his arms for a few breathless minutes, secure in the knowledge that she'd chosen him over Michael. Then he would walk away, go to Aldabaran, and begin a new life. One that was far simpler than the chaotic, unhappy existence he been living here in London.

The music swirled around them as he led her into the simple steps of the waltz. Her hand was warm and welcoming on his shoulder, and he couldn't remember ever being quite so enamored.

He caught sight of Jonathan, lurking behind Michael, and felt a moment of sweet dark triumph. It didn't matter that he'd already promise Michael he would concede the bet. He'd always have the satisfaction of knowing he could have won, if he'd wanted to.

"Your brother has warned you off, hasn't he?" Natalia stared at him, her wide bright eyes drinking him in, as though she wished to memorize this moment, and him, for all time. "Sherbourne told you he plans to offer for me. Or, more correctly, for my dowry."

Dylan nodded, surprised by her accurate assessment of the situation. "The old man has given him strict orders to land you. And I'm supposed to slink off to my estate in Scotland, posthaste, before I tarnish your reputation."

My estate.

He'd waited his entire life to say those two simple words, and the need to share his good news with her overwhelmed him. He longed for a quiet dark place where they could have a few moments alone. He wanted to tell someone about his amazing stroke of good fortune. He wanted to ask her what she thought he should do about the fact that his father had kept his inheritance from him for so long.

Such uncharacteristic thoughts alarmed him. It might be a good thing he'd just given up the right to share anything with her.

A flicker of unmistakable disappointment crossed her lovely features. "So, you're just going to give up on me? Bow to their wishes? Run away with your tail between your legs?"

He frowned, shocked by her audacity, stunned by the cowardly picture she painted. "Why should I stay? You haven't given me any encouragement. No reason to believe you care for me in the slightest."

"Doesn't this dance prove anything? I do care for you. I care for you very much." She seemed surprised by her words, but she didn't try to take them back. Instead, she squeezed his hand, her small fingers lost in his much larger ones. "You said you weren't interested in my dowry."

"I'm not." At least not anymore, he reasoned to himself, once again feeling enormous guilt. He should never have used her weaknesses against her. He felt a sudden intense urge to make it up to her.

"You're a very beautiful woman." He wished she could see herself through his eyes, if only for an instant. "You shouldn't worry that men only want you for the money you'll bring."

She gave him a tremulous smile. "You also said you wanted to make me laugh, to kiss me, and show me passion."

He stumbled, the steps of the waltz forgotten as she repeated his own reckless words. Fear tempered the challenge in her eyes. He doubted she'd ever spoken so incautiously in all her life.

"What are you saying?" He forced himself to move back into the steps of the waltz, pretending nothing was amiss, even though she'd just turned his every expectation of her upside down. Natalia Sinclair had chosen him over his brother. That fact alone made him fall a little bit in love with her. "Are you telling me you want those things as well?" All thoughts of the bargain he'd struck with Michael fled his mind.

"I want to be with you," she whispered, all in a rush, as though she couldn't quite believe her own words. "Alone. Can you meet me in the rose garden in about an hour?"

He knew he should say no. He'd just promised his brother he'd quit pursuing her. But he couldn't walk away without ever knowing if this thing between them was truly as powerful as it seemed. "Of course, I'll be there." How could he say no?

* * *

After dancing with the captain, Natalia waited fifteen endless minutes before approaching her father and Clarice. They were deep in conversation, and Clarice seemed upset. Torn, Natalia was about to turn away, but Clarice saw her hovering and beckoned her near.

"Natalia, darling. Are you having a nice time?" The duchess was obviously glad of the distraction, and Natalia felt terrible about her intended deception.

"Actually, I'm feeling rather ill. I think I'll go up to my room and rest a bit."

Clarice placed one slender, bejeweled hand on Natalia's forehead, her lovely face full of concern. "You don't feel hot. Is it your stomach?"

Natalia nodded and turned to her father. "Would you mind if I left the party early, Father?"

The duke stared at her for a long moment, but her flushed face and the tremors of excitement she couldn't conceal seemed to convince him she was truly sick. "Go ahead, I'll make your excuses."

Hardly daring to believe her luck, she fled the ballroom as quickly as propriety would allow, careful not to glance in Captain Blake's direction even once. She didn't want her disappearance linked to the one he'd make in just a little less than forty-five minutes.

Once inside her room, she dismissed her maid, Cora. She refused to allow the girl to unlace her gown on the pretense she might want to return to the ball later, after she'd rested a bit. Then she sat in a chintz-covered chair in front of the fireplace.

With so much time to analyze her actions, she couldn't help but regret her impetuous actions. Whatever had she been thinking? If she were found out, it would ruin her.

Was it worth it, to risk so much over a man she barely knew?

Closing her eyes, she remembered the way it felt to be in his arms—the intensity in those beautiful gray eyes when she'd told him she wanted to see him in private. He'd seemed so surprised to have finally won her favor, so genuinely glad she'd admitted her feelings.

Hugging herself tightly, she knew she'd risk anything to have that again. To have more than that. A kiss. A caress. Sweet words in the dark…

As Clarice had so eloquently reminded her, she was running out of time. This would be her one act of rebellion. The only thing she'd ever done for herself.

Tomorrow, she would once again become the duke's dutiful daughter. She would marry whomever he decided without one whisper of complaint. She could endure anything, as long as she had memories of a night with Dylan to keep her company.

The minutes crawled by, but at last, the appointed time arrived, and she crept out of her room and down the long silent hall. She descended the back stairs, her heart pounding in her chest as she evaded the busy servants.

Once outside, she breathed in the crisp rose-scented air and made her way to the secluded nook of the garden where she'd arranged to meet Captain Blake. A stone bench covered by a small wooden arbor squatted in the corner against the wall. This area was hidden by an overgrown hedge and was the perfect place for an illicit tryst.

Time passed, and her panic grew as she faced a fear that hadn't even occurred to her before. What if he didn't come?

Thankfully, she didn't have to contemplate such a horrible thought for long. He materialized out of the darkness, a tall lean figure dressed in black. As he rounded the hedge, a shaft of light from the house illuminated his stark male beauty. His pale gaze locked with hers for one heartrending moment before he stepped back into the shadows.

Enchanted, she stood and moved toward him. He caught her in his arms, spun her round and round, and laughed beneath his breath. After a moment, he stopped, and she buried her face against his chest.

"I didn't think you were going to come." She reveled in the simple pleasure of his embrace. Her father was not a demonstrative man, and she couldn't remember the last time anyone had simply held her.

Not that being held by Dylan Blake was like anything she'd ever experienced. His strength and warmth seeped beneath her skin and cradled her very heart. His scent, a clean, crisp mix of soap and leather, overwhelmed her. She didn't want him to ever let her go.

He raised her chin so he could meet her gaze, his own eyes full of rueful amusement. "I shouldn't have. I didn't intend to. But in the end, I couldn't bear to let this moment slip away."

She lifted her hand and touched his cheek with her fingertips. "I'm so glad you're here."

He held her for a moment more and then looked over his shoulder, as though to ensure no one else was around. Satisfied, he pulled her toward the bench, taking them farther out of sight.

She settled beside him, so close her skirts brushed his thigh. Holding her gaze, he took her wrist and unbuttoned her glove. Intimacy wrapped around them like a blanket, and her pulse accelerated as he peeled the glove away. When he finished, he tucked the scrap of silk into his breast pocket and lifted her hand to his lips.

His mouth was warm and surprisingly soft against the center of her palm. She inhaled sharply, and he looked up at her through those extravagant lashes, a troubled frown turning down the corners of his sensuous lips.

"Why me? You're taking a huge risk, meeting me this way. I don't understand."

She didn't really understand herself, but she sensed he wanted far more from her than a glib reply. "I fell in love with the very thought of you," she admitted, embarrassed by the naïve young girl she'd been such a short while ago. "I've read all the newspaper articles of your exploits, and I desperately wanted to meet the hero, Captain Blake."

"I'm not a hero, Natalia." As he spoke, he stroked her palm with the warm pad of his thumb. The sensation melted something deep inside her, and she had a hard time remembering what she wanted to say.

"You risked your life to save someone else's. If that's not the definition of heroism, I don't know what is."

He gave a bitter laugh and shook his head, as though he couldn't believe the extent of her foolishness. "What was I to do? Leave those men to die? There was no heroism involved. Anyone else would have done the same thing."

"No," she whispered. "Most people would have only worried about their own necks. They wouldn't have gone back into the fray three times to drug wounded men to safety."

"Well, if you thought me such a hero and were so eager to meet me, why did you rebuff me the first time I asked you to dance?" He closed his hand around hers and stared into her eyes as though he could somehow see inside her soul. "You realized right away I wasn't the man you thought me to be."

She'd thought she'd managed to hide her true feelings so well. But perhaps that was one of the things she liked best about him—he understood her in a way no one else ever had.

"I was disappointed," she admitted. "You didn't seem sincere, and I thought you were like all the others, the ones who looked at me but didn't see anything but my dowry."

"What changed your mind?"

"I liked your persistence. And once I got to know you a little better, I realized the real you was far more interesting than the Captain Blake I'd read about in the newspapers."

"The real me? Who do you think I am?" Dylan wasn't certain he wanted to hear her answer. She seemed determined to strip away all his masks, and he didn't want her to see what remained. What would she think when confronted with the sniveling coward who was scared to fall asleep at night because of the nightmares that haunted his dreams?

She squeezed his hand. "You're lonely. You want someone to care about, and you want someone to care about you."

He dropped his gaze, stunned by the truth behind her words. "I'm not lonely," he told her sharply. But he was. Oh, he was. "I've had a dozen mistresses since I returned."

"I know you have. I've heard the rumors about the courtesans and the actresses." If he'd shocked her, she didn't show it. She just kept on, relentlessly. "But did you care for a single one of them? And, more importantly, did a single one of them truly care for you?"

He thought of Cassandra and the others, how empty he'd felt in their arms. They'd never pestered him about his past, never made him feel anything at all. Instinctively, he knew if he ever made love to Natalia, it would be the most beautiful experience of his life.

"I never cared about any of them," he admitted, meeting her gaze once again. "But I do care about you."

"Oh, Dylan." Taking a deep breath, she leaned forward until they were mere inches apart. "I wanted to do this so badly the last time I saw you." With a trembling hand, she reached out and cupped his cheek, gently stroking the line of his jaw.

His pulse accelerated at her innocent caress, and it thrilled him that she'd used his given name. Christ, they hadn't even kissed yet, and he was already painfully aroused.

"You wanted to touch my face?" he asked, tenderly amused.

"Since the first time I met you. But that's not what I meant." She wrapped her arms around his shoulders, and then pressed her face against his neck, giving him a fierce hug. "I'm sorry you lost your friends. I wish there was something I could do to ease your pain."

Shocked by her words, his first impulse was to resist her. He tried to duck away, but she hung on, refusing to let him go.

"It's all right." Her soft lips moved against the sensitive skin of his throat. "Just let me comfort you for a moment."

She wants to comfort me. He wasn't sure whether to laugh or cry. In the end, all he could do was put his arms around her and hold on.

Closing his eyes, he sank back against the wall and let her warmth and sweetness surround him, reveling in the pure uncomplicated beauty of the moment. He couldn't remember ever having received such a precious, unselfish gift.

At long last, she pulled away, her cheeks blazing with color, her green eyes hopeful, yet painfully uncertain. God, she was so beautiful. He'd never wanted anything the way he wanted to kiss her.

Leaning forward, he cupped her face in his hands. "Thank you." He smoothed his fingertips over her soft skin, learning her features by touch.

She went still and stared up at him with those exotic trusting eyes, waiting breathlessly for whatever he chose to do next.

"Tell me to stop." He feared once he crossed this line, he could never go back.

"No." She tucked a strand of his hair behind his ear with trembling fingertips. "I want you to kiss me. I've wanted it for so long."

Undone by her words, he closed the distance between them and feathered his lips to hers with infinite restraint. "You are so sweet. I don't ever want to let you go."

The poignancy of the moment, of knowing this was the only time he would ever have her in his arms, was a powerful aphrodisiac. He deepened the kiss, tasted the honeyed sweetness of her mouth, and inhaled her startled breath.

Tentatively, she returned his kiss, and he moaned at her passionate untutored response. Her hands fluttered restlessly over his chest and shoulders. He shuddered to think of what it would feel like if she were to touch him lower, where he needed her so much.

The chill breeze ruffled his hair, and the intoxicating scent of roses mingled with her own sweet fragrance. He kissed her as though he would die if he stopped. One fleeting thought entered his mind—*I'm not lonely anymore.*

Chapter Ten

"Get away from my daughter, you bastard!" The Duke of Clayton's furious voice jolted through Dylan's passion-soaked brain like a bolt of lightning. Ice cascaded through his veins as he glanced up and saw the duke closing in, murder in his eyes.

Natalia jerked away and fumbled with the neckline of her gown, which he'd only just managed to lower. But it was too late. Her father had seen everything.

Dylan lifted a placating hand and searched for a possible explanation. Before he could say anything, the duke blindsided him with a right hook. Dylan reeled backward, stunned by the brute force of the older man's blow.

"Father, no!" Natalia cried, trying to put herself between them, but the duke pushed her out of the way, intent on his goal. She stumbled and fell, hitting her head on a stone bench with a resounding crack.

"Natalia!" Dylan tried to go to her, but as he gained his feet, the duke glanced a punishing blow off his left temple, followed with a swift jab to his gut. Dylan bent forward, gasping and trying to catch his breath.

For a moment, he thought he might lose consciousness, but worry for Natalia eclipsed his pain. When the duke moved to strike again, Dylan lifted his arm and blocked the blow. He deserved every bit of the duke's fury, but enough was enough.

"Just hold on a minute," Dylan growled. "Let me see if Natalia's all right."

"I'll check on her." Much to Dylan's dismay, Michael stepped from behind the hedge and knelt by Natalia's side.

Christ, this was just what he needed. Had all of London invaded their privacy? He kept a wary eye on the duke, ready to fight back if the old man tried anything else. He focused the rest of his attention on Natalia and his brother.

God, he'd made a colossal mess of everything.

Michael pulled Natalia to a sitting position and gently probed the back of her head. He murmured to her in a concerned undertone, but his reproachful gaze locked with Dylan's.

"Are you all right, daughter?" Chagrin replaced the old man's anger when he realized he'd hurt Natalia.

"Yes." Natalia's ragged voice, choked with tears, was not very convincing. "Yes, I'm fine."

Dylan tried not to think about the look of betrayal on Michael's face. The confrontation with his brother would have to wait. The most important thing right now was Natalia. There was only one thing he could do, given the circumstances. And although he realized this was exactly what he'd wanted all along, he hated that it had come about in this manner.

He took a deep breath and turned to face the enraged duke once again. "Your Grace, I apologize for my behavior tonight."

The duke shook his head. "Your apology is not accepted, young man."

Dylan tried again. "I care for your daughter very deeply, sir. I never meant to compromise her. Please, let me make this right. Let me marry her."

"Never. I would die before I allowed my daughter to marry a fortune hunter like you."

Dylan flinched, stung by the duke's contempt. "I may not be titled or wealthy, but I promise to be good to her. I would never hurt her in any way."

Natalia got to her feet and moved to Dylan's side. Her anguished gaze met his, and she lifted her hand to dab a bit of blood from his lip.

"I love you," she said, loud enough for both her father and Michael to hear. "And I'm so sorry about all of this."

Then she squared her shoulders and turned to face the duke. "Please, Father. I'm begging you. Let me marry Captain Blake. I'll never be happy if you force me to wed someone else."

She loves me. All of Dylan's anger, regret, and embarrassment faded away. None of that mattered, not if she truly meant what she said. He reached out and squeezed her hand to let her know how much her words meant to him.

The duke stared at them in brooding silence. Dylan was peripherally aware that Michael had left the three of them alone. Natalia trembled like a leaf in the wind. She held his hand so tightly he could no longer feel his fingertips.

"You shame me, Natalia." The duke's soft words were brutal, despite their lack of heat. "I can't believe you are foolish enough to believe this young man cares for you. Don't you know he only lured you out here to fulfill some sort of rakehell's bet? He's 200 pounds richer because you gave into him so easily."

* * *

A bet. Natalia lifted her gaze to Dylan's, afraid of what she might find. *Please, let this be a lie.* There had to be a mistake. Her father had made it up in order to turn her against the man she loved.

Dylan shook his head, but desperation filled his eyes. So much guilt…

Father's not lying.

Bitter tears sprang to her eyes, and her knees threatened to give way as she confronted the bitter truth. It all made sense now—all his sweet words and relentless pursuit. He wanted something from her, just like all the others.

"It did start out as a bet," Dylan admitted, his voice rough and low. "But I didn't come out here tonight because of that. To win the bet, all I had to do was dance with you twice. If all I'd wanted was the damn money, then why didn't I just convince you to dance with me again?"

"Because you didn't want to settle for 200 pounds?" She put two and two together and reached a sum that destroyed her soul. "Because you realized all you had to do was compromise me, and you could have my entire dowry."

She released his hand, and it seemed as though every ounce of warmth in her body drained away with the loss of his touch. He'd stolen her heart and her innocence. She'd been such a fool.

"It could have been anyone," he whispered. "I could have chosen Emma Marks. Her dowry is even larger than yours. But I didn't want her, Natalia. I want you."

"Do you expect me to be grateful you chose me for your deception?" Self-preservation took over and turned her hurt into angry contempt. She put a hand to her aching temple, feeling as though her head would explode. "I'm sorry I ever met you."

Then she stepped away, crossing the distance to her father's side. Far safer in the duke's shadow. She wondered now why she had been so eager for danger and excitement.

Her father gave her one pitying, exasperated look, then turned his attention back to Dylan. "For the sake of your brother and your father, who are honorable men, I'll let you leave here tonight, but if you ever breathe a word of this to anyone, I'll ruin you. Do you understand me?"

All the emotion bled from Dylan's expression. His eyes became as wintry and empty as they'd been the first time he asked her to dance.

"Of course. I understand perfectly." Then he turned and walked away, leaving Natalia to face her father's wrath alone.

Chapter Eleven

Dylan strode away from Natalia and the duke, disappointment and regret fueling every step. He wanted a quiet place to lick his wounds, needed a few solitary moments to process all the ways in which the evening had gone wrong.

There had to be a way to make things right.

Michael caught up with him near the back of the house, but Dylan didn't even slow down. He wasn't ready to have this conversation. Not on top of everything else.

Michael stopped him with a firm grip on his upper arm. "Don't you dare walk away from me. I think you owe me an explanation, at the very least."

The two brothers stared at each other for a few endless moments. In Michael's eyes, Dylan saw more than mere anger. He saw revulsion and absolute dislike.

Michael had never hated him. Until now.

Dylan looked away first, unable to bear the reproach. "I'm sorry. I never meant to hurt you."

"You didn't think it would hurt me, to find you in a compromising situation with the woman I have to marry?" Michael laughed, a bitter exhalation of sound. "Damn you, Dylan. You gave me your word."

Dylan bowed his head in chagrin. "I know you think you have a chance of winning her heart, but I already told you her father plans to marry her to a prince. And when she asked me to meet her in the garden..." He shook his head in self-reproach. "I should have said no, but I wanted her so damned much."

"Do you think that makes it all right?" Michael stepped away, putting more distance between them. "Not that it's any of your business, but when the duke approached me this evening, he all but implied Lady Natalia was mine if I wanted her." Michael ran his hand through his hair. "You've ruined everything. I'll have to marry that obnoxious little American."

"This doesn't change anything. You can still marry Natalia." Dylan's whole heart rebelled at the thought. But after what had happened here tonight, he knew the duke would make her wed someone else as soon as possible. At least Michael would treat her with respect and kindness. "None of this was her fault."

"You want me to marry a woman I can't trust? Spend the rest of my life worrying that every time I go to my wife's bed, it's you she's imagining beside her?" Michael shook his head. "I think I'll pass on that particular form of hell."

Dylan made a soft sound of frustration. "I said I'm sorry. What else do you want me to do?"

Michael gave him a long measuring look. "We're not children anymore. You can't say you're sorry and make everything all right. It's done. It's over. There's nothing you can do to take it back."

Dylan knew he deserved his brother's harsh words. He nodded once, abruptly, and accepted Michael's judgment.

"I'm through trying to fix your mistakes." Michael shook his head again. "Go to Scotland. Don't ever come back. There's nothing left for you here."

Then the only person who still cared about Dylan turned and walked away, leaving him alone in the duke's garden.

Aching. Knowing he deserved it.

* * *

Natalia's father escorted her back to her room in utter silence. Anger and frustration emanated from him in a wave, but somehow, he managed to restrain from any further recrimination.

Thank God. She couldn't bear to be berated any further. She felt emotionally naked, stripped and laid bare by the evening's events. She'd gone from the heights of joy to the depths of despair, all in a matter of moments, and she was still reeling.

"We'll speak about the consequences of your actions in the morning," he told her gruffly, when they reached her door. "Don't leave this room again tonight."

"I'm sorry. I never meant for any of this to happen."

"I know," he said, softening a little. "Don't worry. We'll find you a husband who's worthy of you. Perhaps Sherbourne or Prince Nikolai will still agree to the match. No one need ever know about the mistake you made tonight." He pressed an awkward kiss on the painful bump on her temple, and then hurried away.

Mistake.

She shut her door and undressed by herself, unwilling to call for her maid when she needed privacy so badly. Her movements were stiff and awkward, and her head still ached from the fall she'd taken.

Father was right; it had been a terrible mistake to meet Dylan in the garden. Her gullibility shamed her, as did her passionate response to his sweet kisses.

He'd played her like a musician strums an instrument, said all the things she wanted to hear, and led her irrevocably into a trap of her own making. She shouldn't have believed his pretty words. After all, she'd heard the rumors about his many affairs. She'd known no woman had ever managed to capture his attention for more than a moment or two.

But she'd wanted to fall in love so badly.

So, she'd constructed a phantom hero, someone who met all her criteria and just happened to be named Captain Dylan Blake. Then, when the actual man came along, she'd tried to force him into a suit of armor that had never quite suited him.

She should have trusted her first instincts and listened to her head, not her heart. She'd known he wasn't the man she wanted him to be the very first night she'd met him. Why hadn't she been more careful? Why hadn't she thought things through before behaving so rashly? She should have chosen someone else on whom to bestow her kisses. Someone manageable like Viscount Sherbourne.

With a sigh, she hung her wilted gown over the back of a chair for the maid to take care of in the morning. Finally, redressed in a warm flannel nightgown, she slipped into her bed and took several long deep breaths, trying to calm her frazzled nerves.

It was no use. She couldn't stop thinking about Dylan, couldn't stop the tears from falling. Merely a trickle at first, they quickly gained momentum as she mourned her lost innocence.

When Dylan looked at her, he had made her feel like the center of his world. She'd been thoroughly taken in by him, so she supposed she deserved whatever fate her father chose to hand her. She couldn't believe she'd fallen for a pair of mysterious eyes and a cocky grin.

Stupid. So very stupid.

When all her emotion was spent and she laid in her lonely bed, staring up at the ceiling with dry burning eyes, all she could think about was that kiss. She couldn't forget the way Dylan's hand had felt upon the tender slope of her breast. In his arms, she'd felt gloriously alive.

Her worst fear was living the rest her life without ever again knowing that feeling.

* * *

After his confrontation with Michael, Dylan returned to his rented rooms. He spent the rest of the night drinking himself into oblivion, trying to forget the utter mess he'd made of his life.

It didn't work. Every time he closed his eyes, thoughts of the people he'd betrayed haunted him. Michael—finally washing his hands of his black sheep brother, once and for all. Natalia—her beautiful green eyes filled with reproach, her professed love turning to bitter anger.

In the end, he didn't even have the bloody 200 pounds to show for the whole debacle. He'd never gotten Natalia to agree to a second dance. Instead, he'd compromised her beyond his wildest dreams, after promising Michael he wouldn't.

He couldn't blame Natalia and his brother for hating him. And he couldn't blame Mrs. Tweed for finely serving him with an eviction notice.

Fumbling in his breast pocket, he drew out Natalia's pilfered gloved. He lifted it to his face and inhaled her faint scent. His life had been empty for a very long time, but until tonight, he'd never realized how much he longed for what he'd glimpsed in Natalia's eyes. Friendship. Love. Hope.

The mere thought of what he'd lost made him sick with yearning, so he made a conscious effort to turn his thoughts away from Natalia. Instead, he distilled his pain into anger and focused it on his father.

As happy as he'd been to learn his grandfather had left him Aldabaran, it killed him to know he'd spent twelve years in the army for nothing. How could his father have kept something like that from him?

He'd struggled all his life to discover the innate flaw that turned everyone who should have loved him away in disgust. Even his mother had abandoned him.

Michael had counseled him to go to Aldabaran immediately, but he knew he couldn't leave London without confronting his father. Perhaps he was a glutton for punishment, but he needed to focus on discovering why the earl had hidden the inheritance— it was far less painful to think about confronting his father than to dwell on the look in Natalia's eyes when she discovered the truth about the wager.

* * *

"Natalia, darling. It's time to wake up."

Natalia groaned, covering her head with the blanket, and tried to ignore Clarice for as long as possible. Her head felt as though it been trampled by a herd of elephants. When she explored her scalp with her hand, she found a large bump near her temple. She winced. How had that happened? Bad memories hovered at the edge of her consciousness, but instinct warned her not to examine them too closely.

"Natalia, wake up." Clarice would not go away. She pulled relentlessly at Natalia's blankets, until there was nothing left to hide beneath.

With a sigh, Natalia opened her eyes and found her stepmother hovering next to her bed. "What time is it?"

"It's just after six." A frown creased Clarice's lovely face. "You look terrible. Are you truly ill, on top of everything else?"

Everything else. Last night's events came rushing back, despite her best attempts to keep them at bay. Natalia buried her face in her hands and wished Clarice had let her sleep. Time to face the consequences of her actions, but she wasn't ready. She'd rather turn back the clock and make different choices. How differently she'd behave, if given the chance.

"I'm not sick." Natalia flinched inwardly at the sound of her own scratchy voice. "But my head is throbbing, and my eyes feel like boiled onions."

"I've had that malady before. It comes from crying yourself to sleep." Clarice sighed and sat down on the edge of Natalia's bed with a rustle of lavender-scented skirts. "Why didn't you tell me Dylan Blake was the man who'd caught your attention? I would never have invited him to the party last night, if I'd known."

Natalia forced herself to sit up and brushed a limp curl of hair from her eyes. "Don't blame yourself. I would have found a way to meet him, with or without your help."

"Dylan Blake." Clarice shook her head. "What were you thinking, darling?"

"Apparently, I wasn't thinking at all." Natalia looked away, unable to bear Clarice's censure.

To her surprise, Clarice leaned forward and dropped her voice to a whisper. "He is one of the most beautiful men I've ever seen. Was it sheer bliss to kiss him? You must tell me everything."

Clarice had done the right thing. She'd married for duty instead of love. She would never understand what Natalia had experienced in Dylan's arms. Personally, Natalia wished she had remained ignorant. She'd learned the hard way that passion only led to a broken heart.

"It was wonderful." She fought a new rush of tears. "He was so sweet, so tender. I love him, Clarice. I thought he really cared about me as well. How could I have been such a fool?"

Clarice gave her a fierce hug. "Falling in love isn't foolish. I just wish you would have chosen someone worthy of you."

"Someone like Sherbourne?" Natalia remembered how kind he'd been to her last night. He undoubtedly felt betrayed by both her and his brother, but he hadn't offered one word of reproach.

Clarice drew away, her blue eyes filled with speculation. "Would you still consider a marriage to Sherbourne? He's not to blame for what his brother did."

Natalia shook her head, unwilling to entertain the thought even for a moment. "I don't want to marry anyone. Not for a very long time."

Clarice frowned. "I'm afraid time is something you no longer have."

Natalia closed her eyes as she came to terms with the gravity of her situation. "Father wants me to marry Sherbourne?"

Clarice nodded. "The duke has made some inquiries, and he's discovered the Earl of Warren is having serious financial problems. Michael Blake needs your dowry, and his reputation is above reproach."

"Everyone needs my dowry." Natalia gave a bitter laugh. "Just this once, I thought I'd found someone who needed me."

"You could still marry Captain Blake, if that's what you want." Clarice watched her closely, as though trying to see into her very soul. "Now that he's had a little time to think things through, I think your father would allow it. He wants you to be happy."

Her father wanted her to be happy? Natalia felt guilty for all the angry thoughts she'd had about the duke in the past. But if he truly gave her a choice in the matter, after what had happened, how could she disappoint him?

Her heart urged her to pick Dylan, despite what he'd done, but she refused to be weak and foolish again. "All right. Tell my father I've agreed to marry Viscount Sherbourne."

At least she didn't have to worry that Michael Blake would break her heart. His brother had already beaten him to it.

Chapter Twelve

Whenever at home, the Duke of Clayton could be found in his library. He'd created a sanctuary out of the huge two-story room with its dark heavy furniture and thousands of leather-bound books. He rarely allowed anyone except the cleaning staff to intrude upon his privacy. Natalia knew it couldn't be a good sign when he summoned her there late that afternoon.

Standing in the hallway outside the library door, she crumpled the note he'd sent her into a tight little ball. Realizing what she'd done, she tried to smooth it back out again then forced herself to take a deep breath and calm down.

It wasn't easy. This would be the first time she'd faced her father since he'd escorted her to her bedchamber door last night.

She shouldn't be so worried. No doubt he'd merely called her down here to inform her Sherbourne had agreed to divest her of her enormous dowry. And that was what she wanted, wasn't it? Gathering every last shred of her courage, she tapped on the wide oak door.

"Come in," the duke called.

She slipped into the room and found her father sitting behind his massive mahogany desk. A pensive frown creased his grim face as he motioned her toward the nearest chair. "Sit down, Natalia."

She did as he asked, relieved to see no sign of Michael Blake. Michael would have to be dealt with, but she wasn't ready to look into his warm blue eyes and see her own sins reflected back at her.

Perhaps she never would be.

The duke stared at her for a long moment, then made a small sound of frustration and shook his head. "I've spoken to Sherbourne. The bloody fool won't have you."

The duke's obvious anger and astonishment might have been amusing, under any other circumstances. She doubted anyone had ever opposed him before. As it was, Natalia didn't know what to feel. Relief, but she also battled with chagrin and uncertainty. Apparently, even her dowry wasn't enough to make a man want her now.

She cleared her throat and tried to remain calm. "We should have realized Sherbourne would balk at this. He has far too much pride to marry someone whose reputation isn't above reproach." Appearances were very important to Michael—as they were to her father.

The duke tapped the end of a quill pen on his desk. "It's of no consequence. I told you I would take care of you, and I meant it."

"What do you want me to do?" Natalia asked, overcome with dread. She hadn't been happy about the match with Sherbourne. But at least she'd come to accept it.

The duke shook his head. "Things have become even more complicated. After leaving Sherbourne, I stopped by my club. While I was there, at least four people asked me if I was going to force Captain Blake to marry you. Apparently, someone else witnessed your tryst in the garden."

Nausea twisted in the pit of Natalia's stomach. Dear God. Everyone knew. It had been bad enough when she thought only Michael and her father had been privy to last night's calamity. How could she ever hold up her head again?

"Who do you think told? Was it Dylan?" Perhaps this was yet another of his underhanded attempts to gain control of her dowry.

"It couldn't have been Captain Blake," the duke admitted. "I sent someone to watch him last night. He went straight home and hasn't left his rooms since."

"Thank God." For the first time today, Natalia felt a glimmer of relief. How humiliating to know someone else had seen her in Dylan's arms, but she couldn't have borne it if Dylan had done this terrible thing on top of everything else.

She didn't want to believe everything about him had been a calculated lie. "Well, regardless of who told, the secret is out, and your life is no longer your own. You have to think about your reputation, do whatever needs to be done to salvage it." The duke tried to smile. "There's still Prince Nikolai Ivanovich.

If we act quickly, we can whisk you away to Russia and have you married before even a hint of the scandal reaches his ears."

Prince Nikolai. The very thought filled her with dread. "Father, isn't there someone else? Someone English? Prince Nikolai frightens me."

"There's no reason to be afraid. Ivanovich is an honorable man. He is your mother's cousin. I'm certain he would never dream of mistreating you in any way."

Dear lord. How could her father be so blind? Couldn't he see the cruelty just behind Prince Nikolai's urbane charm?

She decided to try another tactic. "Please, Father. I don't want to leave England. In Russia, I'll be so alone. I don't know anyone. I don't know their ways."

"I expect you'll learn." The duke sighed and tossed his pen across the desk in frustration. "I know this isn't precisely what you want, but I can't think of any other solution. I've already gone begging to Sherbourne, and I'll be damned if I'll do it again. How would it look if word got around that I'd tried to bribe someone to marry my daughter?" His voice had risen, and he made an effort to control it. "You should have taken all this into account before you arranged to meet Captain Blake."

Natalia felt the heat rise in her cheeks. She bowed her head. He was right. She'd brought all this upon herself.

The duke rose, encircled the desk, and patted her awkwardly on the head. "Don't worry. You'll have the best of everything. You'll be a princess."

A princess. How little he knew her if he thought wealth and position would make her happy.

Seeming to read her mind, he sighed and crouched down so he could meet her gaze. "There is one other option, though I hate to even mention it."

"Is there? At this point, I'm willing to consider anything." New hope filled her. She wanted another choice, any other choice.

"If you'd like to stay here in England, you could marry Captain Blake. He is not what I'd planned for you, but he does come from a good family, and he's a decorated war veteran. It would quiet the gossip, and there does seem to be a certain… affection between the two of you."

Natalia closed her eyes, overwhelmed with a sense of inevitability. *Marriage to Dylan.* Despite everything, her heart leaped at the thought. She'd been so sure she loved him, and perhaps she had, because the emotion didn't seem to want to go away.

Her father, however, seemed to take her silence for dismay. "Forget I mentioned it. I was right to send that opportunist away. You will marry Prince Nikolai. The sooner, the better."

"No." Natalia shook her head. "I'll consider Captain Blake. I just need a few days to think everything through."

The duke pursed his lips. "I'll give you until tomorrow evening."

"Tomorrow?" Natalia was aghast. Perhaps, given time, she might be able to forgive Dylan for what he'd done. But how could she marry him now, when so much anger and betrayal seared her heart?

"Tomorrow," her father repeated. "I want this situation resolved as quickly as possible. There has been far too much speculation already."

* * *

Dylan spent the entire day holed up in his rented rooms at Mrs. Tweed's. Loretta had given him until the end of the week to vacate the premises. He'd thanked her for the extra time and tried to ignore the pity in her eyes.

Then he locked the door and returned to his bottle, determined to remain here and castigate himself for his mistakes until the very last moment. Tomorrow, he intended to pay one last call on his father and then leave for Scotland.

Until then, he planned to wallow in his misery.

He hadn't been sleeping well. Whenever he managed to drift off for a few minutes, nightmares plagued him. Usually, he managed to keep all thoughts of the war buried, but the events of the past few days had freed his demons.

Despite the dulling haze of alcohol, he'd come to the realization that it was time to leave London and all thoughts of Lady Natalia Sinclair far behind him. What good did it do to brood about it, when she'd told him to his face she wished she'd never met him?

And Aldabaran called to him.

Still, he couldn't help thinking of the way she'd held him, or the taste of her mouth against his. She'd offered him a soft sweet haven from the harsh realities of life, made him yearn for things he'd never known existed. She'd said she loved him. Perhaps she'd even meant it, at least until she'd realized he betrayed her.

His self-pitying thoughts ground to a halt when someone knocked on his door. He rose unsteadily, made his way across the room, and muttered profanities beneath his breath as he struggled with the lock. At last, he managed to release the latch, but before he could think ahead to the next step, the door opened from outside.

Stunned, he found himself staring at the last person he'd ever expected to visit his humble abode—the Duchess of Clayton.

"Your Grace. What the devil are you doing here?"

Clarice shook her blond head and entered the room, shutting the door. She stared at him for a long, tense moment, and then wrinkled her pert little nose. "I've come to discuss a matter of great importance with you, Captain Blake. Unfortunately, you don't seem to be in any condition to discuss anything."

Dylan grabbed the nearest chair, cleared it of a pile of dirty laundry, and shoved it in her direction. "Please. Sit down. Can I offer you a drink?"

If there was one thing he had plenty of, it was gin. As he spoke, he poured himself another shot. The shock of her visit had sobered him to an alarming extent.

"No, thank you." The duchess settled herself on the edge of the proffered chair, her posture painfully perfect. Dylan took the seat across from her, his heart pounding as he saw a way to make amends.

"I don't know what you want from me. But I'll do it. Whenever you want. As long as you promise to tell Natalia I never meant to hurt her. Please, just let her know that when I kissed her, I wasn't even thinking about that infernal bet."

"Do you love her, Dylan?"

Clarice's soft question sucker-punched him, forced him to examine the emotions he'd been unwilling or unable to name. Self-preservation took over and he managed a casual shrug. "I care for her. Far more than I've ever cared for any other woman."

He couldn't bring himself to admit any more than that. Not as things stood.

"Well, I suppose that will have to do."

"Why don't you get to the point, Clarice?" Under any other circumstances, he never would have presumed to call the duchess by her given name, but she had initiated the intimacy of informal address. He poured himself another shot, but she put her hand over the glass and barred him from drinking it.

"Drinking yourself into oblivion won't solve anything. Besides, you'll need all your wits about you if you're going to be of any help to Natalia."

Dylan felt a glimmer of anger. "If you're here to get me to convince my brother to marry her, you can forget it. Michael's not talking to me."

"That's not why I'm here." Clarice closed her eyes for a brief moment, as though praying for patience. "The duke has already spoken to Viscount Sherbourne. Your brother refuses to wed Natalia."

Dylan wasn't surprised. Michael would hate to be anyone's second choice. He had so little experience, after all. "Surely, the duke can find another suitable match. It isn't as though everyone in London knows what happened."

Clarice leaned forward. "That's exactly what it's like. Your brother and the duke weren't the only ones who followed you out to the garden. Lord Jonathan Taylor was there as well. He's told everyone who will listen how thoroughly you compromise my stepdaughter."

"What a mess." Dylan put his head in his hands. His stomach clenched with nausea as he realized the full extent of the damage he'd caused.

"Yes," Clarice agreed. "How do you plan to fix it?"

"What *can* I do? Natalia hates me, and the duke won't let me near her to change her mind."

His alcohol-soaked brain formulated a sudden plan to hunt down Jonathan Taylor and tear him limb from limb. Natalia might not appreciate the gesture, but it would make him feel ever so much better.

"Well… The duke is running out of options." She surprised Dylan by grabbing his drink and downing it herself. "Natalia is furious with you, it's true. But she spoke to me before all of this happened, and I know how much she cares for you."

She might be telling the truth, but if so, Natalia had changed her mind during those last few minutes in the garden. *"I wish I'd never met you."* Those words haunted him, echoed in his head until he thought he'd go mad.

"You must act quickly," she continued. "Or she'll be forced to marry Prince Nikolai Ivanovich."

"Ivanovich?" The mere sound of the Russian's name sent a chill down Dylan's spine. Christ. *Ivanovich* was the Russian prince Natalia was to marry?

Dylan had fought opposite Prince Nikolai at Balaclava. In fact, Ivanovich had delivered the saber wound that almost killed him.

Clarice nodded. "Have you heard of him? I believe he was a general in the Russian army."

"Yes, I know of him." He got up and walked across the room to where his Victoria Cross rested on a bed of crushed velvet in a small ivory box. He'd never felt he deserved the medal, and his current situation compounded his sense of worthlessness. He closed the box with a snap. "The man is a monster. He won't be happy until he's crushed Natalia's spirit."

"I haven't met him yet, but Natalia told me the same thing. She's trying to be brave, but Prince Nikolai terrifies her. She says he's cold and cruel. She's afraid he'll punish her for this gossip once he hears about it."

"Over my dead body." Anger filled Dylan when he thought of Natalia at Prince Nikolai's mercy. He couldn't bear for Natalia to pay for his mistakes. "I won't allow Ivanovich anywhere near her." He'd follow them to Russia if need be, rip the bastard's heart out with his bare hands...

"Then you must marry Natalia yourself." Clarice's voice brooked no discussion. "You were the one who compromised her. If you married her, the gossips will find something else to talk about."

"I'd like nothing more." Dylan gave a humorless laugh. "I asked her to marry me. She said she wished she'd never met me."

"She had good reason for those angry words, don't you think?"

"I never meant—" Dylan tried to defend himself, but Clarice held up her hand, cutting him off.

"Things have changed. I think she could be persuaded now that her choices are so limited. She must marry either you or the Russian."

"So, I'm the lesser of two evils?" Dylan smiled. Hardly flattering, but it was something. It was a chance. He could accept that.

"We'll see." Clarice returned his smile. Apparently, he'd managed to win her over. "Natalia has agreed to let you plead your case before she makes her final decision. You're welcome to come over tomorrow evening and try to do so, but only if you sober up." She wrinkled her brow. "And bathe. And shave."

"Of course." Dylan ran his hand over his beard-stubbled chin, shamed and embarrassed by the depths to which he had sunk during the last two days. Natalia's rejection had hit him harder than anything in recent memory, even his father's final repudiation.

"Natalia and I are very close." Clarice leaned forward, her tone confiding. "The duke had planned to come himself, but I convinced him to let me do so in his stead. I wanted to see for myself if you are worthy of her."

Dylan eyed the duchess cautiously. "And what have you decided"

"You're not, of course. But in my opinion, no man ever could be." Clarice stood abruptly, handing him the empty glass. "Seriously, I think you care for her more than you want to admit. Don't prove me wrong, Captain Blake."

"I won't," Dylan vowed, as he saw her to the door. He only hoped Natalia would give him the second chance he needed to keep his promise.

Chapter Thirteen

"Here you are! I've been looking for you for hours."

Natalia looked up from her embroidery to find Clarice in the doorway of the cozy little parlor where she'd taken refuge. For the first time ever, Natalia was less than happy to see her stepmother.

She wanted to be alone with her thoughts and had been sitting in near darkness for hours. Only the roaring fire and a small gas lamp shed light on her embroidery, but it didn't matter. Her fingers worked independently of her mind as she tried to make the most important decision of her life.

"I wanted to be by myself for a while." Hopefully, Clarice would get the hint and go away.

Clarice grinned, turned on another lamp, and settled in the chair across from her. "You shouldn't do needlework in the dark. You'll ruin your eyes."

Natalia laughed. "I think poor eyesight is the least of my present worries."

"You may have a point." With a sigh, Clarice relaxed into an uncharacteristic slouch. "Have you made up your mind?"

Natalia stabbed the needle through the material with excessive force. "How can I make such a decision without hearing what both men have to say? It's been years since I saw Prince Nikolai. Perhaps Father is right and my childish opinions of him were wrong. He might be completely suitable."

"Children are usually far more perceptive than adults," Clarice pointed out. "And haven't you wondered why Prince Nikolai is so determined to marry you? The man is twenty years older than you and hasn't seen you since you were a child. Something is wrong with this situation."

"A lot of things are wrong with the situation." Natalia realized she'd lost all sense of the design and tossed the fabric away. "Prince Nikolai's intentions are no mystery. I imagine he wants my dowry, like all the others."

Clarice shook her head. "It can't be that. He's got more than enough money of his own."

"Really?" For the first time, Natalia actually considered the Russian. "Do you think it's possible he might want me for myself?"

"How could he? He doesn't even know you. He has no idea what kind of woman you've become."

Natalia blinked and tried to hold back a sudden rush of tears. Clarice had a point, but that didn't stop the disappointment. Was it too much to ask, that someone might love her for something besides that bloody money?

"Oh, Natalia. You're being so dramatic." Despite her harsh words, Clarice leaned forward and squeezed Natalia's hand. "Quit feeling sorry for yourself because you're an heiress. I was one, too, you know. But unlike you, I always considered my dowry a blessing."

"A blessing?" Natalia gave an unladylike snort. "Didn't you ever find that the money defined you, kept everyone from seeing who you truly were?"

"No, I never felt that way." Clarice met Natalia's gaze sadly. "You're the only person I've ever met who put such a low value on what you have to offer. Why is that, do you think? What happened to make you think no one could ever love you for yourself?"

Clarice's words made Natalia wonder that herself. When had she started thinking no one would ever want her for anything except her fortune?

"I suppose it must've been in school. The other girls were so cruel. There was one... Amelia Lansdowne. She told me it didn't matter what I looked like. She said I could be the ugliest girl in the world—implied I was—and all the men would still want to marry me."

"Amelia Lansdowne?" Clarice shook her head and gave a small incredulous laugh. "Whatever made you listen to anything that little cat had to say? Surely, you realize she was just jealous?"

Natalia flinched. Clarice had managed to make her worst fears seem so ridiculous. "My father has never loved me. All my life, he's made it clear he wishes I'd been a boy. He wants an heir more than anything."

"Nonsense. The duke loves you a great deal. He's just not very good at showing it." Clarice's voice filled with disdainful challenge. "You'll have to do better than this, darling. So far, all you've done is make me wonder why *I* like you so much."

Natalia sank back in her chair, feeling as though she been slapped. "Do I really sound that pathetic?"

"You have a family who loves you. You're smart. You're witty. You have such luminous unusual beauty." Clarice ticked off each point on her fingers as she went. "Yet all you can do is whine about how unfair it is that your father is giving you a half-a-million-pound dowry."

Well, when you look at it that way…

"I suppose I have acted a little bit ungrateful," Natalia conceded, shamed.

"I'm not trying to hurt you." Clarice squeezed her hand. "I'm just trying to show you there's far more to you than you think."

Natalia leaned forward and hugged her stepmother tightly. "You're such a good friend. I understand what you're trying to do, and I appreciate it. You've given me a lot to think about."

"I just want you to be happy." Clarice hugged her in return and then pulled back. Unshed tears filled her bright eyes, but she managed a smile. "I went to see your Captain Blake today."

"You did?" Natalia stared at Clarice in stunned surprise, all her previous defensiveness rushing back. "Why on earth did you do that?"

"I wanted a chance to talk to him myself. To see if he truly cared for you, or if you are right, and it was only the money that interested him."

"What did you decide?" Natalia feared the answer. Had Clarice been preparing her for bad news?

A mysterious smile played at the corner of Clarice's mouth. With a sinking heart, Natalia realized Dylan had managed to charm her stepmother. "The man is a wreck. He looks as though he hasn't slept in days. He's been drinking heavily, and the first thing he did was beg me to tell you he never meant to hurt you. He said, 'Tell her when I kissed her, I wasn't even thinking about that infernal bet.'"

Natalia closed her eyes, overwhelmed by the picture Clarice painted. She wanted to believe Dylan was devastated about losing her. She wanted to believe it more than she'd ever wanted anything in her life.

Clarice stood and brushed her fingertips lightly over Natalia's cheek. "I'll leave you alone. I know you have a lot to think about."

By the time Natalia opened her eyes, Clarice had reached the door. "Wait," she called, almost frantically. "What would you do, Clarice? What would you do if you were me?"

"I'd marry the man I loved." Clarice gave her a gentle smile. "And then I'd do everything in my power to make him love me in return."

Long after Clarice left, Natalia stared into the dying flames in the grate. Until tonight, she'd always thought of herself as an unselfish and caring person. But Clarice had shown her another side of herself, and she hated what she'd seen. She had a lot of growing up to do, a lot of things to learn.

How could she expect any man to love her, when she didn't even love herself?

* * *

When Dylan arrived at the Duke of Clayton's townhouse the next evening, the butler led him to an elegant reception room on the first floor. "His Grace will be with you shortly."

Dylan sighed moodily, dreading his coming conversation with Natalia's father. He'd hoped to talk to Natalia first. Not that he blamed the duke for putting him through the wringer. He supposed he should be grateful Clayton was considering the marriage at all.

Nearly half an hour passed before the duke finally entered the room. Dylan did his best to hide his annoyance. "Good evening, Your Grace."

The duke frowned at Dylan with obvious distaste. "Captain Blake."

Dylan felt like a recalcitrant schoolboy who had been called in to face the headmaster. He forced himself to remember he'd given the duke plenty of reason not to trust him.

"Thank you for allowing me this opportunity to try to change Lady Natalia's mind. I appreciate it more than you could ever know." When the duke continued to frown, Dylan swallowed and tried again. "I understand your misgivings, but I assure you, your daughter means a great deal to me. I would never hurt her."

"You already hurt her. You broke her heart and destroyed her reputation. Those hardly seem like the actions of a man who cares about a woman."

Dylan flushed and looked away, unable to hold the duke's penetrating gaze. "I've made some grave mistakes. But I plan to spend the rest of my life trying to make it up to her… If you'll let me."

The duke sighed. "You give me little choice. My only other option is to send Natalia to Russia, to marry one of her Ivanovich cousins. And although that was my original plan, I find that I can't bear the thought of having her so far away."

"You're making the right choice," Dylan told the older man. "Nikolai Ivanovich is a cruel, heartless bastard. Eventually, he would hear about the scandal. I'm afraid he'd make Natalia's life a living hell if he felt you'd deceived him."

The duke looked startled. "I wasn't aware you knew Ivanovich."

"He nearly killed me at Balaclava. Might as well have. I certainly wasn't any help to my men after he wounded me. Spent two months on a rat-infested hospital ship fighting the infection."

The duke seemed a bit rattled as he folded his arms across his chest. Dylan wondered if Clayton had even considered the fact that eventually, the prince would learn about the scandal.

"Ivanovich could never care for her as I do. He doesn't even know her."

"And you do know her? What do you know of my daughter, Captain Blake? Other than she's lovely to look upon, and her dowry will make you comfortable for the rest of your life?"

Dylan held out his hands in hopeless entreaty. "She's sweet and honest and kind. She made me feel loved, Your Grace."

"Well, I must admit you seem sincere." The duke gave Dylan a long piercing look. "But I'm afraid you'll have to be a hell of a lot more eloquent if you wish to convince my daughter."

Relief washed over Dylan as he realized he'd passed the first test. "Thank you, Your Grace. All I've ever wanted is a chance."

The duke smiled. "I'll send her in."

Chapter Fourteen

Natalia paced her bedchamber, her nerves frayed to the breaking point as she waited for her father to conclude his interview with Dylan. It seemed an eternity had passed since Dylan's arrival, which she'd witnessed from her window.

On one hand, she hoped her father berated Dylan for all his many sins. But she also feared her father would be too harsh and ultimately send Dylan away. In truth, she didn't know if she wanted him to stay or go. The mere thought of seeing him again created such conflicting emotions; she was afraid to examine them too closely.

A brisk knock interrupted her thoughts. She rushed to the door and found her father waiting on the other side. "Your young man is here." The duke seemed in rare good humor. "Are you ready to speak to him?"

Natalia nodded, unsure what to think of her father's smile. "Yes, Father. I'm as ready as I'll ever be."

The duke took her hand and escorted her down the hall. "Don't fret, my dear. I consider myself to be a fairly good judge of character, and I believe Captain Blake cares for you a great deal. You could do worse."

Natalia's eyes widened, but she held her tongue. She'd expected Dylan to charm Clarice, but never the duke.

"Did you know Prince Nikolai wounded Captain Blake in the Crimea?" The duke shook his head in amazement. "Forgive me for even thinking of marrying you to that Russian, Natalia. You're far better off with Captain Blake."

Ivanovich had wounded Dylan during the war?

Before she could even begin to process that information or steel herself against Dylan's lethal appeal, her father opened the reception room door. Natalia followed the duke and found Dylan waiting inside. Despite her hurt and anger, Natalia couldn't tear her gaze away from him. Though still breathtakingly handsome, he looked pale, and dark circles rimmed his clear gray eyes. Apparently, these last few days had been hard on him, too.

"Lady Natalia." Dylan stepped forward, captured her hand, and brought it to his lips. "I'm so glad you agreed to see me."

The heat of his mouth against her skin sent frissons of desire skittering down her spine. She quickly snatched her hand away. She didn't want to be reminded of the passion they'd shared.

The duke cleared his throat. "Well, I'll leave the two of you alone. I know you have a lot to discuss."

Before Natalia could protest, her father withdrew and left her to face Dylan by herself.

Dylan shifted restlessly and gestured toward a small sofa. "Would you like to sit down?"

She nodded, perched on the far edge, and then glanced at him from beneath the veil of her lashes as he sat down beside her. Although the length of the sofa separated them, he seemed far too close. His unique scent washed over her. She fought the urge to lean closer and simply breathe him in.

He stared at her for a long moment then sighed. "What must I do to make this up to you? What can I say that will prove I never meant to hurt you?"

Nothing. There's nothing you can say that will make this right. All the excuses in the world couldn't make her trust him again.

"Just tell me one thing, and please, tell me the truth." Natalia gathered all her courage and forced herself to meet his pleading gaze. "Did you follow me out into the garden with the intention of compromising me? Did you arrange for us to get caught, just so you could win my dowry?"

A frown pulled at the corners of his beautiful lips. "I swear I never intended to try to win you for myself. You know I promised my brother I'd step aside that very evening."

"Then why did you agree to meet me? Why didn't you keep your promise?" Angry tears stung her eyes, and she struggled to control them, determined not to let him see her cry.

He clenched his fists at his sides and looked away. Perhaps he didn't want to face her while he told her yet another lie.

"Because you chose me, Natalia. *Me*, not him." The raw sincerity in his voice almost convinced her. "You were the first person in my life who seemed to like me better than Michael."

"I *did* like you better than Michael." Her voice trembled with longing as she thought of the easy friendship they'd lost. "I liked you better than anyone I've ever met."

"Does that mean you don't like me now?" He shook his head. "I don't believe that. I think you still care for me. At least a little."

Their conversation had barely begun, and she'd already betrayed herself. She wanted to wipe that confident look off his face but couldn't bring herself to say the hurtful words that would accomplish it.

"Oh, Dylan." She buried her face in her hands, unable to look at him. "I thought you were different than the rest. I thought you cared about me, not the money. Don't you know how badly it hurt to find out you'd gambled on my affections?"

"I'm not sorry about that bet. If Jonathan hadn't goaded me into pursuing you, I'd never have gotten to know you. And I did get to know you, Natalia. I like you for a hundred reasons that have nothing to do with your blasted dowry."

She wanted to trust him, but if she opened herself up to him, he'd inevitably hurt her yet again. So, she said nothing. She merely lifted her head and stared at him, wishing he could be the man she'd once thought he was.

Dylan could see he'd failed Natalia miserably. Despite everything he'd said, she still believed his kiss had been mercenary. "We both know why I'm here. If you don't want to marry me, then go ahead and say so. If you really wish you'd never met me,

I'll walk out that door, and you'll never have to see me again."

He held his breath and stared deep into her exotic green eyes, feeling as though he'd been waiting his entire life for this moment. He needed this. He needed her. "Please, Natalia. I want to marry you." He realized he was begging and made an effort not to sound so needy. "I owe you that much, at least. For all the hurt I've caused."

He knew he'd said the wrong thing as soon as the words left his mouth. "So, you're only doing this to save my reputation?" Natalia shook her head. "You still can't tell me the truth, can you?"

Dylan bowed his head, unable to meet her knowing gaze. "I want to marry you. God, I want it so much."

"You should let me go. We're no good for each other." But as she spoke, she leaned forward and touched his cheek with her fingertips.

Her actions gave him a faint spark of hope. How could she say such a thing, yet touch him so sweetly? He met her gaze and willed her to hear the truth behind his words. "You are wrong, love. You're the best thing that's ever happened to me."

Natalia stared into Dylan sooty gray eyes and knew she'd lost the battle. Unfortunately, Dylan was motivated by guilt and greed—she by sheer desperation. How could a marriage built on such a shaky foundation do anything but crumble? He would break her heart again. But the alternative—Prince Nikolai—was unthinkable.

"All right," she whispered. "I'll marry you, Dylan."

Her only comfort lay in the knowledge that she wasn't making the biggest mistake of her life.

She'd done that when she kissed him.

* * *

When Dylan and Natalia emerged from the reception room a few moments later, Clayton was waiting for them in the hallway. He'd probably heard their entire conversation, given his close proximity to the door.

Dylan and his future father-in-law stared at each other for a long moment, but then the duke extended his hand. "I assume congratulations are in order, young man?"

"Yes, Your Grace." Dylan cast a quick look at his less-than-enthusiastic fiancée. "Natalia has done me the great honor of consenting to become my wife."

"Under the circumstances, I couldn't be more pleased." The duke squeezed Dylan's hand a little more firmly than necessary. In warning, no doubt. Dylan's respect for the man grew. He obviously cared for Natalia a great deal. She was lucky. He would do anything for a father who loved him so deeply.

The duke released Dylan's hand and turned to his daughter. "And you, Natalia? Are you pleased?"

"Yes," Natalia murmured. "Under the circumstances."

Which wasn't exactly the response Dylan had hoped for. Still, she'd agreed to become his wife. They had an entire lifetime to regain what had been lost.

"Well, come along then." The duke seemed satisfied with her answer, which gave Dylan one less thing to worry about. Having the duke on his side meant half the battle was won. "We'll join the duchess for dinner. I'm sure she'll want to have her say in the wedding plans."

* * *

Numb, Natalia followed her father and Dylan down the hall toward the dining room. Everything had happened so quickly. How could her father expect them to sit down to a celebratory dinner? Did they have to plan the wedding this very second? Couldn't her father give her even a moment to think about all that had happened?

When the three of them entered the dining room, they found Clarice pacing. When she saw them, her face lit up and she quickly directed one of the servants to set another place. Duty done, she hurried over and gave Natalia a swift hug. "I knew you'd make the right decision. Everything will be fine. You'll see."

Natalia held her stepmother for a long moment and tried to draw comfort from Clarice's faith. "I hope you're right."

Clarice squeezed her shoulder, then stepped away and took her place at the duke's side. "Please, sit down. Dinner will be served in just a moment."

With a wry smile, Dylan moved forward and offered Natalia his arm. "Shall we?"

Natalia nodded and rested her hand on her future husband's forearm. As they walked toward the table, his muscles moved and flexed beneath her fingertips. Soon, she would have the right to touch him whenever she wanted.

The thought both frightened and tantalized her. What would it be like, to have him in her life, in her bed? Would it be worth the inevitable heartbreak?

Just a few short days ago, she'd been willing to risk everything to find out.

Dylan solicitously pulled out her chair. After she sat, he took the one beside her. A million questions danced in Clarice's bright gaze as she sat down across from Natalia. The duke took his place at the head of the table, while the servants poured the wine and served the first course—a rich turtle soup.

"Well," Clarice began, sounding far too enthusiastic. "It seems we have a wedding to plan, don't we?"

"We certainly do." Dylan matched Clarice's tone. He glanced over at Natalia. "First, we need to set a date. When do you think would be best?"

"I should think we'd like to get this over as soon as possible," the duke replied, giving Natalia no chance to answer. "You'll need to obtain a special license. But I don't think that will be a problem, given my connections. How about one week from today?"

One week. Natalia hadn't realized her father would insist upon such haste. She'd assumed once she'd made her decision, she'd have the normal amount of time to prepare for the wedding. A few months at least, during which she and Dylan could try to repair their relationship.

Dylan squeezed her hand beneath the table in an obvious attempt to offer comfort. "That's very soon, Your Grace. Hardly time to plan a proper wedding."

"He's right," Clarice chimed in. "That's not even time to have a dress made, let alone plan a menu, order flowers, send out the invitations—"

"No need for invitations. It will be a small ceremony, just immediate family." The duke gave Natalia an apologetic glance. "I refuse to invite anyone who will come merely to speculate."

Dylan tightened his grip on her hand. "Natalia deserves to have the wedding of her dreams, Your Grace. I don't want to take that away from her."

Natalia extricated her hand. She didn't want his comfort. "I don't deserve any such thing." She stirred her soup and wished the interminable supper would end. "It doesn't matter. Next week is fine."

The duke frowned, but since she'd gone along with his wishes, he couldn't argue.

Clarice looked near tears. "Of course, you deserve a real wedding, darling." She gave her husband a furious look. "I insist you allow us all the time we need."

"No." Natalia spoke up again, before the duke and duchess could begin a full-fledged argument. "June third is fine. As Father said, it's best to get this whole thing over as quickly as possible."

Dylan shifted beside her, sighing. Apparently, he didn't like the way she spoke of their wedding—as though it were something distasteful. Something which needed to be gotten over with. She didn't care. It served him right.

"Fine. June third, it is." The duke turned his attention toward Dylan. "You'll want your father and brother to come, I suppose." His grudging tone indicated he still hadn't forgiven Michael for refusing her.

Dylan shook his head. "I'm not on easy terms with either of them. But I would like to invite Basingstoke."

Dylan's request startled her. She hadn't realized Dylan and the Earl of Basingstoke were such good friends.

"I suppose that will be all right." The duke steepled his fingertips and looked around the small gathering. "Is there anything else we need to discuss?"

"There is one more thing." Dylan cleared his throat, and Natalia felt his sudden tension.

"Well, speak up." The duke's tone made it more than obvious he didn't want to hear any more surprises today.

A servant entered the room with the second course, but the duke waved him away. "Give us a few more minutes," he instructed sharply. "We haven't even finished our soup."

Dylan waited until the servant left and turned to Natalia. "I recently found out I inherited a small estate in Scotland. I have no idea what shape it's in, but I plan to make Aldabaran my home."

"Out of the question," the duke thundered. "I won't allow you to drag my daughter off to some rotting castle in the middle of bloody Scotland."

Dylan flicked the duke an annoyed glance, then returned his attention to Natalia. "It's beautiful there. Quiet and peaceful."

Natalia was taken aback by the passion and sincerity in his voice.

"I've had enough of London. I think you have, too. But I wanted you to know my plans. There's still time for you to change your mind. If you don't think you'll be happy living a quiet country life, you should tell me now."

He wanted to take her to Scotland. To a quiet peaceful place that meant a great deal to him. His offer sounded wonderful but confused Natalia more than ever. That kind of life did not require a fortune like the one she possessed.

When had he found out about this estate? She wanted to ask him but decided to leave the question for another time. When they did not have an audience. "Scotland sounds wonderful. And if we go there, we'll be able to escape all the gossip. Perhaps the *ton* will find some other scandal to savor, once we're no longer around."

The duke perked up a bit at that. "Perhaps you're right."

"You will bring her back to visit us from time to time, won't you, Captain Blake?" Clarice sounded forlorn. For the first time, Natalia realized her marriage would forever alter her close relationship with Clarice.

Even if she remained in London, they'd no longer share a home and wouldn't see each other on a daily basis. What would she do when she couldn't turn to Clarice with all her troubles and triumphs?

"Of course, I'll bring her to visit," Dylan agreed. "As often as she likes."

"Then it seems as though everything is settled." The duke lifted his wine glass with obvious satisfaction. "Let us drink to a long *fruitful* marriage."

His emphasis on the word *fruitful* did nothing to calm Natalia's fears. Was this the reason for her father's good cheer? Did he hope she'd start popping out children within the first year? *Dear lord.* The mere thought of what that would entail made her weak in the knees. She wasn't ready. She wasn't ready for any of this.

Dylan cleared his throat, and she realized she was the only one who hadn't lifted her glass.

"Sorry," she muttered and awkwardly joined the toast.

Four crystal glasses clinked musically together, sealing her fate.

Chapter Fifteen

After leaving the duke's estate, Dylan headed for the Earl of Basingstoke's residence. He was in dire need of someone to talk to and hoped his friend hadn't already gone out for the evening.

He and Julian had been friends since they'd met in boarding school, and once Dylan told him the way of things, Basingstoke could be counted upon to act with discretion. Dylan didn't want the *ton* to learn about the wedding and descend upon them like buzzards scenting a fresh kill.

He arrived at his friend's huge Georgian townhouse just as evening blanketed the city. The butler opened the door promptly, and he gave the man his card.

Fortunately, Basingstoke was still at home.

The butler showed Dylan into Julian's walnut-paneled office and disappeared to fetch the master of the house. Dylan sank into a stiff leather chair to wait. He shook his head as he took in the newly redecorated nautical theme of the room. Julian yearned for adventure, but his many business interests kept him firmly anchored in London.

Basingstoke broke into a wide grin when he entered the room. "Blake! What on earth are you doing here? Have you run out of virgins to despoil?"

Dylan sighed and raked his hands through his hair in dismay. "Not you, too."

Basingstoke's grin faded. He crossed the room to the small sideboard and poured them both a healthy glass of brandy. "That was meant to be in jest." He handed Dylan a drink. "Given the look on your face, I assume it was in poor taste."

Dylan nodded, but he couldn't contain a small contented smile. "Natalia agreed to marry me tonight."

"You're marrying Lady Natalia Sinclair?" Basingstoke sank into the chair across from him. "Bloody hell, Blake. Good for you! However did you manage it?"

Dylan leaned back in his chair and stared at the ceiling. "I lied to her, of course. And then there was that spectacular scene in the garden, when I made damn sure no one else would ever want her."

Basingstoke laughed. "A bit upset with you, is she?"

"Upset doesn't even begin to describe the lady's emotions." Dylan shook his head and met Basingstoke's amused gaze. "It's not a laughing matter. I can assure you."

"Don't worry. She'll come around eventually, and if she doesn't, you can spend all her money on the fair Cassandra."

"Natalia is worth ten of Cassandra."

"Ah." Basingstoke stared at him speculatively. "Forgive me. I didn't realize you'd fallen in love with the girl."

"I'm not in love with her." Dylan denied it automatically, but his words felt false. Would it be so wrong, if he were to fall in love with his own wife?

Only if she doesn't love me back.

"I think you *are* in love with her." Basingstoke chuckled. "I never thought I'd see the day." Still laughing, he reached forward to touch Dylan's glass with his own. "It's nothing to be ashamed of. I'm happy for you, my friend. I truly am."

Dylan downed his glass, more at ease. He could always count on Basingstoke to say the right thing. "Will you stand beside me at the wedding?"

"Of course," Basingstoke agreed, but he looked troubled. "As long as you're certain you wouldn't rather have Michael do the honors."

Dylan shook his head and tossed down the rest of his drink. He concentrated on the slow burn of alcohol, instead of the ache in his heart. "Michael wanted her for himself. As you can imagine, he wasn't too pleased with the way things turned out."

Basingstoke shook his head. "Rough luck on his part. But you need the girl far more than he does. I'm sure he'll get over it."

Dylan made an impatient gesture. "His anger is more than justified. I'm surprised he didn't write me off long ago."

"He'll come around. Michael's not a bad sort under all that conservative bluster."

Dylan doubted his brother would ever forgive him, but he held his tongue. He'd never gotten anywhere in an argument with Basingstoke.

"I have one other bit of news," Dylan told his friend, in an effort to change the subject. "Before our row, Michael told me my grandfather left me Aldabaran."

"Well. That's news worth celebrating." Basingstoke smiled and poured Dylan another drink. "I know how much you love that place."

"Father has known all along but chose not to tell me. I can't imagine his reasons. You'd think the old bastard would have sent me there with his blessings, merely to get rid of me."

Basingstoke didn't seem surprised by the old man's perfidy, but then he'd been privy to all Dylan's many fights with the earl over the years. "You haven't confronted him?"

"No." Dylan gave a rueful laugh. "I've had my hands full with confrontations during these last few days."

Basingstoke chuckled. "Yes, I suppose you have."

"Michael thinks I should wait. He says I should go to Edinburgh first, make sure everything's in order."

"Michael's probably right." Julian shook his head. "If there's a way for the old man to keep you from having what's yours, I'm sure he'll try to find it."

Dylan ran his hand through his hair in agitation. If both Michael and Basingstoke thought he should wait to confront his father, perhaps he should take their advice. He had enough to worry about already, without adding another acrimonious scene with his father into the mix.

Still, he burned with the need to make his father pay for all the pain he'd caused. He wanted to look in the old man's eyes and see his fury when he realized Michael had betrayed him and told Dylan the secret hidden for so long.

But that could wait for some other time. Right now, he needed to secure his estate and regain Natalia's trust.

"I'll send some inquiries to the solicitor in Edinburgh in the morning. See if anyone's been taking care of Aldabaran during the last twenty years. I expect to find it in ruins. Natalia will probably be disappointed. She's accustomed to far more comfortable accommodations."

"Well, you'll have all the money in the world to make improvements. Let her help. I've heard even the most recalcitrant woman gets a smile on her face when there is expensive remodeling to be done."

Perhaps Basingstoke was right. Natalia might feel more at home at Aldabaran if she helped to restore it. And they could definitely afford anything she might suggest, thanks to her dowry.

With a sigh, Dylan finally got around to the part of this visit he'd dreaded. "I have one more favor to ask of you, Julian."

Basingstoke leaned forward, his face troubled; Dylan hardly ever called him by his given name. "Anything, Dylan," he muttered, returning the more intimate form of address. "All you have to do is ask."

Dylan looked away, embarrassed. "Can I stay with you until after the wedding? I've been evicted."

Basingstoke laughed, a deep relieved sound of amusement. "Bloody hell, I thought you were going to ask me to help you get rid of Jonathan Taylor's body."

Dylan stiffened at the reminder of the wrongs Jonathan had committed against his future bride. Yes, his father could wait. At the moment, he had other fish to fry. "Not yet. But I wouldn't count it an impossibility."

Still laughing, Basingstoke nodded. "Well, just let me know if I can be of service. And of course, you can stay. You're welcome to stay as long as you like."

* * *

The May evening was still young, but exhaustion pulled at Natalia like a dead weight. Her emotions were shredded. She felt strange, disconnected from what was happening around her.

As soon as Dylan departed, she headed toward her bedchamber. She wanted nothing more than to slip beneath her covers and go to sleep for a very long time.

"My lady, I didn't expect you so soon." Cora, Natalia's freckled little maid, jumped up from the window seat and tried to hide the book she'd been reading while she waited for Natalia to return.

"It's all right," Natalia assured the girl with a weary smile. "If you'll just help me undress and brush out my hair, you can have the rest of the evening off."

Cora's blue eyes lit up, and she hurried to assist Natalia out of her gown. After changing into her nightdress, Natalia sat down at her dressing table, while Cora released the many pins that had held her intricate hairstyle in place. Giving herself over to the soothing nightly ritual, Natalia let her mind drift away.

Scotland. She'd always loved the wild beauty of the Highlands. Apparently, Dylan did, too. He obviously craved the serene peaceful setting enough to risk letting her go in order to live there.

Once again, he confounded her. Who was the real Dylan Blake? Was he a fortune-hunting cad or a tender hero? A warrior or a lover? She feared he was all that and more.

Why had he pursued her for her dowry? She suspected all he'd ever wanted was a place of his own, a home.

A home. That was all she'd ever wanted, too. Somewhere cozy and comfortable instead of grandiose and echoing. A place where children could run and play without worrying about breaking some precious artifact.

Perhaps she would finally find the home of her dreams in Scotland.

As Cora continued brushing her hair, Natalia let her thoughts drift to her future husband. Exactly what did Dylan expect of her? Was this to be a marriage in name only? Or did he want her to be his wife in truth?

The mere idea of making love to him, of leaving herself vulnerable to those strange exciting emotions, terrified her. But she couldn't bear the thought of spending the rest of her life at arm's length, watching him flip between mistresses while he treated her with polite indifference. Oh, anything but that.

If marriage to Dylan was to be her lot in life, she had to figure out a way to either trust him more or love him less. Trusting him again might take more courage than she possessed but loving him less seemed impossible.

Chapter Sixteen

During the next few days, Dylan busied himself with wedding details and preparations for the move to Scotland. He arranged a special license and spoke to the minister who had agreed to perform the ceremony. He also sent a message to his grandfather's solicitor in Edinburgh to inform the man he would arrive to collect his inheritance within the month.

Every evening, he paid a call to the duke's residence to report his progress. He dined with his future bride and her parents. The four of them pretended nothing was wrong, but the looming wedding wasn't the happy occasion it should have been.

Natalia treated him with eerie politeness. She smiled and said all the right things, but he could see the panic building in the depths of her emerald eyes.

She made certain he had no further opportunity to speak to her in private.

Dismayed by the way things were progressing, he wanted to reach out to her and recapture the essence of that evening in the garden. Those few moments had changed his life—given him a glimpse of heaven on earth—but as time wore on, he feared he'd only dreamed it.

This proper, demure girl, who hardly ever spoke and never met his gaze, couldn't possibly be the same sweet hoyden who'd begged him to kiss her.

So, on the third evening of his engagement, he sent his regrets. Drinking and gambling at the club with Basingstoke seemed far preferable to another night at Clayton's mansion. What good did it do to sit beside his future bride and worry and wonder? The arrangements had been made. The die was cast. All he could do was hope things would get better after the wedding when he had her all to himself at Aldabaran.

The moment he and Basingstoke arrived at the club, Dylan knew he'd made a mistake. Clayton had been right about the gossip and speculation. As they moved through the crowd, Dylan caught enough of the whispered buzz to realize Natalia's fall from grace was still the main topic of conversation. His protective instincts rose in proportion to every vicious insult he overheard.

"I shouldn't have let you talk me into this," Dylan muttered as Basingstoke led him to an empty table in the corner of the smoking room.

"You're a legend, my friend." Basingstoke lit a cigar and took a few puffs before expounding. "Very few men ever attain this sort of notoriety. But don't worry. It will pass. They'll find someone else to talk about."

"Well, I hope it's *you*. Then you'll understand what I'm going through." Dylan ignored the drink the waiter place before him. He no longer felt like drowning his sorrows.

In fact, the whole vice-ridden atmosphere no longer held much appeal. The heavy cloud of smoke choked him, and the ribald jokes and laughter hurt his ears.

Basingstoke laughed at his willful expression. "I wouldn't mind, my friend. Not if it meant ending up with what you've got—a bride you can't stop thinking about."

Dylan smiled, but his momentary good humor faded as he spied Jonathan Taylor on the other side of the room. He and his wastrel friends whispered and pointed in Dylan's direction.

"That little bastard." Dylan suddenly remembered his vow to make Jonathan pay for the disgrace he'd brought upon Natalia. "If he'd only kept his mouth shut, no one would have ever known what happened."

Basingstoke winced and laid a steadying hand on Dylan's shoulder. "Just ignore the little bugger. Don't let him goad you."

"You don't understand." Dylan thought his voice sounded surprisingly calm, considering the maelstrom of emotions within him. "I have a score to settle with our friend Jonathan. And I might take you up on that offer to act as my second."

Basingstoke shook his head. "Don't waste your energy. In case you've forgotten, you've a wedding to attend in less than a week."

"Don't worry about me. Worry about him." Dylan surged out of his chair and strode across the room.

Basingstoke groaned and hurried to catch up as Dylan made his way through the suddenly quiet crowd. "Just don't kill him. I refuse to come visit you in Newgate."

Dylan ignored his friend's warning and concentrated on the task before him. Besides, he didn't intend to kill Jonathan—he just planned to make him sorry he'd ever been born.

Jonathan paled a bit as Dylan approached. His slimy confederates quickly slipped away, leaving him alone to face Dylan's fury. "Blake," he said, with false enthusiasm. "Good evening."

"Cut the bloody civility," Dylan snapped. "You know why I'm here."

Jonathan cast a quick glance toward Basingstoke, expecting him to intervene. But Julian just shook his head disapprovingly. Frowning, Jonathan returned his attention to Dylan. Apparently, he'd decided to brazen it out. "Have you come to pay your debt? I only saw you dance with the lady once."

"Yes, but you saw me do far more than dance with her, didn't you? And you made damn sure everyone in town heard about it." Dylan kept his voice low. He refused to give the rest of the spoiled young gentlemen who crowded the room any more gossip.

Jonathan smiled. "I may have mentioned your little rendezvous to a few people. Can you blame me? Don't tell me you weren't secretly glad to see her ruined, especially after she refused your proposal and told you she never wanted to see you again."

"Oh, you heard that, did you? Well, I'm sorry to disappoint you, but she's changed her mind. She's agreed to become my wife."

"That's impossible." Jonathan paled. "I don't believe you."

"Believe me. I guess the better man won, after all."

Jonathan gritted his teeth in impotent frustration. "There's still the matter of the 200 pounds you owe me."

"You're not getting a shilling of it. And if I find out you said even one more damaging word about my bride, I'll call *you* out." Dylan took another step forward, intimidating Jonathan with his superior height and fiercest glare. "I won't back down the way you always do."

Jonathan flinched. "Are you threatening me?"

"Hell, yes."

Jonathan glanced once again at Basingstoke.

Basingstoke grinned. "Blake is the least of your worries. You're lucky Clayton hasn't gone after you. He's ruined men for far less."

Jonathan went white as a ghost. While Dylan might be able to hurt him physically, Clayton could hurt him socially. To a parasite like Jonathan, that was even worse.

Jonathan made to leave, but Dylan stopped him once more. "I want you to retract everything you said about her. Publicly. Do you understand?"

"Yes," Jonathan muttered, but his eyes promised hellish retaliation for the humiliation Dylan was causing. "I understand."

Dylan gave his nemesis one last threatening glare and reluctantly turned away. He'd have felt much better if he'd beaten the little prick to a bloody pulp.

Sometimes, it was hell being a gentleman.

* * *

"Oh, Clarice. It's starting already." Natalia reread Dylan's brief note for the tenth time, then crumpled the fine parchment into a tiny ball and tossed it into the fireplace.

She felt only a tiny spark of satisfaction as she watched the paper burn to ashes.

The two women waited in Natalia's bedchamber for the overworked seamstress to arrive. Madame Toussaint had promised to have Natalia's wedding gown done on time; her people were working on it around the clock and charging the duke an exorbitant fee.

"What's starting already?" Clarice didn't seem the least bit upset by the fact that Dylan hadn't shown up for dinner this evening.

"Dylan. We're not even married yet, and he's already finding excuses to avoid me." Natalia flung herself into the nearest chair. At first, she'd been hurt, but she'd quickly moved beyond that paltry emotion. Fury consumed her now.

"Who's avoiding whom?" Clarice shook her head. "When he's here, you make every effort to ignore him. I know there are things he wants to say to you, but you've done your best to ensure the two of you are never alone."

Natalia felt heat rise up in her cheeks. Clarice was right, but that didn't excuse Dylan's behavior tonight. "I'm not trying to avoid him; I just don't know what to say when we're together."

"You could start by forgiving him. Perhaps he'd want to spend more time with you if you gave him the least little bit of encouragement."

"I'm afraid to forgive him," Natalia admitted. "Because once I do, once I let myself start caring for him again, he's bound to break my heart. What he's done tonight proves it."

"What has he done, darling?" Clarice seemed honestly confused. "The fact that he didn't come for dinner doesn't prove anything, as far as I'm concerned."

"Don't be absurd. We both know he's gone to visit one of his actresses." *There.* She'd said it. Her worst fear.

Clarice gave her a sympathetic glance. "Perhaps he has. And even if he hasn't, it's likely someday he will. Most men of our class keep mistresses. I'm sure your father does. But you can't think about that. Not if you want anything resembling a happy marriage."

Natalia blinked away a film of threatening tears. "I can't bear to think of him touching anyone but me. If I'm going to be his wife, I want to be his entire world."

"That's what every woman wants," Clarice whispered. "But very few of us ever get it."

They sat there, lost in their own miserable thoughts, for several endless minutes. Devastated by the picture Clarice painted of marriage, Natalia's eyes welled with tears. Was there no hope then? Was she destined to spend the rest her life watching Dylan flit from woman to woman?

"Oh, Natalia. Don't cry." Clarice gave a shaky laugh. "Just because my marriage is unhappy doesn't mean yours will be, too. I'm far too pessimistic about the whole matter. Besides, I've seen the way that man looks at you. If any woman on earth has a chance at keeping her husband at her side, it's you."

Clarice's words rang with truth, and Natalia clung to the possibility like a lifeboat. "How do I do that? Tell me how to keep him from looking elsewhere."

Clarice blushed bright red. "Well, I'm obviously not an expert on the matter. But I know a few things that might help."

"What kind of things?" Natalia immediately conjured up an image of Dylan leaning over her, his face drawn with passion, his breath hot against her skin. There was so much she didn't know, so much she wanted to learn.

Perhaps, if she could learn to please him, to do the things his mistresses did, he wouldn't be so eager to look elsewhere for his pleasures.

"Maybe we should start at the beginning." If possible, Clarice turned even redder. "Tell me, Natalia, what do you know about making love?"

Chapter Seventeen

The following afternoon, Natalia took her afternoon tea in the garden. She hadn't left the house in nearly a week and felt horribly confined. She longed for the freedom of her weekly ride, but once the gossips caught sight of her, she'd regret the indulgence. Women she'd once thought of as her friends were bound to cut her dead.

Clarice offered to join her outside, but Natalia wanted to be alone for a while. After finishing the tea the servants had set on a small table near the conservatory doors, she wandered toward the rose arbor, unable to resist the lure of the place where her life had changed so dramatically.

In the light of day, the back corner of the garden didn't seem a place of mystery and intrigue. In fact, the overgrown rose bushes needed a good pruning and the stone bench seemed forlorn and desolate.

With a deep sigh, she sank down on the bench where Dylan had kissed her. Wistfully, she placed her fingertips to her lips as though a trace of that magical moment lingered.

"Thinking of your lover, Lady Natalia?"

The mocking words startled her. She whirled around and then froze when Lord Jonathan Taylor strode toward her from the back of her father's property. Unease settled in the pit of her stomach.

"Lord Taylor." She strove for an imperious tone. Jonathan had spread the gossip that had ruined her. For the first time, she wondered if he were bitter because she'd rejected him. "What are you doing here?"

"Why, I've come to offer you my congratulations, of course. You see, I just heard about your forthcoming marriage." His pale, sharp-featured face bore an angry menace. As he spoke, he moved closer, until less than a yard separated them.

"That's very kind of you." Natalia rose from the bench and edged toward the house in an effort to put the maximum amount of distance possible between her and her former admirer. "I'm sure my father will be glad to know you called. Shall I fetch him for you?"

Jonathan shook his head. "We both know it's you I've come to see."

Natalia frowned, anger eclipsing her fear. "No, Lord Taylor. In fact, I can't imagine what makes you think you have the right to approach me in such an inappropriate manner."

"Inappropriate? How dare you speak to me of what is appropriate? I saw you kissing Dylan Blake. I saw you moaning at his touch like a cat in heat."

Natalia shook her head, embarrassed and furious. "I'm not going to stand here and listen to this." She turned her back, her pulse racing as she quickened her steps in an effort to be away from him. Surely, he wouldn't try to stop her.

She hadn't gone five steps before he grabbed her from behind, trapped her arms, and pulled her against him with an unexpected wiry strength.

"You weren't supposed to want him."

Terror rose in her throat as he turned her in his arms and shoved her onto the stone bench. Straddling her thighs, he pinned her in place. She bucked wildly, trying to dislodge him. Laughing, he grabbed her hair and twisted until she cried out.

She stilled, glaring up at him as she struggled to catch her breath. "What do you want from me?"

"I want some of what you were so eager to give your future husband. Don't you know you've ruined everything, you stupid bitch? You were supposed to put him in his place, not marry him."

Natalia intensified her struggles, but he wrenched her arms behind her back until she thought they would snap. His face loomed above hers; his breath rank with the scent of brandy.

He was drunk, she realized, her terror growing. He must be out of his mind, to come here like this, to threaten her and put his hands on her so brutally.

Unless he doesn't plan to leave me alive to tell anyone what happened.

"Let me go." She tried to make her words into a command, but they came out as a breathy quiver.

He shook his head. "I'll make you want me. I'll make you forget about Blake."

Natalia let out a piercing scream right before his mouth descended upon hers and choked her cries with a punishing kiss.

* * *

When Dylan arrived at the duke's townhouse, the duchess greeted him warmly and directed him out to the garden, where Natalia had taken her afternoon tea.

"Why don't you join her?" Clarice suggested with a smile. "Dinner won't be served for several hours, and I know you two have a lot to talk about."

Dylan gave the lovely young duchess a grateful smile. "Thank you. I feared I wouldn't get another chance to talk to her in private until after we were married."

"Be patient with her," Clarice advised. "She's still angry and upset, but I think she'll forgive you eventually."

Heartened by his future mother-in-law's words, Dylan slipped out into the garden, only to find the small table abandoned, the tea grown long cold. He frowned. Had Natalia—?

A woman's scream cut through the quiet afternoon and stopped him in his tracks. The sound seemed so out of place, given the formal splendor of his surroundings, it took him a moment to comprehend.

The scream choked off, as though brutally silence. Dylan's heart plummeted with fear as he recognized the voice. *Natalia.*

Cursing beneath his breath, he sprinted through the hedges, praying she'd slipped or been surprised by some insect. He reached the back corner of the garden in record time, only to skid to a sharp halt.

Jonathan Taylor had Natalia trapped against the stone bench with the full weight of his body. Natalia struggled to get away, her panic and disgust evident. As Dylan started toward them, Jonathan drew back his hand and slapped her viciously across the face.

"Be still," Jonathan snarled. "Quit fighting me."

"Get your hands off her." Dylan found it hard to speak past his fury. "I'll kill you for this, you bastard."

Jonathan whirled around, his pale skin flushed with passion and anger. "I'm only taking what should have been mine all along—"

Dylan punched Jonathan into silence. The force of the blow reverberated all the way up his arm, giving him a moment of sweet satisfaction.

Jonathan stumbled. Dylan hit him again, his fury and confusion driving several more punishing blows.

Peripherally, he was aware the duke and several male servants had come outside. Natalia cringed against the hedge, her mouth buried in her hands, her eyes wide and horrified as she watched the violent scene play out before her.

Is she all right? His momentary inattention allowed Jonathan to land a blow of his own. Dylan staggered and tried to shake off the unexpected pain in his jaw.

"I wanted you to fail." Jonathan caught Dylan under his chin with another quick jab. "All my life, you've beaten me, but I thought that little bitch would finally be the one to put you in your place."

"Don't call her that." A red haze of fury obscured Dylan's vision. Jonathan would pay for daring to put his hands on her…

"Stop, sir. You're going to kill him." The calm and soothing voice pulled Dylan out of his murderous rage with an abruptness that left him reeling.

Dylan blinked, disoriented. As his mind focused, he found himself straddling his enemy's prone body. Jonathan was unconscious, his aristocratic face battered nearly beyond recognition.

"It's all right, sir." Clayton's butler crouched, his face carefully neutral. "We'll handle the matter from here."

Dylan glanced around. Clayton's servants, none of whom would meet his gaze, surrounded him. In the corner, the duke tried to calm Natalia. She trembled, her face buried against her father's chest.

"Tie him up and take him down to the cellar," Clayton instructed his men as he stroked his daughter's dark hair. "I'll send for the magistrate. We'll let the authorities deal with this piece of filth."

Dylan stood and found he, too, trembled. Clenching his hands, he pressed them behind his back so they wouldn't betray him.

His own violence stunned him, sickened him. He'd tried so hard to lock this side of himself away, afraid of what he was capable of when he gave into the demons of battle that haunted him. But as he stared down at Jonathan's inert form, he couldn't be sorry.

The bastard had dared to put his hands on Natalia. Death was too good for him.

* * *

Natalia knew she couldn't hide from her brutal attack. Her cheek and lips stung from Jonathan's angry slap, but she wasn't really hurt. Just frightened and overwhelmed by the violence of the last few minutes.

Tentatively, she lifted her face from her father's chest. Her gaze locked on Jonathan's battered form. Unconscious, he'd obviously taken the worst of the battle.

Dylan stood beside her attacker, looking rather dazed. His beautiful mouth was bloody, and his dark hair fell over his desolate gray eyes, giving him the wild, dangerous appearance of a pirate or highwayman.

Although she'd been horrified by the violence, his actions comforted her. He'd protected her in the most primal way. Every time she thought she knew him, he did something completely unexpected. His complexities both frightened and intrigued her.

"Come along, Natalia. You certainly don't need to see this." The duke tried to lead her away, but she shook off his hand.

"No. I want to talk to Captain Blake." When her father looked as though he meant to argue, she gave him a tremulous smile. "Please. It will be fine."

The duke gave a deep sigh as the servants dragged the unconscious man toward the house. "I don't know how he got close enough to you to do such a thing. I refused to allow him to court you a few weeks back, but I never dreamed he'd try something like this."

"No one could have," Natalia assured him. "But I'm fine now, and Captain Blake and I have a lot to discuss."

"Certainly." The duke squeezed Dylan's shoulder in passing. "Well done, young man. I owe you a great debt."

Dylan shook his head, seeming beyond speech. As soon as the duke disappeared, Natalia sank down on the edge of the bench, certain her weak knees would no longer support her.

"Did he hurt you?" Dylan advanced toward her, then stopped uncertainly a few feet away. "Christ, when I saw that man touch you…"

"You rescued me." She gave a lost laugh. "You really are a hero, aren't you?"

"No." He shook his head, holding her gaze. "Not a hero. I'm so sorry for what he did to you. I feel as though it's my fault."

He reached out, and they both noticed the blood on his hand. Grimacing, he scrubbed his palm against his thigh, trying to wipe the crimson stain on his trousers.

"Stop it," she whispered. "Come with me. I'll help you."

He frowned at her imperious tone but obediently followed her inside. She led him into the conservatory and gestured for him to sit in the nearest chair, then doused a clean handkerchief with a generous amount of brandy from the sideboard.

A soft hiss of pain escaped his lips when she touched the first of his split knuckles, but he quelled the sound. "You don't have to do this."

She threw him a chiding look. "And you didn't have to keep Jonathan Taylor from molesting me. But you did."

The undamaged corner of his mouth quirked into a smile. "If you keep this up, I might almost believe you care."

Natalia scrubbed his bloody knuckles with unnecessary force and wondered how she could survive touching the lush curve of his mouth after she

Diana Bold

finished with his hands. "Of course, I care. But don't start thinking I've forgiven you, because I haven't. In fact, I don't' know if I ever will."

He sighed and raked the hand she'd already tended through his disheveled hair. "All I want is a chance to earn your trust back, Natalia. How can I do that if you won't even talk to me?"

She frowned and took his other hand. As she wiped away the blood, she tried to forget how tender he'd been that night in the garden. "You're right. I can't very well avoid you forever."

"I'm glad to hear it." Some of the tension seemed to flow out of him. She couldn't help but wonder if the last few days had been as horrible for him as they had been for her.

She finished his hand then boldly sat down on his lap so she'd have better access to his poor battered face. She tenderly dabbed the small cut on his upper lip. "You're going to have a fat lip for our wedding."

At her touch, his breath hitched, his gray eyes burning with intensity. He wrapped one arm around her waist and pulled her closer. With the other, he took the bloody cloth from her hand and tossed it aside.

"If you really want me to feel better, just let me hold you for a while." As he spoke, he pressed her head against his chest and enfolded her in his strong embrace. He pressed a tender kiss to her temple and squeezed her tight. "Now, tell me honestly. Are you all right?"

God, it felt so good to be in his arms again. She let out a breath and a shuddering sigh and relaxed against him. "I am now." Her voice sounded muffled against the broad wall of his chest. "He scared me, more than anything. It seemed so unreal. I couldn't believe he was actually attacking me in my father's garden."

Dylan made a soft angry sound deep in his throat. "I can't believe it, either. When I saw him…"

She lifted her gaze to his and saw how much his own violence had upset him.

"I would have killed him if someone hadn't stopped me. I completely lost control."

Natalia cupped his face and stared deep into his eyes. "You protected me, Dylan. I'm so glad you were there. Lord knows what he would have done if you hadn't heard me scream."

"I went too far," he insisted. "Ever since I returned from the war, my anger is far too close to the surface."

"That's understandable. And I don't think you would have truly killed him. I imagine he'll be fine in a few days."

Dylan huffed out a sound of disgust and buried his face against the crook of her neck. "I don't know how he expected to get away with it."

Natalia shuddered at the memory. "I think he was drunk."

"That's no excuse."

"Don't think about it anymore. It doesn't matter. No harm was done."

Dylan lifted his head, a troubled look in his eyes. "You seem far more willing to forgive him than you are me."

His words shattered the fragile truce the afternoon's unsettling events had forged between them. Natalia pushed off his lap and stared down at him in dismay. She refused to admit his words had merit, even though they struck a chord deep within her. She told herself it wasn't unreasonable to nurse her anger and hurt, even when faced with his tenderness. "Perhaps, that's because I hardly know him. I never trusted him the way I did you."

Dylan let his head fall against the back of the chair and closed his eyes as though he couldn't bear to look at her. "I deserve that. But it's still hard to hear."

She stared at him, at this beautiful wicked man who'd stolen her heart, and she wanted to weep with the hopelessness of it all. Where did they go from here? Was it even possible to start again?

"I'm sorry. It wasn't my intention to hurt you." With a sigh, she leaned forward and pressed her lips against the cut he'd suffered in her defense. "Thank you for rescuing me. Why don't you rest for a while? I'll send someone down to tell you when dinner's ready."

Then she turned and hurried away, trying to pretend she didn't wish he'd asked her to stay.

* * *

As soon as Natalia left the room, Dylan went to find his future father-in-law. Something had to be done about Jonathan. Clayton had the power and influence to ensure the slimy worm never hurt Natalia again.

He couldn't believe Jonathan's hatred and jealousy ran deep enough to attempt an assault on the Duke of Clayton's daughter. He shuddered to think of the lengths Jonathan might have gone to in order to keep Natalia from naming her attacker.

One of the servants informed Dylan the duke was in the kitchen with Jonathan. Dylan headed in the direction the man indicated and found Jonathan stretched out on the floor, still unconscious. The duke paced around his prone body.

"I should have let you kill him," the duke muttered without preamble. "That bastard would wake up on a slow boat to China if he weren't the Marquess of Langley's son."

It doesn't matter whose son he is," Dylan asserted. "He has to pay for what he's done."

The duke nodded. "You're right. I'll insist Langley banish him. The marquess won't be happy about it—Jonathan is his heir—but I'm sure he'll agree it's the only possible way of making amends. God forbid we should have to drag this matter into the courts."

"God forbid," Dylan agreed. Enough scandal and gossip surrounded Natalia already. A sensational trial would only make things worse.

Clayton nudged Jonathan's hip with the toe of one polished black boot, as though he wanted to kick him a few times. "Well, let's just try to put all this unpleasantness behind us, shall we? The wedding is in less than two days."

Chapter Eighteen

On the morning of June third, Dylan stood before the mirror in Basingstoke's guest suite and struggled to arrange his recalcitrant cravat. Julian had offered him the use of a manservant, but after about two minutes of the man's stiff and unsmiling company, Dylan had sent him away. He was nervous enough already.

"Do you need a hand with that?"

His brother's voice jarred Dylan out of his nervous thoughts. Stunned, he let his hands fall from the starched fabric. He met Michael's gaze in the full-length mirror, instantly defensive. "What are you doing here?"

"Basingstoke told me about the wedding. I hope you don't mind if I attend? After all, it isn't every day a man's only brother gets married."

Dylan forgot all about his neckpiece and turned around. He met his brother's gaze head on and realized how much he'd hated to be the cause of the rift between them. "I thought you never wanted to see me again."

Michael shrugged and shook his head. "Words said in anger. I didn't mean them."

Dylan managed a smile of his own, divested of his tremendous load of guilt. "I'm glad to hear that, Michael. God, you can't imagine how happy I am that you're here."

"I couldn't let you go through the most important day of your life without a single member of your family by your side." Michael stepped forward and tied Dylan's cravat with crisp efficiency. "I'm sorry, but Father refused to come. He's still furious you managed to do what I couldn't. I told him it's his own fault he's lost Natalia's dowry. That if he hadn't driven you away, you might have been willing to help him."

"What about you?" Dylan picked up the light gray morning jacket that completed his wedding ensemble and shrugged into it, careful not to meet his brother's gaze. "Are you still angry with me?"

"I regret having to marry Emma Marks." Michael gave a bitter laugh. "But I feel nothing for Lady Natalia. We really don't suit. She would never have cared for me the way she cares for you."

"Perhaps you should take a closer look at Miss Marks." Dylan flashed his brother a speculative look and wondered if the flamboyant American was exactly what he needed. Maybe she could get him to bend a little. Michael needed to have a little fun and learn not to take everything so damned seriously. "I met her, you know. She's a very interesting woman."

Michael snorted, the most ungentlemanly sound Dylan had ever heard from him. "I suppose so—if crass, low-bred commoners appeal to you."

Dylan grinned. "You're such a snob, Michael. The girl can't help not being born an aristocrat."

"You're right." Michael gave a reluctant laugh. "I haven't made much of an effort to get to know her. We've never even spoken."

"Well, perhaps you should introduce yourself. You never know what might happen." Dylan went back to the mirror and gave his appearance one last critical glance. "I think it would be a very fine thing, being in love with your own wife."

He hoped such a thing was possible—prayed Natalia could learn to care for him again.

"Well, I doubt that will happen in my case, but it seems as though you've got something special with Lady Natalia. I wish you all the happiness in the world."

Dylan smiled at his brother once again. Until this moment, he hadn't realized how much Michael's absence pained him. Bless Basingstoke for his interference. "Thank you for coming. It makes all the difference."

* * *

Natalia's wedding was supposed to be brief and impersonal, performed by a clergyman in her father's extravagant gold salon. But when Natalia entered the room on her father's arm, she discovered Clarice had managed a small miracle, given the short amount of time.

Thousands of white roses accented the gold and white décor. Elegant floral arrangements covered every surface and filled the heavy air with their sweet perfume.

Although still morning, dozens of candles burned on the small altar where the clergyman waited. They provided a romantic ambiance with their flickering light.

Only Michael, Basingstoke, Clarice, and Natalia's father were in attendance. The Earl of Warren had not come, and she wondered what sort of man refused to attend his own son's wedding.

But all thoughts about the guests, or lack of them, drifted away when she caught her first glimpse of her future husband. Dylan stood to the clergyman's left, dressed in an elegant morning suit of the palest gray. His dark hair had been ruthlessly tamed, and his pale eyes glittered with appreciation as he took in Natalia's elaborate, beaded white gown.

"You take my breath away," he told her as the duke gave him her hand.

His sweet words held a ring of truth. "Thank you," she whispered. Heat rose in her cheeks as Dylan's strong fingers closed on hers.

The clergyman smiled and then cleared his throat. Solemnly, he read the words that would bind Dylan and Natalia together for the rest of their lives. All too soon, he reached the heart of the ceremony.

"Do you, Dylan Patrick Blake, take this woman to be your lawfully wedded wife?"

Patrick. His middle name was Patrick. Natalia tucked that little bit of information away for future reference. This was yet another thing she hadn't known about her future husband.

"I do." Dylan held Natalia's gaze, the moment fraught with promise. Natalia found herself drowning in the depths of his turbulent gray eyes.

"Do you, Natalia Anastasia Sinclair, take this man to be your lawfully wedded husband?"

"I do." Natalia promised to love and honor Dylan Blake in a trembling voice. Such a huge vow to fit inside two tiny words.

"You may kiss your bride," the clergyman announced, breaking the spell.

Dylan blinked, and then slowly lowered his mouth to hers. The tenderness of his chaste kiss took her breath away. The small crowd of guests gave a spatter of applause.

She was now Mrs. Dylan Blake.

* * *

Dylan couldn't tear his gaze away from his beautiful bride, who was resplendent in white lace and satin. Her intricate hairstyle left longer silky tendrils curling down her back. Diamonds sparkled at her throat and neck, but her emerald eyes far outshone such paltry treasures.

He still couldn't believe she was actually his.

There had been a moment, there at the altar, when she'd given him an unguarded look filled was such sweet promise… And kissing her again had been sheer heaven.

As they turned away from the clergyman to accept the congratulations of their small circle of guests, Dylan held fast to her hand, unwilling to let her go.

Excitement pulsed through him at the thought of the night to come. Unfortunately, he still had to get through the wedding breakfast and then the first leg of the long trip to Edinburgh. He regretted having decided to start the trip today, but he wanted to get to Aldabaran as soon as possible.

* * *

Natalia drifted through the wedding breakfast in a daze. The fine champagne Basingstoke had provided for the celebration went straight to her head and relaxed her for the first time in days.

She was grateful for the tipsy detachment. Otherwise, she would have burst into tears. All her life, she'd imagined her wedding day, and this wasn't at all how she'd planned it.

She'd expected her special day to be a huge formal affair, with hundreds of people laughing and wishing her well. Instead, only these few friends and family members had attended, and the atmosphere was far from festive.

Even her groom was quiet and subdued. Although, every time she turned her head, she found him watching her.

At last, the interminable breakfast came to an end. The small group adjourned to the parlor, where her father and the duchess presented her with an intricately carved ivory box that contained all her mother's jewels. The gift touched her, but it still didn't make the whole thing seem real.

Then the moment she'd dreaded arrived. Dylan wanted to leave directly for Scotland, and she was forced to say goodbye to her father and Clarice.

She embraced the duchess tightly. "I'll miss you so much," she whispered as she inhaled Clarice's scent of lavender and sweetness.

"Everything will work out for the best," Clarice promised her. "Write me every day."

"I will." She tried to smile through her tears.

Her father came next, looking worried and grim. "I hope you made the right choice, daughter. God knows I intended so much more for you."

"He's a good man." Natalia found herself defending Dylan despite everything that had happened. "Don't worry, Father. I'll be fine."

He nodded, then returned to Clarice's side.

Sherbourne approached her next, while Dylan and Basingstoke said their goodbyes on the other side of the room. "Congratulations. You've managed to achieve something people in our class rarely do. You've married for love."

Love. She looked away, embarrassed. This man had heard her say those damning words. He'd seen her locked in Dylan's passionate embrace.

He should have been at her side today. She almost wished he was. At least with him, she would have always known where she stood. He would never have made her heart race and her breath catch. He was far too proper to feel such a crass emotion as love.

"Dylan married me for my dowry. It had nothing whatsoever to do with love."

"I wouldn't be so certain of that. I've seen the way he looks at you." Sherbourne lowered his voice. "He has a good heart. He just needs someone to care about. I know he's hurt you, but I think if you give him a chance, he'll never let you down again."

"I wish that were true." The picture he painted of his brother resembled the one she secretly held in her heart, and she desperately wanted to believe he knew Dylan well enough to be right.

Impulsively, she leaned forward and kissed him on the cheek. "Thank you for your kind words. They mean a great deal to me."

He flushed, obviously taken aback. "My brother is a lucky man. A very lucky man."

Chapter Nineteen

Natalia and Dylan set off for Aldabaran in a fine coach that Basingstoke had loaned them. Dylan was grateful for his friend's generosity. It would have been impossible to have a meaningful conversation with his wife if they were surrounded by strangers.

Unfortunately, it wasn't easy to have a meaningful conversation when they were alone, either. Before they even reached the outskirts of London, Natalia turned her face away, curled into a protective little ball on the opposite seat, and went to sleep.

At least she pretended to sleep. He had his doubts. She was probably faking it to avoid talking to him.

In truth, he could use a nap as well. He'd spent the previous night pacing in his suite of rooms, wondering if he'd made the right decision. Could he ever earn Natalia's forgiveness?

How could he bear it if she kept him at arm's length forever? Perhaps her reticence would not hurt so much if he'd never gotten to know her. But they'd had that one magical evening together, and he feared he'd spend the rest of his life trying to recreate it.

Would she even allow him to consummate their vows? God, what would he do if she turned him away? Would he be forced to eventually turn to another woman?

His heart rebelled at the very thought. He didn't want to take a mistress. He wanted his wife.

He sighed, and then shifted in his seat in an attempt to wake her, but she didn't move a muscle. In the end, her utter stillness gave her away. If she truly slept, her body would sway in rhythm with the coach.

He stared out the window for a while, but his frustration grew with each passing mile. He couldn't stand her silence. He had to do something.

"I think there are a few things we need to talk about." He spoke casually, as though they'd been in the middle of a conversation. She flinched, and he grinned with satisfaction. "I know you're not sleeping," he continued. "And I wish you'd stop pretending you were."

For a long moment, she didn't move. He had to restrain himself from reaching across the coach and shaking her. At last, she sat up, brushed a few wayward strands of hair out of her remarkable green eyes, and met his gaze. "You're right. I didn't mean to be so rude."

Mollified, he searched for the right words. "I'd like to work this out, Natalia. Just tell me what you want me to do."

"You don't need to do anything. I realize this fiasco isn't entirely your fault." She sounded bitter and resigned. So unlike the vibrant happy girl he'd met just a few short weeks ago.

"It is my fault. All of it." He hated this feeling of helplessness. He had no idea what to do or say that could make things right.

She shook her head. "It was my own choices, my own decisions that brought me to this. I was such a fool." She blinked rapidly, as though trying to hold back tears. "I'm afraid to trust myself."

It slew him to know she felt that way. He didn't want her to feel foolish about herself. He wanted her to regain her wonderful impetuous spark. He wanted her to trust herself again. He wanted her to trust *him*.

"It's not wrong to be impulsive and passionate. Do you think you're the only girl who ever stole away from a party to kiss a man in the dark?"

"Perhaps not. But I should have known better."

He raked his hand through his hair and laughed. "I should have known better, too. I should've walked away the moment I realized Michael wanted you."

"But you couldn't." She broke eye contact and sank back against the velvet seat, staring out the window at the passing scenery. "You had your precious wager to think about."

He'd known this was coming, sooner or later. Perhaps it was better to have the wound out in the open, where the blister could be lanced. They'd already let things fester and boil beneath the surface for too long.

"I never meant to hurt you." He wanted to reach out to her, hold her the way she'd held him. He wanted to show her he could offer comfort as well as passion.

"What did you think would happen? You knew I'd find out. You didn't even try to keep it a secret." Her anger was a vast improvement over the bitter resignation.

"The gamble seemed harmless enough at the time. I only had to dance with you a few times. Nothing that would harm your reputation. I planned to collect my winnings and never look back. But then I met you, and I knew I couldn't do it. I wanted far more than that."

"Why?" She held his gaze, her green eyes filled with reproach. "I've heard the rumors. I know about all your conquests. No woman has ever captured your attention for more than a moment or two. All you wanted was my dowry."

"No," he murmured. "You sell yourself short."

"Admit it," Natalia insisted. "In a few weeks, you'll want someone else, and I'll be nothing but a burden to you."

He shook his head and prayed she was wrong. He needed this marriage to work. The alternative—an endless, empty future—was too awful to contemplate. He couldn't bear to go back to the way things had been. He needed his life to have some meaning.

For better or worse, she was it.

"Despite the circumstances, I didn't take our wedding vows lightly. I won't look elsewhere. Not unless you intend to shut me out completely." He met her gaze head-on. "Do you?"

She blushed and closed her eyes. "No. I didn't take those vows lightly either."

"Good." He sighed and tried to relax. The entire conversation had taken much more energy than he'd expected, but there was still one more thing he wanted her to know. "I knew you were different the moment we met. When you looked into my eyes and really saw me. Not the hero my father wanted on display for his parties. Not the fearless captain my men looked up to, but the real me. The one no one else had ever tried to see before."

She gave him a wistful smile. Then she crossed the aisle in a swish of silk skirts and sat beside him. Threading her fingers through his, she stared deep into his eyes. "Show me that man again. I miss him."

"I will." Her generosity stunned him. He knew how much it cost her to move those few feet.

They passed the next few hours in silence, watching the scenery pass, but she never took her hand away.

He held on tight. As far as meaningful conversations went, this had definitely been a good beginning.

* * *

By the time they reached the inn, Natalia was dripping with exhaustion. Although Basingstoke's coach was well sprung, the road had been rough. Her entire body ached from the jarring ride.

Dylan went inside to procure them some rooms while she remained in the coach. She needed a few moments alone to gather her thoughts. The hours spent holding his hand in companionable silence had rattled her far more than she wanted to admit.

After an entire day in such close quarters, she should've gotten used to Dylan's masculine presence. But the constant temptation only made her long for more.

He'd been so sweet this afternoon, and he'd broken through her defenses with astonishing efficiency. Perhaps it was the captain in him. Perhaps she was merely another battle to be won. No matter how cynically she tried to look at the matter, she had to admit he'd done and said all the right things. And this was their wedding night.

Dear God, she needed a little more time.

He returned a few moments later, opened the coach door, and smiled up at her. "Are you ready?"

She nodded, but her entire soul cried, "No!"

She wasn't ready. She'd never be able to maintain the proper distance. Once he kissed her, she'd be lost.

With every passing moment, she fell more deeply in love with him. When he walked away from her this time, it would be lethal.

Dylan usurped the coachman and helped her down to the street. He held her against him for just a moment too long, and she shivered at the contact.

Oh, this was a bad, bad idea.

"God, you feel so good." The soft whisper tickled her ear and then his lips brushed her temple. "I feel as though I've waited for this night my entire life."

She stared up at him, unable to speak. His pale gray eyes held such passion and promise. All Clarice's advice about lovemaking tumbled to the forefront of her mind. Could she really do such things in an effort to bind him to her forever?

"Come with me," he urged. "I don't want to wait any longer."

Turning, he led her through the inn's front door into a raucous common room, where people danced and drank with abandon. The scent of cabbage mingled with ale and sweat. She glanced around in awe. The laughter and music were infectious.

At a corner table, a couple kissed ravenously, unconcerned by their audience. Natalia blushed and hurried to keep up with Dylan's long-legged strides.

They mounted a few flights of stairs and, on the third floor, Dylan ushered her inside a surprisingly nice suite of rooms. The small sitting room boasted a lovely overstuffed sofa placed near a crackling fireplace. A large bedchamber was visible through an arched doorway.

Natalia glanced at the huge canopy bed, and her heart nearly stopped. *Only one bed.* Tonight, she would sleep in Dylan's arms.

Natalia paced while the footman carried up their luggage. When the man had finished, Dylan shut the door. He smiled and looked around in satisfaction. "Basingstoke recommended this place. It's nice, don't you think?"

"Yes, very nice. But there's only one bed." Natalia blurted out the words before she had a chance to think them through. Then she stood there, dying a thousand deaths as she realized how childish she sounded.

Dylan's smile faded. "I only meant to have one bed. This is our wedding night, Natalia. And after what you said in the coach, I didn't think you'd turn me away."

"I meant what I said. But not tonight. It's too soon. I need more time."

"More time?" He sighed in frustration and crossed the room to the sofa. A bottle of champagne chilled in a bucket of ice, and he gave her a pensive look as he picked it up. When he popped the cork, the sharp sound made her flinch. "How much time do you need?"

As he spoke, he poured them both a glass of the bubbly liquid. He offered her one, and she took a few hesitant steps, closing the distance between them. When she reached for the glass, his hand touched hers. His heat stunned her.

"A few weeks. A month perhaps." She dropped her gaze and brought the glass to her lips.

"That's too long." The words exploded out of him.

She stepped back. Had she gone too far? Would he resort to violence? Her heart pounded frantically in her chest, while she waited for whatever he chose to do next.

To her relief, he took a deep breath, as though trying to calm himself. Then he sat down on the edge of the sofa and rolled the stem of the glass back and forth between his long elegant fingers.

She stared at his hands, transfixed. Why postpone what would undoubtedly be the most amazing experience of her life?

"All right, I'll give you a little time. I understand that you're still angry with me, and you didn't really want this marriage. I agree not to exercise my marital rights until after we leave Edinburgh."

His marital rights. She shuddered at his reminder that she'd vowed to give him unlimited access to her body.

"You said we'd only be there a day or two."

He brought the champagne glass to his lips and drank deeply before he answered. "It could be longer, though I hope not. In any event, I want us to spend our first night at Aldabaran as husband and wife."

"We're already husband and wife," she reminded him, in growing exasperation.

"No," he said, his gaze locked with hers. "We're not."

She decided not to push the matter any further. At least she'd won one small victory. She wouldn't have to deal with him tonight, while her emotions were still so bruised and battered. She had a little while to resurrect her defenses. A week at the very least.

"Very well. We'll consummate our marriage the first night we spend at Aldabaran."

He relaxed. "Sit down. Finish your drink. I'm not going to attack you."

She sank down on the edge of the sofa. "Are you going to get another room?"

He shook his head. "I already told the innkeeper this is our wedding night. I'll be damned if I'll go back down there and ask for another room now."

"But where will you sleep?"

"Right bloody here, I imagine." He patted the sofa.

Men were impossible. "Don't be ridiculous. You're far too tall. Wouldn't it be better to just swallow your pride and ask for another room? Why do you care what the innkeeper thinks?"

He downed the rest of the champagne and poured himself another glass. She watched him nervously, wondering if he became volatile when he was intoxicated.

"I'm not getting another room. I do have a little pride."

"Fine," she muttered. "Be uncomfortable. I don't care."

He leaned toward her, with the pretense of refilling her glass. Her champagne had somehow disappeared during the last few tension-filled minutes. Now only inches separated them.

He stared at her as though he'd like to wring her neck. Or devour her. Or both.

"Don't you?" He brushed her cheek with his fingertip, the touch feather light and at odds with his simmering anger.

"Don't I what?" His nearness made her feel breathless and strange.

"Don't you care for me, Natalia? Not even a little?" He ran his index finger over her lips, his gaze frighteningly intense.

"Please," she whispered, but she didn't know what she was asking for. Did she want him to keep touching her, or did she want him to leave her alone?

He kept stroking her lip, and she felt a growing urge to open her mouth, to kiss the soft little pad of skin on the tip of his finger. The champagne seemed to have inhibited her ability to keep from giving into her urges, because before she could stop herself, she'd done exactly that.

Eyes widening, he inhaled sharply as she tasted the softness of his skin.

"Yes. Kiss me. At least give me this much. A wedding present. A real kiss, not a dutiful little peck like this morning."

He wanted to kiss her. Suddenly, it didn't seem like so very much to ask. It was their wedding night, after all.

She leaned forward, holding his gaze until the very last second. Then she closed her eyes and fell into his embrace.

This time, he was not sweet. He was not gentle. He devoured her mouth and pressed her against the back of the sofa as if he'd like to pin her there for all eternity.

Weak and dizzy with longing, she let him consume her, drowning in the taste of him—man, heat, and sweet champagne. She speared her hands through his silken hair and pulled him even closer. A maelstrom of passion ignited within her and centered in the pit of her stomach with pulsating urgency. She wanted to press against him until they became one shape, one body.

With a muffled groan, he pulled away. He rested his forehead against hers and his big body trembled as he obviously fought to control his own raging need. "If you don't want to make love to me, you'd better get the hell out of here."

She blinked owlishly, blinded by a haze of lust.

"Run away," he urged sharply, then he gentled. "Or don't. Stay, love. Let me take off your clothes and touch you. Taste you." He spread gentle, tender kisses over her brow, and then ran his tongue around the delicate shell of her ear. "Let me come inside you, Natalia. Let me make you my wife."

She shuddered at the images his words conjured. For a long second, she let herself dangle on that dangerous precipice. Oh, how she wanted to stay. She loved him so much…

She wrenched out of his arms. She couldn't do this, not now, when everything inside her demanded that he love her in return. She might beg. She might plead. She might say those damning words again.

I love you, Dylan.

"I'm sorry," she whispered. Then she raced for the bedchamber door, slamming it shut and locking it behind her.

Chapter Twenty

The solicitor, Mr. James Byrnes, kept a suite of offices near the Royal Mile, in the very heart of Edinburgh. Dylan went there alone after they arrived in the city, leaving Natalia at the inn where they'd spend the night.

If his finances were as desperate as he thought, he didn't want her with him. His poverty would only give her more ammunition the next time she wanted to argue about her dowry.

The long trek from England had passed pleasantly, for the most part. They talked on and off again in the coach during the day, but at night, he'd taken to procuring separate rooms for them. He kept hoping that as they got to know each other better, she'd realize how ridiculous it was to keep putting off the inevitable, but to his dismay, she'd seemed all too eager each night to take her leave of him.

He'd sent word ahead, and when he arrived, the secretary ushered him directly into the elderly gentleman's office. Mr. Byrnes was a slim man with spectacles and a friendly smile.

"Captain Blake. So good of you to stop by."

Dylan returned the smile and shook the old man's proffered hand. "I hope you have good news for me."

The old man returned to his place behind his desk and gestured for Dylan to take the leather chair that faced him. "Oh, very good news, young man. I'm sure you'll find everything in order. The estate has posted a profit for several years now." Still smiling, he handed Dylan a leather-bound account book.

"A profit?" Dylan's excitement grew as he glanced through the pages. "Someone has been taking care of the place?"

"Of course." The old man gave Dylan a disgruntled look. "I knew your mother's family very well, Captain Blake. The old Laird and I were great friends. I've done my utmost to ensure your inheritance."

"Forgive me. But since I wasn't even aware I had an inheritance until last week, I had my doubts."

The old man looked abashed. "I feel terrible about the misunderstanding, but I've been sending quarterly reports to the Earl of Warren since you were a child. I had no idea he hadn't seen fit to inform you the estate was yours."

Dylan relented. He could hardly blame the old man for not trying to contact him directly. No doubt the earl had told Mr. Byrnes that Dylan was simply too much of a wastrel to want the responsibility.

"And what of the house?" Dylan asked, thinking of Natalia's promise. "Is it in good order?"

"Oh, yes. I believe so. The rooms might need a good airing out, but the caretaker has assured me many times it could be ready for you immediately if you ever expressed interest in a visit."

Dylan smiled. "Well, I intend to do more than visit. I brought my new bride. We plan to make Aldabaran our home."

"That's wonderful news." The old man's eyes lit up at the prospect. "Your grandfather would have been so pleased. Would you like me to send word ahead, have them prepare the rooms?"

"No. That won't be necessary." Dylan's mind already raced ahead. "I plan to leave first thing in the morning."

* * *

Aldabaran sat upon a high rocky cliff, overlooking the churning sea. The keep had been built 500 years ago with defense in mind. A sturdy square building, five stories high, the keep's pale stone walls gleamed in the afternoon light.

Dylan swung out of the coach and took a deep breath of the familiar salty air. His troubles fell away, at least temporarily. *Home at last.*

Turning, he helped his wife climb down and examined her face as she got her first look at their new home. His intense desire for her to love Aldabaran frightened him.

But she didn't disappoint him. She took a long slow look around, her green eyes missing nothing. "It's beautiful. Everything you said it would be."

Smiling broadly, he took her hand and started toward the gate, sparing the coachman a wink and a wave. "I'll help you with the bags in a minute, mate.

Right now, I need to carry my bride over the threshold."

The coachman nodded, and Dylan dragged Natalia along behind him, excitement pulsing in his veins. To his utter surprise, the inner courtyard looked exactly as it had twenty years ago. Flowers bloomed, and the stones were meticulously swept.

As they approached the front door, a scowling man strode from the direction of the stables. "What is your business here?" he demanded as he intercepted them.

Dylan gave the stranger an annoyed glance, but on closer examination came recognition.

"Patrick Macpherson!" He changed direction and shook the other man's hand. "Dear God, it's good to see you after all these years."

Long dormant memories flooded him. Patrick, not the earl, had taught Dylan to ride, hunt, and fish. How could he have forgotten, even for a moment?

Patrick hadn't aged at all. Even though he must be in his fifties, and his dark hair had gone gray around the temples, he was still fit and lean.

"Dylan," Patrick said, his voice gone hoarse. "Have you really come home at last?"

Dylan smiled, and the tension flowed out of him like water through a sieve. "Aye," he told Patrick in the brogue that had once been second nature. "It took me a while, but I finally found my way back,"

The older man's face bore a look of extreme emotion. For a moment, Dylan thought Patrick might embrace him. Then a mask fell over Patrick's features, and he took a step back. "I'm sure you'll find everything in order, sir. Mother and I have taken good care of the place while you've been away."

Patrick had once been the head groom, but apparently, he now ran the entire estate. By the look of things, he'd done a damn fine job of it.

Remembering his manners, Dylan drew Natalia forward. "Lady Natalia Blake, may I present Patrick Macpherson, a dear old friend. Patrick, this is my wife. We married less than a fortnight ago."

Patrick gave Natalia a long assessing look then grinned. "You'll do fine, my lady. Just fine." Turning to Dylan, he gestured toward the house. "Mum wasn't expectin' you, but I'm sure she'll have the rooms made up in no time at all."

Room, Dylan thought fiercely. Tonight, they would share the same room, whether Natalia liked it or not.

"Very good," he said, relieved. "I'm sorry we didn't send word ahead."

Patrick shoved his explanations away. "We're just glad to have you back, lad. This place has been quiet and empty for far too long."

* * *

Natalia followed her new husband and Mr. Macpherson toward the keep. As the two men spoke of the past, she noticed an eerie resemblance between them, with their dark coloring, startling blue-gray eyes, and animated gestures.

When they reached the massive oak entry, Dylan turned and swept her up in his arms, giving her no chance to protest. He grinned down at her, gray eyes full of mischief. "I told you I'd carry you over the threshold."

"Yes, you did." She clung to him, thrilled. His heat and strength surrounded her, a blatant reminder of the night to come.

All too soon, they were inside. He let her slide down his muscled length. But his rueful smile assured her he didn't want to let her go.

Still flustered, she gazed around at her new home. She'd expected the inside of the keep to be dark and musty, but to her delight, it been renovated, probably when Dylan was a child.

They stood inside a huge great hall, which stretched the entire length of the building. Bright sunlight filtered through dozens of mullioned windows fitted with sparkling glass, and the dark wood shone with signs of a fresh polish.

On the walls hung a vast assortment of weapons—swords, daggers, and claymores—arranged in such intricate patterns they looked like works of art. Huge fireplaces stood on each side of the hall, both large enough to cook a full-sized boar. The ceiling soared twenty feet overhead and depicted scenes of the mighty Camerons in bloody battle.

A very male room, to be sure, but despite its immense size and bloodthirsty décor, the great hall made her smile. The room suited Dylan, somehow. And the small, rather cozy groupings of upholstered chairs near both fireplaces kept it from being too overwhelming.

Dylan's face was lit up like a little boy's. "What do you think? Do you like it?"

"Yes, I do," she replied honestly. "I like it very much." Aldabaran seemed like a home, far more so than any of her father's grandiose estates. Perhaps this was the place she'd been looking for.

Before she could say anything else, a small elderly woman emerged from a door on the far side of the room.

"Patrick?" Her voice was old and faded. As she came closer, Natalia decided she looked like a grandmother out of a storybook. Plump, with white hair and red cheeks, her blue eyes sparkled despite her age. She approached slowly, a puzzled frown on her lovely old face. "Do we have guests, son?"

A wide grin split Patrick's handsome weathered face. "It's our boy, Dylan. He's come home, Mum. Home to stay. And he's brought his new bride."

"Dylan?" The old woman shuffled a few steps closer and stared at Dylan's face as though he were the savior. Her eyes filled with tears. Reaching up, she touched his cheek tenderly, as though afraid he'd vanish into thin air. "Oh, my sweet boy."

"How are you, ma'am?" Dylan smiled gently, but he shifted uncomfortably, as though uncertain how to handle such unconditional acceptance. Natalia wondered if he even remembered the old woman. He'd said he hadn't been back here since he was seven.

Apparently, he'd been a wonderful little boy, or these people wouldn't be so glad to see him.

Now it was her turn to shift uncomfortably, because she'd always known this side of him existed. But if she'd married a truly kind and generous man, where did that leave her and her anger?

"We kept everything nice for you." The little woman blinked away her tears. "Patrick thought you'd never come back. But I always told him that you would. This is your home, isn't it, dearie?"

Dylan nodded and brought the old woman's hand to his lips, kissing it with a tender smile. "It certainly is, Mrs. Macpherson. I always wanted to come back, but I didn't find out my grandfather left Aldabaran to me until recently."

"Didn't the earl tell you, then?" A thundercloud settled over Patrick's face, and he muttered something wicked-sounding in Gaelic. "I never should have—" He broke off, once again managing to control his emotions. "Well, that's neither here nor there. We're just glad he finally told you."

Natalia laughed at Patrick's audacity. Until now, she hadn't known the earl had kept Dylan's inheritance away from him.

Dylan glanced down at her, a small smile curving his well-formed lips. "You have a lovely laugh. I hope to hear it more often."

Her own smile faded. She realized this was the first time she'd laughed in a very long time.

He sighed, his disappointment obvious, and turned back to Patrick. "My father and I have never gotten along very well. He never had much use for me, after my mother died."

Patrick shared a swift pained look with his mother, and then placed his broad hand on Dylan's shoulder. "Don't fash yerself, lad. Come along. I'll show you some of the changes I've made these past twenty years. There's much I'd like your opinion of."

Dylan glanced over his shoulder at Natalia. "Will you be all right with Mrs. Macpherson? Perhaps she can give you a tour of the old place."

Natalia nodded. "I'll be fine." In truth, she was grateful to have a few moments to collect her thoughts. She hadn't forgotten the promise she'd made to him on their wedding night. He obviously hadn't forgotten it either.

The two men departed through the open door and walked back to the coach side by side. Once again, their similarity struck her. They were the same height and had the same muscular build. Amazingly beautiful men, she thought with a sigh.

Mrs. Macpherson seemed to be thinking similarly; as she watched, her face shimmered with wistful yearning. She finally turned to Natalia. "Come with me, lass. I'll show you the rest of the house."

"That would be lovely." Natalia hoped the bedchambers were as charming as the great hall. She followed the old woman through the dining area and into a large, surprisingly modern kitchen, which was also on the first floor. She didn't know much about kitchens, having rarely even entered one, but it looked well equipped and sparkled with cleanliness.

"You've been taking care of this great big house all by yourself?" she asked, as they ascended a set of wide spiral stone steps toward the upper levels.

Mrs. Macpherson scurried up the stairs with the speed of a woman half her age. "My Patrick helps, of course. When he's not taking care of the gardens and the tenants."

"The tenants?" Natalia grew more impressed with Dylan's caretakers by the moment.

"Our dear Dylan owns all the land hereabouts. There's a small settlement over the ridge. Good people, mostly. We haven't had a bit of trouble with them paying their rents. Patrick goes to Edinburgh once a year to deposit the sums."

With Dylan having been such an absentee landlord, the Macphersons could have easily let the place go and skimmed the profits for themselves. But they seemed to care for Dylan and were strangely eager to please him.

"We'll have to see about getting you some help, perhaps a cook or a maid," Natalia mused, as she hurried to keep up.

Mrs. Macpherson cast her a grateful glance. "I am gettin' up in years. A little help would be greatly appreciated. I can think of several village lasses who would do just fine." *Lasses.* They were certainly informal around Aldabaran. Even Natalia had been addressed as lass. Still, she couldn't work up the energy to be insulted. In fact, she rather preferred the informal atmosphere. At the duke's home, no servant would even dream of meeting an aristocrat's eyes, let alone addressing one with such familiarity.

Mrs. Macpherson led her up yet another flight of stairs. A large library, which doubled as an office, and a cozy sitting room comprised the second floor, while four large bedchambers and two antiquated bathrooms were on the third.

They briefly visited the servants' quarters on the fourth floor. The Macphersons already occupied several rooms, but plenty of space remained for any others she might hire.

Huge, barren, and sunlit, the tower solar was the only part of the keep that hadn't been renovated. Natalia strolled across the dusty wood floor and wondered how she could use it.

The tour complete, Mrs. Macpherson led her back down to the third floor for a closer inspection of the bedchambers.

Natalia wandered through the four rooms, amazed by their simple beauty. Two were decidedly feminine, one decorated in various shades of green, the other pale peach. There was also a master suite, which she assumed had belonged to Dylan's grandfather.

The last room had obviously belonged to a little boy, Natalia stared at the fanciful paintings of jungle creatures on the walls and felt the strangest ache. One day very soon, her own child might fall asleep with lions and elephants watching over him.

"I'll have the master bedchamber made up for you and your husband in no time, lass." Mrs. Macpherson had let Natalia explore the rooms at her leisure, but now the old woman seemed anxious to get to work.

Despite the extra work it would cause the old woman, Natalia wasn't brave enough to share a room with Dylan. She and her husband had come to a fragile truce, but in order to maintain it, she needed to keep him at a distance.

She would share her bed with him tonight, because she couldn't think of any way out of the promise she'd made. But after she'd done her marital duty, she needed at least the illusion of privacy.

"I'd prefer to have my own bedchamber." Seeing the old woman's crestfallen face, she explained hurriedly, "I'll air out the green bedchamber myself. You need only worry about the master suite."

Mrs. Macpherson seemed a little mollified by the offer, but she continued to frown. "I'm grateful for the help, lass. And it's a good choice. Dylan's mother used that room when she was a girl, and then later, when she'd return for the summers, after she married that dreadful man."

Only half listening, Natalia turned back to the green bedchamber, wondering where on earth she should start. She'd never cleaned her own room in her life.

Mrs. Macpherson stepped in front of her, shaking her head as she peered up into Natalia's face. "Are you sure you don't want stay in the master suite, lass? Dinna young Dylan say the two of you were newlyweds? Surely, you want to spend some extra time with the lad?"

"I'm afraid our marriage is one of convenience," she told a woman in order to quash any romantic fantasy the woman might have.

"Ah. Highborn, are you, lass?"

"My father is a duke." Natalia felt uncomfortable with the old woman's curiosity but couldn't see the harm in answering her questions.

"A duke!" Mrs. Macpherson chuckled. "Imagine that! Our little Dylan, marrying a duke's daughter."

"He married me for my dowry." Natalia related the news bitterly, wanting to deflate Dylan's saintly image in some way. "All he cares about is the money."

"A duke's daughter, and a large dowry, too?" Mrs. Macpherson couldn't have been more delighted. "I must tell my Patrick. He'll be so pleased."

Still muttering happily under her breath, the little old woman wandered down the hall, leaving Natalia alone.

Mrs. Macpherson didn't seem to care that Dylan had married her for her money. Embarrassed, Natalia realized she'd wanted the other woman's sympathy. Why didn't anyone else find the circumstances of her marriage as horrible and demeaning as she did?

She flopped down on the bed, then sat bolt upright, coughing and choking at the cloud of dust she'd released. Resolutely, she stood and stripped off the covers until only the mattress remained. With a deep sigh, she gathered the blankets and carried them outside. Perhaps she'd be able to work out her frustrations by beating them into submission.

Chapter Twenty-one

Patrick led Dylan on a very satisfying tour of Aldabaran's grounds. The spotless stables contained magnificent blooded horses, and the outbuildings were in excellent repair. The dairy and chicken coop looked prosperous, and the gardens and flowerbeds bloomed profusely.

After completing the tour, Patrick took Dylan to the village to meet some of the tenants. Dylan spent a few wonderful hours getting to know the people who called Aldabaran home.

The afternoon flew by, and he noticed the sun sinking over the stormy sea in surprise. As he and Patrick returned to the keep, Dylan reflected that nothing else on earth could have diverted him from spending the evening in Natalia's arms.

For all intents and purposes, this was his wedding night, and with that thought in mind, he hurried his steps and earned a wide grin from his companion. "Eager to get back your pretty young wife, are you, lad?"

Dylan nodded. "Aye, I am. I hope she isn't too upset that I've left her on her own for so long." In truth, he imagined she'd been glad for the respite. But he couldn't admit such a thing to Patrick.

"I imagine Mum has kept her occupied. The lass will want to explore her new home."

They crested the hill and Aldabaran stood before them, its stone walls glowing blood red in the last rays of the setting sun. Dylan paused for a moment, overwhelmed by the sheer beauty of his new home.

Patrick turned to see why he'd stopped. Then he stilled, too, and stared at Dylan's face with an arrested expression. "You look so much like your mother. She'd always get the same look on her face whenever she returned home from London."

Dylan tore his gaze away from the keep, stunned by the yearning in the older man's eyes. And in that one naked unguarded moment, Dylan understood why Patrick had stayed here all these years.

"You loved my mother, didn't you?" The words escaped before Dylan could think better of them.

Patrick flinched and turned away. "Of course, I did," he muttered, as he strode up the path that meandered along the edge of the cliff. "Everyone who knew Fiona loved her."

Dylan stared after him for a moment then hurried to catch up. "That's not true," he told the other man with a bitter laugh. "My father didn't."

Patrick cast him a quick pained look. "Can we not talk of Warren, lad? The very thought of the man incites me to a murderous rage."

Dylan chuckled at Patrick's audacity. He felt the same way about his father, most days.

About a hundred yards from the keep, Patrick turned toward him once more. "I wanted to tell you, lad, how proud I was to hear of your accomplishments in the army. I followed your career as close as I could, Aldabaran being so remote."

Dylan blinked, caught off guard once more. A curious sense of warmth stole over him. Patrick had just gifted him with the very words he'd waited in vain to hear from his own father.

He cleared his throat, embarrassed. "Thank you. I appreciate that."

Patrick squeezed his shoulder and then smiled. "Let's get up to the house. Mum should have dinner ready by now."

"Sounds good. I'm starving." Though welcome, Patrick's praise had embarrassed Dylan, and he was glad to bring the conversation back to the mundane.

Within minutes, they'd reached the keep. When Dylan opened the wide front doors, an assortment of wonderful smells greeted him. Crystal and china covered one end of the massive table, and his lovely wife waited for him in one of the armchairs before a roaring fire.

Her dark hair shone like satin in the firelight. She'd obviously bathed and changed since this morning. Now she wore a lovely, yet simple, green gown, which complemented the extraordinary color of her eyes. She couldn't hide a momentary flicker of pleasure at the sight of him, and he grinned, thoroughly pleased.

Life couldn't get any better than this.

Mrs. Macpherson bustled up to meet them, urging Dylan to take his place at the head of the huge table. "I've made some haggis," she exclaimed, beaming at him. "I remember how much you liked it."

Dylan remembered no such thing, but he smiled back, charmed. "I'm sure it will be wonderful." Glancing back at Natalia, he held out his arm. "I missed you," he murmured, as he led her to her chair.

She blushed a bit but made no comment. After she was seated, he took his own place. When the Macphersons turned to leave the room, he protested, "Have dinner with us. There's plenty of room."

Patrick looked as if he'd like to agree, but Mrs. Macpherson pulled him toward the door that led to the kitchen. "Nonsense, young man. We wouldn't dream of it. Have dinner with your lovely wife."

And so, at long last, Dylan was alone with Natalia.

"How was your day? Did Mrs. Macpherson show you around?" As he spoke, Dylan began offering her the covered dishes spread in front of them.

Natalia served herself, skipping the haggis. "Mrs. Macpherson was very helpful. This house is wonderful, Dylan. Truly. I like it very much." She gave him a shy smile that warmed his heart.

"Anything you'd like to change?" He hoped not, but he was more than willing to give her the opportunity. He hadn't forgotten Basingstoke's advice.

She shook her head. "Everything is perfect, just the way it is. However, the solar is empty."

"Any thoughts on what you'd like to do with it?" Dylan smiled, amazed at how right it felt to have this boring little domestic discussion.

"What was it used for when you were a child?"

He thought for a moment, and an image came to him. He remembered racing around the great empty space, while his mother stood in a pool of light, her face and clothes covered in paint.

"My mother was an artist. She used the solar as a studio." How could he have forgotten such a thing? It unsettled him to realize how much of his childhood he'd locked away in the far corners of his mind. "I wonder if there are any of her paintings still in the house."

"We'll look first thing tomorrow," Natalia promised him. "It would be a way to get to know her better, wouldn't it?"

Once again, she surprised him. He reached across the table and squeezed her hand in an attempt to let her know how much her offer meant to him.

"How old were you when you lost her?"

Her question chased away the happy memories and brought forth the ones he tried so hard to forget. "I was seven." He released her hand and returned his attention to his plate. "It was a long time ago. I don't remember much about her."

"I was four when my mother passed away."

Natalia's soft comment reminded him he wasn't the only one who'd dealt with loss.

"She died in childbirth, trying yet again to give my father a male heir." Her voice held a subtle prompt. She obviously wanted to know how Fiona Blake had died, but his mother's suicide still hurt too much, so he changed the subject.

"Did you have our things taken to my grandfather's bedchamber?"

Natalia looked away, and her cheeks flushed. "Your things are there. But I put my own in the green bedchamber."

Dylan mentally counted to ten, determined not to let his anger and disappointment get the best of him. "Separate rooms? I thought we'd reached an understanding in Edinburgh."

"We did." Natalia turned even redder, if such a thing were possible. "I won't turn you away tonight, should you still wish to come to me. But I'd like you to leave afterward." Her voice turned accusatory. "Or am I too have no privacy at all?"

She won't turn me away. For a moment, nothing else registered. His immense relief briefly blocked the rest of what she'd said. But then the words sank in, and he glared down at his food in an attempt to keep from turning his anger and disappointment on her. So, she wanted privacy, did she?

More likely, she just wanted to maintain the distance she'd tried to impose between them. She knew it would be impossible once he held her in his arms all night.

Hopefully, she would change her mind after they'd made love.

In any event, he decided not to argue the point. She'd been remarkably accommodating so far, but the stubborn set of her jaw convinced him she wouldn't bend on this point.

"I will come to you tonight. But I'll leave afterward, if you're sure that's what you want."

He no longer had the slightest interest in his meal. He was starving for something, but it wasn't food.

Natalia made one last desperate attempt. "You won't change your mind and give me a little more time?"

"What do you think?" He refused to let her make him feel guilty. She was his wife, and tonight he meant to have her. "I'm going to take a bath, Natalia. When I'm finished, I expect you to be waiting for me."

Then he pushed away from the table and stomped out of the room.

* * *

Natalia sat on the edge of the immense featherbed in the green bedchamber, running a brush through her loosened hair. Her nerves were frayed to the breaking point, and she hoped this familiar routine would calm her.

It wasn't working.

Every small sound made her jump, and she clutched the edges of her thick flannel nightgown more tightly around her throat. She'd worn the ugly prudish garment in an attempt to cool Dylan's passion, but she knew her efforts would prove futile…

Perhaps she *hoped* they would prove futile.

The conversation she'd had with Clarice filled her mind. But the things her stepmother had told her seemed so strange. She still wasn't sure how the whole thing could even be possible.

After a brief knock, Dylan slipped inside her room and locked the door behind him. She froze, the brush still tangled in her hair, her heartbeat accelerating at the sight of him.

Fresh from a bath, with his dark hair slicked back from his face, he wore nothing but a midnight blue robe. Belted at his lean waist, the heavy satin gapped to reveal a thin slice of his chest. She stared, mesmerized by all his silky golden skin. Realizing what she was doing, she looked away, jerking the brush free and taking a few strands of hair with it.

"You should have waited for me to answer the door." She tried to make her voice cold and haughty, instead of weak and needy. "It was very rude to enter without permission."

He shook his head, refusing to be baited. His intense gaze never left hers as he strode toward her. "God, Natalia. You're so beautiful. I've dreamed of seeing you like this, with your hair all loose around your shoulders."

"Don't do that." Natalia felt breathless and uncertain, seduced in spite of herself. Was he lying or telling the truth? She didn't know. Didn't want to know.

"Do what? Compliment you?" He came closer, until he stood directly in front of her. So close his thighs brushed her knees. "You're determined to make this as difficult as possible, aren't you?"

"Why should I make it easy?" She tried to move back, but he leaned forward and trapped her with the seductive heat of his body. She inhaled deeply—a mistake, because he smelled wonderful. Clean, with the barest hint of sandalwood and something that went even deeper, something that was pure Dylan.

"Well, if you meant to make it hard, you've succeeded." He laughed, a deep rich sound.

Her gaze flew to his, reading his silky amusement, yet unsure what she'd done to cause it. "What are you talking about?"

"Let me show you." Holding her gaze, he lifted his hands to the belt of his robe.

She made a sharp shocked sound but couldn't find the words to tell him to stop. After all, this was what she'd been waiting for, wasn't it?

He hesitated, his gaze locked with hers. When she said nothing, he smiled and continued. As much as she feared falling under his spell, she couldn't resist following the path of his large elegant hands. She watched as he untied the belt and the heavy material fell away. The fabric slid from his broad shoulders and pooled with a silky swish on the floor at his feet.

Then he stood before her. Naked. Proud. Aroused.

She stared, overwhelmed by his masculine beauty. His shoulders were immense, much broader than any gentleman's should be. Fascinated, she let her gaze drift over the sculptured swells of his chest, and then drop to the muscled ridges of his flat stomach. He was lean in the hips—she skipped over what came next, not daring to let her gaze linger— and his legs were long, powerfully built.

Unable to resist, she glanced back up, focusing on the part of him that thrust from a thick nest of dark hair. *Hard.* Now she understood. Her limited knowledge of what transpired between a man and woman turned upside down.

"It will never work," she whispered with complete certainty.

He chuckled. "Oh, love. It will work. I promise."

Before she could protest any further, he reached for her hand. Holding her gaze with ferocious intent, he closed her fingers around his thick shaft.

They both gasped at the intimate contact.

She'd never thought it would feel like this, so incredibly hot and hard. It was also silky soft, vulnerable in some way. "You go too far."

"No, Natalia." He squeezed her hand more tightly. "I haven't gone nearly far enough."

She tried to pull away but only succeeded in stroking his thick length from base to tip. This seemed to inflame him even more. She could feel his pulse, thundering beneath her hand.

"Listen to me," he whispered feverishly, all in a rush. "You know how much I want you. I think you want me, too. You can hate me later—God knows I deserve it. But for now, for tonight, can't you love me just a little bit?"

Love him a little bit? As if she'd ever done anything by half measures. Therein lay the problem. She loved him far too much already.

A hysterical laugh bubbled up in the back of her throat. Lord, she was so lost. "Let go of my hand, Dylan."

He shook his head, every muscle in his big body tensing, as though what she asked was physically impossible. Then, with a small, soul-deep groan, he let his fingertips slide from her wrist.

She supposed she should shove him away, order him out of her room, and tell him what she thought of him for forcing her to do such a vulgar, unprecedented thing. But she didn't. It was enough to know he would have let her.

They might as well get this over with. At least then she wouldn't have to worry and wonder any longer. And she had to admit she was curious. She wanted him; she always had.

So, instead of pulling away, she stroked him again, exulting in the look of pure bliss that settled upon his stark chiseled features. Her touch stunned him into immobility. For this moment at least, he was completely under her control.

She took the opportunity to examine his gorgeous body once more. This time, her gaze lingered upon a small imperfection. An ugly, six-inch scar slashed across his hipbone and the top of his thigh. Prince Nikolai Ivanovich's work, she remembered, overcome with tenderness.

"My beautiful hero." Leaning forward, she pressed her lips against the pale delicate line. He'd taken this at Balaklava, risking his life so someone else could live.

Dylan shuddered; the unexpected sweetness of her actions almost brought him to his knees. He'd never expected this, that she'd touch him so sweetly. She stroked him with gentle, untutored awkwardness, and it was the most exciting, arousing thing he'd ever known.

"Oh, Natalia," he murmured, smoothing the dark hair from her temples. "You have no idea how good that feels."

"I like touching you." She blushed. His charming, virgin bride.

Reluctantly, he became aware of his selfishness. He should be pleasuring her, making this so good she'd let him repeat it on a regular basis.

He closed his hand around hers once more, but this time, he brought her fingertips to his lips and kissed her palm with lingering heat. Then he sat down on the bed beside her and pulled her into his lap. "Let me kiss you, love. I want to kiss you until the whole world falls away."

"Yes." She lifted her mouth to his. "Yes, I want that, too."

He drowned in his wife's warmth and sweetness, wondering how he'd ever find the strength to go slow. Kissing her was sheer bliss, but he wanted to do more.

So much more.

After an initial hesitation, she responded to him with all the fervor and passion he remembered. He knew how difficult it must've been for her to let go of her anger. Still, he was frustrated beyond belief. He didn't want to hold back. He'd never been this aroused, and he hadn't even touched her breasts yet…

God. He lifted one trembling hand to her flannel-covered chest, lightly grazing her nipple through the thick fabric. She gasped, and her fingernails dug into his shoulders.

"Easy," he whispered, touching her again. "Relax, love. I won't hurt you."

Gradually, she gentled her grip. He kept his touch light, letting her get used to his caress. At last, he slid his fingertips beneath the neckline of her gown and filled his hand with her voluptuous, quivering warmth. He moaned at the silky texture of her skin, such a contrast to the hardness of her nipple.

Breaking the kiss, he drew back the tiniest bit, just enough to catch a glimpse of her pale creamy flesh. He only allowed himself one glance, but even that sent a fireball of heat to his already painfully hard groin. Holding her gaze, he rubbed his thumb across her sensitive nipple.

"How does this feel?" His voice was low and rough with desire, barely recognizable.

Natalia's pale skin flushed with healthy color and her emerald eyes were unfocused. She blinked at his question, not answering, but when he moved to her other breast and repeated the motion, a soft sigh escape her lips. "Good. So good."

He grinned at her answer and slid the gown from her shoulders, baring her feminine curves to his hungry gaze. "I have never seen anything as beautiful as you." He lowered her to the bed and then buried his face against her chest, smiling in pure bliss when she hugged him to her, instead of pushing him away.

For a long moment, he just lay there, with his head against the delicious softness of her breasts, trying to regain control.

Tentatively, she ran her fingertips through his hair. He shuddered, wondering how he'd ever lived without this. Turning his head, he captured her nipple with his mouth. Her gasp of pleasure was the sweetest sound he'd ever heard.

He sucked her with growing fervor, until she shifted restlessly against him, her movements compounding his pleasant agony. Perhaps she was ready.

If he went very slowly, if he was very gentle...

God knew, he was past the point of rational thought. He wanted to touch her, to see if she was wet for him. If she was...

He slipped his hand from her breast and started inching his way down her stomach, unbuttoning her gown as he went. At last, she was free of the hideous concealing fabric—her beautiful body bare to his hungry gaze.

Her green eyes were wide and uncertain, her mouth ripe with his kisses. Her dark hair tumbled across her shoulders, her breasts full and lush. He found her tiny waist, generous hips, and short slender legs incredibly perfect.

"My wife. My sweet lovely wife." She was his, completely. No other man had ever touched her this way; no other man ever would. A surge of protectiveness overwhelmed him.

Natalia grasped Dylan's broad shoulders, desperate to pull him even closer. He lowered his mouth to her breasts, and tendrils of his dark damp hair fell across her pale skin as he suckled her with tender passion.

She'd almost gotten over the newness of the exquisite sensation, had started to relax and simply enjoy it, when his hand began to roam over her body. Gently, he stroked her stomach and the upper curve of her thigh.

A soft gasp of dismay and delight escaped her lips as he delved between her legs, touching her in the most private place. She clenched her legs shut, resisting the invasion, but he persisted.

"Please," he whispered. "Let me do this, love. Let me touch you all over."

Unable to resist such a heartfelt plea, she let her thighs fall apart, allowing him to continue his sinful exploration. Somehow, her body had become damp and moist. His fingertips pressed deep within her. She moaned and pushed against his hand, seeking more, wanting something she couldn't even name.

Then he brushed his mouth down her body, spreading sweet hot kisses everywhere his hands had been. His tongue swept across her core, and she cried out his name in alarm. She buried her fingertips in his hair, unsure whether to push him away or pull him closer. In the end, she could do nothing but ride the waves of pleasure that crashed over her.

Chapter Twenty-two

Dylan held Natalia while she recovered. Watching her face as she found release for the first time had been the most beautiful thing he'd ever known.

At long last, Natalia blinked up at him, her face flushed and her hair adorably disheveled. She touched his cheek, the emotion in her eyes making him feel as though he could fly.

"Did you like that?" His voice was rough and husky. He wanted her to know how good it could be between them, how much he wanted to break down her defenses. But he was far past the last vestiges of restraint. He must have her, now, or die in the attempt.

Natalia nodded, her eyes wide as an owl's. "I had no idea."

He gave a shaky laugh. "Just imagine how it will feel when I'm deep inside you." Just saying the words sent a soul-deep shudder through his already overheated body.

She let her hand trail from his face to the upper contours of his chest. "I love the way you feel."

He covered her hand with his own. "Then touch me again, love. I'm dying to feel your hands on me." He held her embarrassed gaze for a moment, then closed his eyes and let go of her hand.

Natalia ran her fingertips over his chest and shoulders, gentle as a butterfly's wings. The rapid cadence of his breath intensified to a harsh, uneven pant.

When he couldn't stand her sweet torture any longer, he placed his hand over hers and guided her again to the place where he desperately needed her touch.

Her hand trembled, but she explored his rigid length, wringing a soft moan of need from his lips. She started to pull away, but he tightened his grip and showed her how to pleasure him. "Please. Like this."

She got the hang of it in no time at all. He released her and fisted his hands in the blankets beneath him, while his body strove for release.

It embarrassed him a bit, coming now, but he realized it was better this way. They had all night, and he needed the edge taken off his desire. Orgasm ripped through him, turning him inside out with blinding intensity, and he spilled his seed in her hand.

"Did I hurt you?" Natalia's horrified voice cut through the haze of bliss.

He managed to stir himself enough to open his eyes and look at her. "No," he whispered. "Of course not."

She waved her hand helplessly. "Then what's this?"

He struggled to hide a weak smile. "That's how babies are made, love."

Pushing himself up on one elbow, he reached over and grabbed her hideous nightgown from the foot of the bed and wiped off her hand. "Do you want children?"

He liked the idea of her pregnant with his child. He liked it very much. The mere thought of having a family of his own made him weak with longing.

What transpired between them tonight could very well result in the son he'd secretly dreamed of for years. He would never make the mistakes his own father had made. He'd love his own children more than life itself. His throat tightened painfully as he waited for her answer.

"I don't know."

He could see all the old anger resurfacing. She wasn't ready for this, and he cursed himself for revealing so much.

"Shh," he whispered. "We'll talk about all that later. For now, just let me make love to you."

Natalia looked at her husband and nodded. She was no longer afraid. He'd done everything he could to make this easy for her. Now she ached for him to finish what he'd begun.

He was right. They had the rest of their lives to talk about the future.

He smiled and gave her a lingering kiss, while his hands once more worked their magic on her body. Before long, he was poised between her thighs and a heavy pressure replaced his fingertips.

"It might hurt a bit, but only for a moment, and just this once." His face was full of concern as he worked himself against her, making her head spin with the strange feelings that had claimed her before.

"I'm ready," she assured him, hoping it was the truth. She'd touched the satin length of him, felt its size and power. Despite his reassurances, she still couldn't see how this was going to be possible.

He dipped his head to kiss her again then thrust deep within her. The abrupt forceful motion rent her maidenhead and filled her completely. She cried out, stunned.

"Are you all right?" He held himself still, but his big body shook like a leaf in the wind. "God, Natalia. I'm so sorry."

"It's all right," she whispered, trying to ignore the stinging pressure. "I'm fine."

"Good." He pulled back slowly and then thrust again, seeming to brush her very womb.

She sucked in a breath at the feel of him, seated so deeply inside her. She'd never known it would be like this—so primal, so intense. The pain eased, and as he began to move, a delicious friction grew between them.

"Put your legs around my waist," he coaxed.

She did, granting him even deeper access to her body. She clung to his broad back as his thrusts became harder and faster, filling her entire world. There was nothing but Dylan, and the way he made her feel. She reached for the same pinnacle she'd known before.

Then her entire body convulsed in a shuddering explosion of sensation and emotion. She sobbed with the beauty of it, while Dylan shuddered deep inside her.

* * *

In the aftermath, they held each other, their bodies so tightly entangled Dylan wasn't certain where he stopped and she began. He felt strange, undone. But in a good way.

My wife.

A small smile tilted his mouth, and he pressed a tender kiss to her temple. Making love to Natalia had been everything he'd hoped it would be. She'd given herself with artless generosity, and hope swelled within him. How could she continue to hate him, when they shared this?

She stirred against him, and he ran his hand down the smooth contours of her back, trying to soothe her. She was bound to feel awkward after they'd been so intimate, and he wanted to forestall her withdrawal as long as possible.

Her hand drifted up his chest, and she tilted her head back so she could meet his gaze. "Oh, Dylan. You were so right to insist we do this."

"I'm glad you think so." He lowered his lips to hers and kissed her with lingering heat before he pulled away. "I'll cherish the gift you gave me tonight for the rest of my life."

"You should." She snuggled even closer, resting her head in the crook of his arm. "I'd like to stay just like this, forever."

Oh, this was good. This was very, very good.

"Let me stay with you for the rest of the night. Please. I want to wake up with you in my arms."

For a moment, she didn't say anything. He feared he'd ruined it. Perhaps she'd forgotten she wanted her privacy. Now that he'd reminded her, she'd probably send him away.

"I'm so afraid," she whispered instead. "I'm afraid this will pass. I'm afraid I'll grow used to having you beside me, and then you'll leave."

"That won't happen. I'll never leave you. Never."

Dylan's promise rang with truth, and Natalia wanted to believe him. His lovemaking had been so beautiful, so breathlessly tender. She no longer wanted to maintain her distance. What good did it do, to deny her heart's desire? She couldn't love him any deeper, couldn't hurt any less if he walked away.

"I believe you." The time had come to take a leap of faith. In retrospect, her last attempt hadn't worked out so badly. The road had been difficult, but her decision to dance with Dylan had been a defining moment in her life.

She didn't want to live in fear of what might have been. Life was too precious not to live each day to the fullest. So, she would trust in him, believe in herself, and see where it took them.

* * *

Dylan awoke in pitch dark. His heart raced, and sweat drenched his entire body.

"What's wrong?" Natalia's soft voice startled him. It took a moment to realize where he was.

He'd fallen asleep, in Natalia's bed, after an amazing night of lovemaking.

"I'm all right. I just had a bad dream."

Natalia drew herself up on one elbow beside him and brushed the damp hair off his forehead. "You're trembling." He could barely see her face in the dark, but he could sense her concern.

"Don't worry." He reached over and lit the candle with unsteady hands, desperate to chase away the dark. "Go back to sleep."

"Do you want to talk about it?" She shifted closer and stroked his brow with her soft, cool hands. "Were you dreaming of the war?"

He supposed it would be impossible to live with her, to sleep in her bed every night, and not expose her to his nightmares. Still, his weakness embarrassed him, made him want to snap at her and flee. But that would ruin the closeness the night had brought, so he took a few calming breaths and tried to relax.

"No, this one wasn't about the war." He sighed and reached for her free hand, needing something to hold onto. This nightmare dated from his childhood, but it had been years since this particular vision of hell had come to haunt him. He'd hoped never to experience it again. The blood and guts of the Crimea didn't terrify him nearly as much as this silly childhood terror. He supposed it made sense he'd have it here, during his first night back at Aldabaran.

"Tell me about it. I want to know everything about you. Especially the things that hurt you."

He tried to remember why this particular dream had frightened him so badly as a child. More importantly, why did it still have the power to frighten him now?

"I'm here, at Aldabaran," he began. "There's a bad storm brewing at sea." With a groan, he leveraged himself to a sitting position. "I don't want to tell you this. It sounds ridiculous."

"I won't laugh," she told him solemnly. "I promise."

He snaked one arm around her hips and gave her a sharp tug so she fell across him, straddling his thighs. "Let me make love to you again." He buried his face between her bare breasts, trying to distract her. "That will make me forget all about it."

She gave a breathless laugh as he stirred to life beneath her. "All right," she agreed. "But first, tell me about the dream."

Her nipples were already hard. He stroked one with his tongue. God, she was so sweet. He could make love to her every night for the rest of his life, and it still wouldn't be enough.

Her breath caught, and she threaded her fingers through his hair. "I know what you're trying to do," she whispered, shifting against him. "And it's working."

"Good." He rolled his hips, and she gasped and clung to his shoulders. This was much better. The nightmare was fading already.

"No, it isn't good." She tilted his head, so he had to look at her. "I love making love to you. But I want there to be more between us than that. I want you to take me into your confidence. I want you to tell me things you've never told anyone else and trust me to guard your secrets after you do."

"I already have. I already do."

"Then tell me this. Rob it of its power to haunt you."

He sighed. In truth, he supposed he did want to tell her. This closeness she spoke of—the sharing of secrets—he craved it even more than the ecstasy of being inside her.

And he knew then that he loved her. He'd loved her all along.

"I'm standing at the edge of the cliffs." His voice grew husky with his new knowledge. "Rain is pouring down my face, and lightning is flashing across the breakers crashing on the beach far below."

Natalia ran a soothing caress over his shoulders as he spoke.

"Then, out of the corner of my eye, I see a man come toward me out of the darkness." He shuddered and bowed his head. How could she fail to think less of him after hearing such a cowardly tale?

"Who is this man? Does he have a face?"

Her question gave him pause. He tried to think, tried to conjure the man's image in his mind, but something inside him shied away from taming his demons.

"No. It's just a man in a dark coat. I can't see his features."

Natalia didn't look as though she believed him, but she didn't argue the point. "Are you a man in your dream or a child?"

He stared at her, impressed by her questions. Perhaps it would help to take the dream apart and examine its pieces. He was willing to try anything to take away its power. "I'm a child," he realized. "That's why the man frightens me."

She smiled, as though he were a not-so-bright student who had just given the right answer. "What happens next?"

"I back away, desperate to escape him. He starts chasing me, and I scramble over the rocks, slipping and sliding, losing my footing again and again." As he recounted the story, he got an uncomfortable feeling. Was this a nightmare, or was it an actual memory? It felt so real.

"Does he catch you?"

"No, I hid in the smugglers' cave, down by the beach, and waited for him to tire of searching." His words surprised him. There wasn't a smugglers' cave in the dream. In his nightmares, the chase just went on and on. He ran until his lungs were ready to burst, then woke up in a cold sweat.

"What happens after the cave?" Natalia could be quite relentless.

"That's all there is to it," he lied. "See, I told you it was silly."

She leaned forward and kissed him with infinite tenderness. "Thank you for telling me. I hope it helps."

"It did. I'm glad you're here." Actually, she'd left him unsettled, with more questions than he'd had before, but he didn't want to hurt her feelings.

"Wasn't there something else you wanted to do now?" Smiling, she reached between them and stroked his rigid length.

He gasped and pressed himself more fully into her palm, letting the bliss of her touch eclipse everything else. This was right. This was real. Nothing else mattered.

Chapter Twenty-three

Dylan remained awake long after Natalia drifted back to sleep in his arms. Soon, dawn poked tendrils of light through the narrow window. Sighing in frustration, Dylan slipped out of bed, careful not to wake her. He pulled on a robe, then went to the room's lone window and stared down at the rocky cliffs, at the sliver of restless sea far below. The sight made him uneasy, and he wondered why. As a child, he'd loved to watch the tide come in.

Maybe this bad feeling could be attributed to the lingering effects of that stupid dream. But, more likely, it was because his mother had thrown herself off these very cliffs. He'd told Michael it didn't bother him that their mother had killed herself here, but somewhere deep down, it did.

Natalia had consumed his thoughts for the past few weeks, so he really hadn't had time to think about his mother's death. Now he forced himself to think about those dark days.

And for the first time, he wondered why she'd brought him with her that summer, if she'd known she was going to take her own life. Had something happened, something she hadn't foreseen when she left London? Something so terrible she couldn't face the consequences?

In his memory, his mother was beautiful, happy, and always laughing. What could have happened to make her feel life wasn't worth living?

How could she have left him alone, with a father who hated him?

He didn't remember much about that last summer. They'd only been here a few weeks before his mother's death. He couldn't even recall how he'd found out she was gone or who had told him.

Perhaps Patrick would know, although Dylan really wasn't sure he wanted to remember. What was the point in dredging up the past?

Fiona Cameron Blake was gone. Nothing would bring her back.

* * *

The next morning, Natalia made her way down to the kitchen, feeling irritable and out of sorts. It was late, nearly noon, she guessed, though there had been no clock in her room, so she wasn't sure.

She'd expected to wake up in Dylan's arms, but he was gone, his pillow cold. Her disappointment had been as intense as her embarrassment about what had passed between them during the night.

Surely, no decent woman would behave so wantonly. But wanton or not, all she could think about was his exquisite body in the firelight. The tenderness of his touch. The beauty of their intimacy.

Just love me a little bit.

How she longed to say those words back to him. If she somehow managed to find the courage, would he repay her in kind?

Voices echoed from the direction of the kitchen. Pausing for a moment in the passageway, she tried to school her features into a semblance of calm. How would she ever face him after the things she'd done last night? Should she greet him as though he were a passing acquaintance, as though he'd never joined his body with hers in the dark?

Taking a deep breath, she entered the room. To her intense disappointment, Dylan was nowhere to be seen. Instead, Mrs. Macpherson and a much younger woman were busy cleaning up after breakfast.

"Good morning, ma'am." The second woman bobbed her head nervously, drawing Mrs. Macpherson's attention.

"Ah, there you are, lass. We were wondering if you were going to sleep all day." With a wink, Mrs. Macpherson hurried to Natalia's side, bringing a tray loaded with assorted pastries and meat pies. "You mentioned yesterday we might hire a cook, so I sent for my niece, Shannon. She arrived this morning to make breakfast—an audition, of sorts. Young Dylan said she would do fine, but he left the final decision up to you."

Mrs. Macpherson offered her a plate then both women watched with hope-filled eyes as Natalia took a pastry and bit into it. An audition? For the first time, she realized she was in charge of running this household, a responsibility that made her nervous. She wanted to please Dylan, but she had little experience in domestic matters. Fortunately, the pastry was light and flaky, filled with a sweet cherry sauce. If this was a sampling of Shannon's work, she'd do just fine. "It's absolutely wonderful, Shannon. When can you start?"

"See, lass, I told you everything would work out." Mrs. Macpherson enveloped her niece in a huge hug, and then the two of them danced a little jig right in the middle of the kitchen.

Natalia couldn't remember ever laughing with the help. No one who worked for her father had so much as cracked a smile in her presence, let alone danced about. But their exuberance pleased her, and her bad mood lifted.

How nice to be among such friendly people.

Shannon came forward, her blue eyes sparkling. She shared Dylan's striking coloring, and it was easy to see she was related to the Macphersons. In her early thirties, and very attractive, she was far too thin to be a cook. "I promise you won't regret hiring me, ma'am. My husband passed away last year, and I've three wee bairns, so this job is a Godsend."

Such gratitude made Natalia uncomfortable, but she was glad to give the woman the assistance she needed to support her young family. In fact, knowing the woman's story, she would've hired her even if the food had been horrible.

"We're glad to have you." When she had a private moment with Mrs. Macpherson, she'd ask the older woman about Shannon's living situation. If Shannon needed to bring her family here to live, there was still plenty of room in the servants' quarters. This big old house needed a few children laughing and playing in the hallways.

The thought made her remember the longing in Dylan's eyes when he'd asked her if she wanted children of their own. She'd been too overwhelmed to think about the possibility last night, but now she realized how much she wanted a family.

What a wonderful father Dylan would make.

A strange little thrill went through her at the prospect. Unobtrusively, she placed her hand on her stomach. Amazing to think a child could be growing inside her this very minute.

"Where is my husband?" she found herself asking, after the servants had finished their little impromptu celebration.

"Oh, he was up with the sun this morning, lass." Mrs. Macpherson sat down in the nearest chair and gave Natalia a speculative look. "Looked as though he hadn't slept a wink, poor lad. Patrick took him down to the village to meet the rest of the tenants."

"Oh." Natalia sat down at the kitchen table to finish her pastry. Heat spread across her cheeks as she thought about what had kept him awake.

There was passion between them. No doubt about that. But she wanted more. She wanted his love, and she had no idea how to go about earning it.

If only Clarice were here.

She eyed Mrs. Macpherson and Shannon and wished she knew them better. She'd love to pour her heart out to someone. These women were older and presumably wiser. Might they have some tidbit of information that would help? Some trick to winning a man's heart?

Now that Natalia had hired Shannon, the two servants were chatting merrily as they went about their work. They were so caught up in their village gossip they seemed to have forgotten their employer even existed.

Besieged by loneliness, she longed for Clarice's companionship. She had so many questions. About love. About marriage. About sex. Perhaps she would write her stepmother a letter. It lacked the immediacy she craved, but it would be a way of expressing her confusing emotions. Plus, she wanted to tell Clarice how wrong she had been about lovemaking.

As far she could tell, there was nothing distasteful about making love to Dylan. Then again, her husband was beautiful, tender, and kind. Regretfully, Clarice's was none of these things.

Glad to have a plan, Natalia finished up her breakfast, bid the women farewell, and went back to her room.

* * *

"Mrs. Macpherson? Can I have a moment?" Later that afternoon, Natalia found the old woman in Dylan's childhood room, briskly stripping the small bed.

"Of course, lass. What can I do for you?" Mrs. Macpherson straightened, put her hands on her hips, and arched one brow in curiosity.

After writing her letter to Clarice, Natalia had spent the rest of the day wandering the keep, looking for Fiona Blake's paintings. So far, her search had proven fruitless. No trace of Fiona's art remained in the solar or any of the living areas. She figured anyone would know where to find something at Aldabaran, it was Mrs. Macpherson.

"Dylan told me his mother was an artist. Would you happen to know if any of her paintings remain at Aldabaran?"

Mrs. Macpherson turned away and gathered up the heap of blankets, her motions jerky with some strong emotion. "Our dear little Fiona. She was always dabbling with her paints and brushes. Such beautiful pictures that lass could paint."

Which didn't answer Natalia's question. Reining in her impatience, she tried again. "Yes, but did she leave any of the paintings here? I'd like to see them, and so would Dylan."

With a deep sigh, Mrs. Macpherson let the blankets fall back on the bed. "Aye, she left some behind. If you'll wait here, I'll go find them."

The woman's evasive behavior didn't sit well with Natalia. Something strange was going on, and she was determined to find out what. "Oh, that won't be necessary. I'll come with you."

Mrs. Macpherson hesitated, casting Natalia a pained look. "I'd prefer to fetch them myself, lass."

"I want to go with you." Natalia refused to back down and a long, tension-filled moment passed between them.

At last, Mrs. Macpherson shrugged. "I'll take you then. But you must promise you won't think poorly of Patrick for keeping them. He never meant no harm by it."

"Of course not," Natalia agreed, but her mind spun. Patrick? Why on earth did *he* have Fiona's paintings?

Gesturing for Natalia to follow, Mrs. Macpherson led her up to the fourth floor. She stopped before a room at the end of the corridor and opened the door. Natalia stepped inside and caught her breath as she saw what lay within.

Sparsely furnished, with only a neatly made bed and a small armoire, the room's walls were covered with paintings of every conceivable size and shape. Some were expensively framed, others mere canvases, and some weren't even finished. The result was a kaleidoscope of color. Natalia turned slowly, trying to take it all in.

Dylan had said his mother was an artist, but the word didn't begin to describe the depth and beauty of her work. Fiona had painted from her heart; that much was obvious.

Many of the paintings were of Aldabaran. She'd painted her home from every angle and season. There were also pictures of the forbidding rocky cliffs, and the churning sea far below.

But the portraits were by far the most arresting. Natalia took a few steps toward one of a small boy, his gray eyes sparkling with laughter. "Dylan." She reached out to touch her husband's painted cheek, enchanted by the image of the carefree boy he'd been.

"Aye." Mrs. Macpherson's wistful voice startled Natalia, so lost had she been in her own reverie. "That was always my favorite. I found it a great comfort, during all those years when the lad was gone."

Natalia raised a brow, still struck by the obvious affection the old woman had for Dylan. "The countess was very talented. How sad to think of her dying so young."

"Sad, indeed," Mrs. Macpherson murmured. "Not a day goes by that we don't mourn her loss."

"How did she die? Was it childbirth?" Another portrait caught Natalia's attention, and she moved toward it. This one was also Dylan, but, strangely, in this one, he was full grown.

"Oh, if only she had." The old woman shook her head. "How much easier that would have been for all of us who were left behind."

Natalia turned, reluctantly looking away from the picture of Dylan. "What happened to her?" she asked, wondering if she really wanted to know.

Mrs. Macpherson approached, and she, too, seemed captivated by the picture Natalia had been examining. "She used to come home every summer. But that year, the earl came early to fetch her back to London. They had a terrible row, and later that night, she fell from the cliffs."

A cold chill travel down Natalia's spine. "She fell?"

Mrs. Macpherson blinked back a rush of tears. "They say she jumped, took her own life. But I've never believed it. Not our Fiona."

Dylan had never said anything about his mother's death, and now Natalia knew why. He'd been so young. A mere child. How had he dealt with such a devastating loss? Perhaps he hadn't, which would account for the nightmares that left him trembling and drenched in sweat.

She returned her gaze to the portrait. In it, Dylan stood at the edge of the cliffs his mother had fallen from. Wind whipped his hair and clothes. But his pale eyes shone with love.

She wanted him to gaze at her this way. As though she were the only thing in the world that mattered to him.

"How did she know what he would look like?" The accuracy of the painting amazed her, given the fact that Fiona had never lived to see the man her son would become. Had Fiona painted this portrait after she decided to kill herself, perhaps in an effort to imagine the grown man she'd never know?

"Why, he posed for it. Fiona always did love to paint Patrick." Mrs. Macpherson gestured to another painting, which Natalia hadn't examined yet. "I've always like that one, of the two of them together."

Patrick? Upon closer examination, she realized the portrait *was* of Patrick. The resemblance between the two men really was remarkable. Still trying to fit the pieces together in her mind, Natalia turned to look at the other painting Mrs. Macpherson had indicated.

The two of them together.

The dark-haired man and boy stood on a grassy hill, the man's hand resting on the boy's shoulder. The man smiled down at the boy was such love, such pride, and the little boy looked up at the man as though he'd hung the moon. Patrick and Dylan.

Father and son?

It all made sense now. Dylan's resemblance to Patrick—his lack of one to Sherbourne. The Macphersons' absolute delight upon seeing Dylan again—the Earl of Warren's shameful lack of interest.

Why should the earl care for Dylan, if Dylan wasn't truly his son?

Natalia glanced back at Mrs. Macpherson, who obviously realized she'd said too much. "Shall I continue to call you Mrs. Macpherson? Or shall I call you Grandmother?"

The old woman's eyes welled with tears. "Oh, no. You mustn't. The lad must never know."

"Why not?" Natalia asked. "I think he'd like to know. I think it would make him very happy."

"Does it bother you, lass?" Mrs. Macpherson shook her head, as though she couldn't believe

Natalia's easy acceptance of what she'd learned. "To find the man you married is not the aristocrat he seemed? That he is only a Scottish groom's son?"

"No," Natalia whispered. "It doesn't matter to me. Not at all."

It was the truth. From the beginning, she had cared for him because he wasn't like the vain, foppish aristocrats she'd known. And this revelation didn't change that. If anything, she loved him even more.

How hard it must've been for Dylan to believe his own father hated him.

"Patrick has always wanted young Dylan to know the truth. But he couldn't give the boy the kind of life the earl could." Mrs. Macpherson rubbed her eyes with the back of her hand. "But keeping the secret meant losing his only son. It almost killed him when the earl took the lad away."

"How terrible." Natalia ached for both men. How lonely they'd both been, when their pain could so easily have been avoided.

"Patrick thought he'd never see Dylan again. That's why he brought Fiona's paintings down here. So he could see the lad's face each night before he fell asleep."

Tears stung Natalia's eyes as she looked around at the paintings. Each one was a glimpse into Fiona Blake's life. She'd told Dylan seeing his mother's work would be a chance to get to know her, but she hadn't realized how truthful the statement had been.

She understood Fiona far more than she wanted to.

Fiona had been forced to marry a man she didn't love. And the man she did love had been forbidden to her. How easily Natalia could have shared her fate.

But Fiona had been strong. She'd found a way to continue to see Patrick. During those months she'd spent at Aldabaran, she'd been free. Her friendship with Patrick flourished, while her marriage fell apart. Apparently, Patrick and Fiona's passion had gotten away from them, and Dylan had been the result.

Somehow, Warren must've found out. No wonder he treated Dylan so poorly. Was that the reason he'd come after Fiona the summer she died? What had he said to make her take her own life? Had he threatened to take her sons away from her?

Natalia realized Mrs. Macpherson was worried Natalia would tell Dylan everything she'd learned here today. Natalia wanted to do exactly that, but it wasn't her place. If Dylan were to learn the truth, Patrick should be the one to tell him.

"I won't say anything to Dylan," she assured the old woman. "And I understand why Patrick wanted her paintings. He must've loved her very much."

"Aye, he did," Mrs. Macpherson agreed. "He loves her still."

Was Patrick's son capable of such love? She hoped so.

With a wistful sigh, Natalia turned her mind back to the matter at hand. Somehow, she had to convince Mrs. Macpherson that Dylan needed to get to know his father.

"Patrick should tell Dylan the truth. It doesn't matter anymore. Dylan has Aldabaran and my dowry. No one can take those things from him."

Mrs. Macpherson nodded thoughtfully. "Perhaps you're right, lass. I'll speak to Patrick."

"In the meantime, I did promise Dylan I'd find some of these paintings. Do you think we could take a few of them downstairs? Some of the landscapes and maybe the one of Dylan as a boy? I don't think he should see them all. Not yet anyway."

Mrs. Macpherson gave her a grateful look. "Yes, I think that's a fine idea. We'll take the ones you mentioned down to the laird's room. It will be a nice surprise for the lad when he returns."

Chapter Twenty-four

Dylan remained away from the house most of the day. During the morning, he explored his land, his excitement and sense of possibility growing by the moment. For the first time in his life, he could taste happiness.

It tasted wonderful.

Afterward, Patrick talked him into visiting the village pub. They spent a very enjoyable afternoon, drinking fine dark ale and discussing plans for Aldabaran. Nearly every man in the village stopped by to meet him and share a pint. They laughed and joked and welcomed him back. For long moments, he forgot the uneasy memories lurking in the back of his mind.

But the more Dylan drank, the more last night's revelations plagued him. Was his dream a nightmare or memory?

What secrets remain locked within my mind? He wanted to be rid of them because he sensed they held the power to destroy this fragile peace his marriage and inheritance had granted him.

"Is something bothering you, lad?" Patrick lifted a questioning brow as Dylan signaled for yet another drink. "If I had such a pretty lass waiting, I'd be in a considerable bit more of a hurry to get home."

They were finally alone, since most of the village men had gone home for supper. Only the barkeep, the serving girl, and a few diehard drinkers in the corner remained. Still, Dylan lingered, wondering how to broach the subject of the cave.

"You needn't worry on that account." Dylan gave Patrick a satisfied grin at the mere thought of his lovely wife. "Things between Natalia and I are better than they've ever been."

"Good." Patrick returned the smile. "Glad to hear that. She seems a good sort."

"Very good. The best." Dylan took another deep swig of beer, then wiped the back of his hand across his mouth and gave his companion a considering look. Patrick's reminder of what waited at home gave him the impetus he needed to get to the point.

"Natalia isn't the problem. My worries are of an entirely different sort." He might as well ask the questions that plagued him. Better to know for sure than to wonder.

Patrick frowned and placed his mug on the scarred table where they sat. "Is it something to do with Aldabaran, lad? Is there anything I can do to help?"

Dylan glanced at the few remaining patrons then lowered his voice. "Is there a smugglers' cave in the cliffs below the keep?"

A neutral mask dropped over Patrick's face. "Aye. Why do you ask?"

"Ever since I was a child, I've had these nightmares." Dylan gave a self-deprecating smile, embarrassed to admit such a weakness. "At least, I always thought they were nightmares. But last night, I remembered some things, and it occurred to me that perhaps I've been reliving something that actually happened."

Patrick sat back, stroking his chin. "If you're telling me you don't remember what happened the night your mother died, I'm not certain I want to remind you, lad."

The night Mother died.

Dylan closed his eyes as an image flashed through his mind. His mother, standing on the cliffs in the rain…

"Tell me, Patrick. Tell me what happened."

Patrick shook his head, misery etched in every line of his face. "I don't know exactly what happened that night. I don't know what you saw that frightened you so badly. But when the storm was over, Fiona lay dead upon the rocks, and you were nowhere to be found. I always thought you must have seen her jump…"

"I hid in the cave." Dylan shuddered, overwhelmed by sudden memories of that dark place. He had been so alone. Cold. Afraid. He'd known he'd never see his mother again, and he'd been terrified by what would happen if he gave up the tenuous security of his hiding place.

"It took me three days to find you, lad." Patrick's voice broke, and he swallowed convulsively before continuing. "You were curled up in that cave, whimpering like a wild thing. Half starved, nearly frozen to the bone, and you wouldn't say a word, not one word to me."

Three days?

"Oh, God." Dylan buried his face in his hands, remembering. "My father... He was there that night, wasn't he?"

Patrick was silent a moment, and then laid his hand on Dylan's shoulder. "Aye. The Earl of Warren arrived unexpectedly that afternoon."

"He and my mother argued..."

"Do you remember what they argued about, lad?"

Yes.

Dylan lifted his head, stunned by the words that echoed inside his mind. He met Patrick's eyes—his piercing, blue-gray gaze—and all the pieces fell into place.

He'd seen eyes that color before. He saw them every time he looked in a mirror.

"They argued about her lowborn lover. About the bastard child she'd tried to pass off as the earl's legitimate son." The words were wrenched from somewhere deep inside him, from that dark place where they'd remained hidden all these years.

"Christ." Patrick released Dylan's shoulder and then groped for his mug. He took a long deep drink. "I didn't think he knew, lad."

"Then it's true. You're my father." What a huge, life-altering thing, to be summed up in so few words.

"Aye, it's true." Patrick lifted his hand, as though to touch Dylan again in some way, then apparently thought better of it. "You mustn't think any less of your mother. She tried to be a good wife to the earl, but nothing she ever did was good enough for him. Summer after summer, she'd arrive with bruises on her face, her lovely spirit nearly broken by his cruelty."

"So you seduced her." Dylan felt numb, as though he were listening to the story of someone else's life, not his own.

"I loved her. I tried to comfort her." Patrick took another drink, then met Dylan's gaze. "And when you came along, I loved you, too. More than life itself."

Dylan gave a bitter laugh. "If you loved me, you would have told me the truth. You wouldn't have sent me to live with the man who hated me, who saw in me a constant reminder of how he'd been cuckolded. He beat me, too, you know. Every time I was within reach."

Patrick flinched and looked away. "I didn't know that. Christ, lad. I'm so bloody sorry."

"I've heard enough." Dylan stood and threw a handful of coins on the bar. Blinded by despair, he made his way through the maze of empty tables and out to the deserted cobblestone street.

Night had already fallen across the sky, but a full moon hung low in the east, dimly illuminating the shadowy landscape. Dylan sagged against a rough wooden post. He blinked to accustom his eyes to the darkness and told himself that it didn't matter.

So, he was the bastard son of a groom instead of the legitimate son of an earl. What difference could it make, at this late date?

But it did matter. *It will matter to Natalia...*

He hadn't even been good enough for her when she believed he was Warren's son. What would she say when she realized how low she'd actually married?

"Dylan, wait." Patrick emerged from the pub seconds later, his broad shoulders filling the doorway. "Please, son. There's so much more I need to say to you."

Son.

"Don't. Call. Me. That." Dylan's anger ignited, and he enunciated each word with deadly fury. "You weren't there for me when I needed a father, and I sure as hell don't need one now."

"Listen to me," Patrick insisted. "It killed me to lose Fiona. But when it seemed I had lost you as well, I was sick with grief. I promised God that if He helped me find you, I'd never ask Him for anything else."

Dylan shook his head. "Then why did you give me up? Why did you give me to the man who killed my mother?"

Patrick drew in a sharp, shocked breath. "Warren killed Fiona? Are you sure, lad?"

"Aye." Dylan gave a tired nod and started walking, leaving Patrick to follow or not, as he chose. The events of that long-ago night flashed before him like distant lightning.

His mother's tear-stained face. The earl's hand, raised to strike. The rain. The sea. The cave. All bright searing glimpses of his haunted past.

"Tell me what you remember," Patrick demanded, hurrying to keep up. "Please, Dylan. I beg of you. Let me put this nightmare to rest."

"I will," Dylan snapped. "But first, I need you to answer the other part of my question."

Emotionally lacerated by the evening's revelations, he needed to know why Patrick, who was everything he'd ever dreamed of in a father, had given him up to a monster like Warren.

"I'll answer anything you want if you'll stop walking for a bloody minute and turn and face me like a man." Patrick's frustrated bellow stopped Dylan in his tracks.

"Face you like a man?" Dylan spun around, grabbed Patrick by the collar, and shoved him up against the crumbling wall of the nearest house. "How dare you say such a thing to me, after what you've done?"

Patrick's eyes filled with anguish, and he did nothing to defend himself. "I know you're hurting, lad. And I'm sorry for my part in it. But I thought I was doing the right thing. Your mother had such plans for you, and I knew I could never make them come true. I wanted more for you than I could give. It seemed a fitting punishment for my sins to have to live without you."

Patrick's words had an unmistakable ring of truth, and Dylan released him. He understood Patrick's motives, misguided as they may have been.

"All the riches in the world can't make up for the lack of love," Dylan told his father.

Patrick let his head fall back against the rough stone wall. "You were loved, lad. Not a day went by that I didn't think of you and wonder how you fared."

A small kernel of warmth blossomed in the vicinity of Dylan's heart, burning away years of pain and disappointment. His choices were simple. He could either hold onto his anger and freeze out this man who was everything he'd always wished his father could be, or he could let the past go and live in the present.

Tentatively, Dylan held out an olive branch. "We've lost so many years... But I don't think it's too late to start again, do you?"

Tears sprung to Patrick's eyes, and he pushed away from the wall, embracing Dylan in a bone-shattering hug. "There's nothing in the world I'd like more, lad."

Dylan gave a shaky laugh, overwhelmed by emotion as his father awkwardly released him. "I lied when I said I didn't want a father. I need one more than ever."

Patrick clamped him on the back, steering him toward the edge of the village. "I haven't much experience, son. But I'll do the best I can."

For a long while, they walked in silence, the full moon lighting the familiar path to Aldabaran. Dylan still hadn't managed to absorb everything he'd learned, but he was very aware that he'd promised he'd tell Patrick what had happened the night of his mother's death.

The words were not easy to find. He'd held them inside for far too long.

Patrick didn't push, did nothing to reveal the impatience he must be feeling.

"My mother was terrified when the earl arrived at Aldabaran," Dylan said at last. "We were in the tower when she saw a coach pull into the courtyard. She sent me to my room, made me promise not to come out until after he was gone. But I didn't listen. I crept downstairs to listen, hoping he hadn't come to fetch us back to London."

"I was crazy with jealousy when I heard he had arrived, so I took myself off to the pub to drown my miseries." Patrick's voice was heavy with regret. "I should have hurried to Fiona's side. But I thought my being there would only cause more harm."

"You were right to leave," Dylan assured him. "If you'd been there, he would have killed you, too. He bribed my mother's maid to report back to him, and he knew every single thing that had ever transpired between the two of you."

Dylan sensed Patrick shaking his head in the darkness beside him. "He drove her into my arms, the fool. If he had given her the least little bit of affection, she never would have broken her vows."

For the first time, Dylan wondered what he would have done if Natalia had been forced to marry Ivanovich. Would he have been strong enough to resist her if she'd return to London for a few months every year? How would he have borne to see her neglected or abused?

He knew the answer. He would have found a way to see her. He would have tried to comfort her. Like Patrick, he would've found himself caught up in a romance destined to end in tragedy.

Tearing himself away from such thoughts, he forced himself to return to the story. "I couldn't believe what he was saying, didn't want to believe it." The terrible betrayal of learning the earl wasn't his father still seemed fresh in Dylan's mind. As a child, he'd been devastated to realize his mother and Patrick had lied to him. "I turned to leave, but before I got very far, he hit her. She sobbed your name and ran from the house, out into the storm."

"You followed them?" It wasn't really a question, and Dylan could tell Patrick was having a hard time keeping his own emotions under control. How must it feel to know the woman he'd loved had run to him, seeking his help, and he had not been there to give it?

"I was afraid of what he might do to her." Even then, Dylan had known what violence the earl was capable of. It hadn't been the first time he had beaten her. "He chased her out to the cliffs, and they fought again."

Dylan had been too far away to hear the last words that had passed between them, but he'd seen the earl's fury escalate and sensed his mother's growing desperation.

"The bastard pushed her, didn't he?" Again, it wasn't really a question. Like Dylan, Patrick had always known the truth. "She never would have jumped. Not my Fiona. She was far too strong to give up on life that easily."

"He struck her again, but this time, she'd had enough. She hit him back, and he went a little mad. He shoved her. She scrambled to keep her footing." Dylan paused in the middle of the trail, leaning forward, his hands on his knees. His breath came in harsh pants. No wonder he'd blocked all this out for so long. "I can still hear her screaming…"

Patrick put his hand on Dylan's shoulder, again trying to offer a bit of fatherly comfort. And it came at great cost, because Dylan knew how hard this was for Patrick to hear. Dylan couldn't imagine how he'd survive if he were to lose Natalia in such a manner.

Gathering his courage, Dylan managed to go on. "I must have made some sound, because he turned toward me… That's when I started running… I don't know how long I ran, or if he even chased me…"

Patrick's hand slid from Dylan's shoulder, and he sank to his knees in the middle of the trail, silent sobs wracking his body. "Forgive me," he managed, his voice broken and lost. "Forgive me for not knowing, for not being there when you needed me."

Now it was Dylan's turn to offer comfort. He lightly touched his father's bowed head. "You're here now. That's all that matters."

Chapter Twenty-five

"Natalia will leave me when she finds out the truth." Dylan spoke casually, as though the imminent loss of his wife's affections didn't really matter, but inside, he died a little at the mere thought.

He didn't want to lose her.

"Then don't tell her." Patrick, too, kept his tone neutral, devoid of any emotion—an excess of which had already been expended this evening.

They'd almost reached Aldabaran, having spent the last few hours catching up on the past twenty years. It was late, past midnight. Natalia would be furious with him when he arrived.

She'd be wondering if the things he'd said—the promises he'd made in the heat of passion—were all lies. She'd assume he'd been unfaithful, drinking and carousing while she worried and waited at home.

In the long run, perhaps it would be better to let her go on thinking those things. Let her believe he was the rake she'd first assumed him to be.

He didn't want her to know the truth—that he was a bastard, so far beneath her in Society's eyes he wasn't even fit to lick her boots, let alone all those sweet pale places he'd kissed and touched last night.

But, dear God, he wanted to make love to her again. He wanted to lose himself in her arms, forget how dramatically his life had changed for just a few blissful moments. She would hold him so tenderly, kissing him with that beautiful soft mouth…

With a defeated sigh, he wrenched his mind back to the matter at hand and his father's ridiculous suggestion. "What do you mean, don't tell her? We can't all live in the same house without her finding out eventually."

Dylan paused near the front door of the keep, where a torch still burned. He gave his father a hard look. He knew what Patrick was suggesting, and he wanted no part of it.

"I gave up twenty years with you, so you could be a bloody aristocrat and marry a woman like the one who waits within these walls." Patrick gave him a weary smile. "I won't have you give all that up so I can hear the word father from your lips now and again."

Dylan shook his head, humbled to know Patrick was once again willing to sacrifice his own happiness for Dylan's benefit. Having a father who loved him was going to take a lot of getting used to.

All of which made him even more determined to do what needed to be done, no matter how much it hurt.

"What am I to do, pretend as though you and Grandmother are mere servants, just so Natalia will continue to think I'm good enough to be her husband?" Dylan met Patrick's eyes, determined not to back down. "I've spent my entire life pretending to be something I'm not, and I'm tired. I don't want to do it anymore."

"There's nothing in this world I'd like more than to claim you as my son, Dylan." Patrick smiled, and Dylan knew he'd managed to say the right thing. "But not if it means you wind up with a broken heart."

"If she looks down her nose at my family, she isn't worth getting my heart broken over." More truthful words had never been spoken, but Dylan knew they wouldn't protect him in the end. After all, Natalia couldn't help her aristocratic sensibilities any more than Michael could.

"I'm glad you feel that way. And if you do, I think you should tell the lass the truth, son. She can't blame you for things you had no control over. It isn't as though you hid this from her when the two of you wed. You never know, she might surprise you."

She might surprise you.

Dylan wanted to believe such a thing was possible, but he'd been disappointed too many times, by too many people. "I'll tell her I've changed my mind, that I think we should live apart. She'll have access to her blasted dowry, and she can live like a queen in London. I'm sure she'll jump at the chance."

"I don't think you're giving the lass enough credit. But then, you know her far better than I."

But that was the problem. Dylan really didn't know Natalia at all.

He let his head fall back against the rough stone, staring up of the starry sky. He tried to imagine

Natalia's reaction to the news, tried to envision a scenario that did not end with her walking away.

His father was right—it would break his heart to bare his soul in such a manner, only to receive the ultimate rejection. No, far better not to give her the chance.

Patrick gave him a little shove. "You can't sleep out here, lad. Best to get it over with."

Dylan nodded in resignation and moved to open the heavy front door. Patrick entered first but paused just a few feet inside. "She waited up for you. That must be a good sign."

Dylan shut the door behind them, then turned to follow Patrick's tenderly amused gaze. Natalia slept awkwardly in one of the overstuffed chairs near the fireplace. She was still fully dressed, her dark hair trailing in a silky pool on the floor. He'd never seen anything so beautiful in his life. His heart squeezed as he realized that if he went through with his plan, he would never see her like this again.

"She looks like a wee angel, son."

"Aye," Dylan agreed hoarsely. "That she does."

"Well, I'll leave the two of you alone, then. But remember what I said." Patrick smiled over his shoulder as he headed for the kitchen. "You're a good man, Dylan, and she knows it."

You're a good man. She'd thought so once, but Dylan knew he'd already destroyed that opinion.

After his father left, Dylan moved toward Natalia with the slow precision of the walking wounded. The only other time he'd been this numb and confused was during the Crimea. After the doctors had dressed his wounds, he'd defied their orders to rest.

Instead, he'd limped back to the battlefield and stared down into the lifeless faces of men who'd been like brothers to him. He'd tried to count them, to put a number and a price on all that had been lost. Their deaths had hurt far more than Ivanovich's saber.

As he stared down at his wife's sleeping face, he once again tried to add up the loss of something irreplaceable.

Despite his initial anger, learning Patrick Macpherson was his father was one of the best things to ever have happened to him. He couldn't wait to get to know his father better, to bask in the unconditional love Patrick had already shown him time and again.

Unfortunately, the only other good thing in his life was Natalia, and he didn't see how he could possibly keep them both.

* * *

Natalia wasn't sure what woke her, but when she opened her eyes, Dylan loomed above her. He said nothing, just stared down at her, looking so troubled, so lost and alone, she forgot her anger.

"Dylan." She scrambled to a sitting position and fumbled to put her hair back into some semblance of order. "What's wrong?"

He shook his head and sank to his knees on the floor in front of her. "I just want to touch you," he breathed, burying his face in her lap. "I want to feel your hands on my skin."

She caught her breath, overwhelmed by his sweet words and unexpected actions. "I missed you today." She brushed his dark hair away from his pensive face. She wanted him to tell her where he'd been, but she didn't want to sound like a shrew, demanding to know his whereabouts every moment of the day.

He turned his cheek into her palm and pressed a warm lingering kiss to her wrist, making her pulse race. Looking up at her through his extravagant long lashes, he reached out and stroked her nipple through the fabric of her gown.

"Make love to me," he demanded. "Right now. I need you, love."

His intensity frightened her. Something was terribly wrong. She wanted him to talk to her, wanted him to tell her what had put that desolate look in his eyes. But if making love to her would give him the same sense of peace and contentment she'd known in his arms last night, how could she refuse?

Without a word, she rose from the chair. Taking his hand, she led him through the darkened house toward the bedchamber.

After he closed the door, he sank into one of the plush chairs and gave her a moody look as he unbuttoned his cravat.

She sat nervously before him and wondered what she should do. She no longer felt as though she knew him. He seemed unapproachable, a far different man than the tender lover who had initiated her into the joys of the marriage bed.

"Tell me what to do," she said, her voice husky and hesitant. "I want to please you, Dylan."

"Do you?" He raised a mocking brow, as though he didn't believe her, as though she had offended him in some way.

Swallowing, she lifted her hands to unfasten her gown. Slowly, deliberately, she let the heavy fabric fall off her shoulders. It caught for a moment on the fullness of her breasts, before pooling at her feet. Clad only in her lace chemise, she knelt between his thighs.

"I don't know what happened to make you act this way." She ran her fingertips across the taut fabric that restrained the thick length of his erection. "But I wish you'd talk to me about it. I want to help you."

Her touch made him gasp and clench the arms of the chair with both fists, but his face remained impassive. Still, he said nothing. The watchful look in his eyes made her think he was testing her in some way.

Testing her... and expecting her to fail.

Holding his stormy gray gaze, she unfastened his trousers with a boldness she didn't feel. As much as she wanted him, she'd rather he confided in her. Lovemaking was a temporary fix, at best.

But perhaps, in the tender intimacy that followed, he would open up and tell her what was troubling him.

She trapped his face with her hands, kissing him with devastating hunger.

He tasted of anguish and desperation. For some reason, she felt those things, too. It seemed as though this was the last time he'd ever hold her, as though he were saying goodbye.

Fumbling in his haste to remove her chemise, he gave up and tore it down the front. Her breasts tumbled free into his hands, as his tongue pillaged every corner of her mouth.

She was completely bare, while he remained fully clothed except for his loosened breeches. The feeling was both frightening and erotic, especially when he pressed more fully against her and his clothing chafed her sensitive skin.

He slid his hands up her thighs. She gasped when his fingers probed her intimately. "You're so beautiful. So passionate." His breath was moist and hot against her throat, and he sounded as though the words pained him.

She feathered her hands through his hair with infinite tenderness. "You're the only one who has ever made me feel this way," she assured him. "The only one."

Lifting his gaze, he stared into her eyes as though all the secrets of the universe lay within. "I don't want to talk. I just want to feel you."

He shifted her weight, thrusting forward at the same time, sheathing himself deep within her. Natalia clung to his shoulders, overwhelmed by his fierce possession. He flexed his hips, a long slow slide.

Gasping at the exquisite fullness, she leaned forward and kissed him, trying to tell him without words that her anger was gone.

Only love remained.

Chapter Twenty-six

Dylan pressed his lips to Natalia's temple, allowing himself this one last moment of intimacy before he said the words that would drive her away from him forever. They lay tangled amidst the blankets upon Natalia's bed, having moved from the chair sometime after the first incredibly erotic episode. Even now, having made love to her twice more during the night, he wanted her again.

God, what a colossal mistake.

He should never have touched her, never should've admitted how badly he needed her. He'd meant it to be goodbye, wanted to create one last memory to cherish.

All he'd done was fall even more deeply in love with her.

He loved that she wanted to please him. He loved that she hadn't questioned or nagged him about the way he was acting. Most of all, he loved the way she'd held him after their passion was spent, touching his face as though he were precious to her.

She'd given him everything and asked for nothing in return.

But all these things only made him more determined to send her away. He wanted to remember her exactly like this—flushed with desire, instead of pale with fury. He couldn't stand to watch the love in her eyes turn to disgust and dismay, couldn't bear to watch the slow and inevitable destruction of their marriage.

Better to end it now, while he still could.

* * *

Natalia laid content in the circle of Dylan's arms, her back pressed against his chest, his thigh flung over her hips. She'd never felt so safe, so loved.

He still hadn't told her what had been bothering him, or why he'd arrived home so late, but she was confident he would. Their lovemaking had gentled him, perhaps even exercised his demons once and for all.

She knew it wasn't easy for him to admit to any weakness. He found it impossible to ask for help. But she was certain if she just kept showing him how much she cared, eventually he'd realize she would never use his secrets against him.

He shifted restlessly against her. To her amazement, she felt him hardening against the cleft of her bottom. Smiling, she turned to face him, only to have the smile fade from her lips as she saw the troubled look on his face.

She wanted to ask him what was wrong, but somehow, she restrained herself. He was obviously struggling to find the words to begin. She didn't want to say anything that might dissuade him.

He would tell her in his own words, in his own way.

Holding his gaze, she brushed a few strands of silky black hair out of his startling gray eyes and prayed she'd be able to say the things he needed to hear. It was time to put the past behind them. She was desperate to rekindle their fledgling friendship, which had been crushed so brutally back in London.

"So," he said at last. "Do you still think I married you for your dowry?"

It was the last thing she'd expected him to say. For some reason, she hadn't thought their marriage had anything to do with his troubles. She'd assumed something had happened to him while he was down in the village, something that had reminded him of the terrible tragedy of his mother's death.

She shook her head. "No. I don't think that. Not anymore." It was the truth. Sometime, within the last few days, she'd come to realize he wanted her for more than her money.

She wasn't sure what she'd done to make him care, but she no longer doubted he did. Beneath the spoiled, self-conscious girl she'd been, he'd somehow seen the passionate loving woman she'd always wanted to become.

"You don't?" He seemed surprised and more than a little annoyed. Frowning, he turned on his back and stared up at the ceiling. "Well, you're wrong."

"What do you mean?" A cold chill traveled down Natalia's spine. He was pulling away from her, and not just physically.

"When I met you, I had nothing. I had no money. No future. No hope. I was almost thirty years old, the earl had written me off, my commission was gone, and I was about to be thrown out of my shabby little apartment down by the river. The only dream I'd ever had—to run an estate of my own—seemed as unattainable as the moon."

She'd known all this, of course, but it made her uncomfortable to hear him say it. She'd never known that sort of desperation, had always had the security of her name and fortune to carry her through rough times.

How naïve she'd been.

"Then I made that wager with Jonathan, and I started thinking you were exactly what I needed. A rich wife would solve all my problems. If I had your dowry, I could buy the finest estate on the market. I'd never have to worry about money again."

He glanced at her through his dark lashes, as though to check that his words were having the desired effect. Natalia met his gaze, refusing to even blink, lest he know how badly he was hurting her.

Something was very wrong. These things he said might hold truth, but she knew him well enough now to realize his motives had never been so cut and dried. He wasn't a heartless man.

No. Dylan cared about people far more than he wanted to. He wouldn't be doing this unless he had somehow gotten it into his head that by pushing her away, he was protecting her.

"You're lying," she said, with utter certainty. "That might have been why you approached me at your father's ball, but it wasn't the reason you agreed to meet me in the garden."

"You're defending me now?" He shook his head. "Just a few short days ago, you were more than willing to believe I'd married you in order to get my hands on your dowry."

"A lot has changed since then." She placed her hand against his heart, loving the slow steady beat. "Seeing you here, at Aldabaran, I've come to realize that a home is far more important to you than any amount of money could ever be. And you knew this place was yours before you met me in the garden."

"As far as I knew, Aldabaran was a crumbling ruin," he told her stubbornly. "I thought I might need your money to rebuild it."

With every cold, calculating word Dylan said, Natalia's confusion grew. What was he trying to do? It seemed as though he was trying to hurt her on purpose.

"All right," she agreed, tired of arguing. "You married me for my dowry. But that doesn't mean our marriage can't succeed. Many marriages start this way."

Dylan pushed himself to a sitting position, his back against the headboard, one knee drawn up to his chest. He gave her a brooding look. "I don't think I'm ready for this. To have you here in my life every moment of the day. Perhaps it would be better if we found you a house in London."

Natalia felt as though she'd been slapped. He didn't want her in his life? She sat up as well, careful to keep the sheet drawn up to her chest, feeling a sudden resurgence of modesty. "You don't want to be married to me? Are you suggesting a… divorce?"

Divorce was practically unheard of. If Dylan actually went through with such a thing, she'd be a social pariah. No one would receive her.

But that was the least of her worries. If Dylan were to do this, to reject her with such cold finality, she would die. She couldn't bear the thought of living without him.

Dylan shook his head, his gaze shuttered and distant. "I didn't say anything about a divorce."

Natalia's hurt faded, replaced by a wave of searing anger. "Then perhaps you need to be a little clearer, Dylan. Because I don't know what the hell you *are* talking about."

He looked a bit taken aback by her profanity. "I think we should live apart. You don't belong here."

If he'd meant to destroy her, he couldn't have chosen a better weapon. She already loved Aldabaran and couldn't bear to think of leaving it. "I don't know how you can decide that so quickly. Give me a little more time. We've only been here a few days."

He shook his head and slid out of the bed, crossing the room to gather up his discarded pile of clothing. His golden skin gleamed in the firelight. She looked away, ashamed by the way his broad shoulders, slim waist, and long, lean flanks could still make her heartbeat accelerate.

"You were made for the glittering lights of London, Natalia." As he spoke, he pulled on his breeches, fumbling in his haste. "And I've been alone for far too long. I can't imagine having you underfoot day after day."

"Have I done something wrong?" Natalia hated herself for asking, hated the way her love for him had made her weak.

The man had just told her he didn't want her. She should be walking away instead of trying to figure out a way to make things right.

He paused for a moment and turned to face her, his shirt gaping open across his broad chest. "Don't make this any harder than it has to be, love. You've done nothing wrong. It just wasn't meant to be."

"So, I'm to go running back to my father? Tell him I made a mistake?" Natalia squared her shoulders, determined not to let him know this was killing her.

"Of course not." He sighed and raked his hand through his hair. "The dowry is yours to spend as you see fit. Buy a fashionable home. Become a bluestocking if you wish. Don't you see? You'll be free to do whatever you want with the rest of your life."

He was the one who didn't see. All she'd ever wanted was here, at Aldabaran. She wanted to raise a family with the man she loved, grow old and die with the sound of the ocean in her ears.

"Will you visit me from time to time, at least enough to keep the gossips at bay? Will you promise to be a decent father if these nights we've already spent together result in a child?" Pride be damned. She couldn't bear to lose him completely.

He shrugged. "I'd rather not. But if that's what it takes to get you to leave, I suppose I could manage an occasional visit."

His indifference managed to hurt her more than his cruelty. Tears stung her eyes, and she blinked to keep them at bay. "You bastard. I've done nothing to deserve this."

Dylan shook his head and left the room, leaving her alone with the shattered remnants of her dreams.

Chapter Twenty-seven

The next day dawned gray and gloomy, a perfect setting for Natalia's mood. She'd cried herself to sleep, and when she awoke, her head throbbed, and her eyes burned. Clad only in a robe and slippers, she drifted to the narrow window and stared down at the churning sea. A storm was brewing, which meant Dylan wouldn't be able to send her away just yet.

She didn't know whether to laugh or cry.

No matter how many times she replayed all the horrible things Dylan had said last night, she couldn't believe he truly meant them. Everything he'd said and done had been so out of character. She couldn't help thinking she'd missed something.

There must be an answer. There must be a logical explanation. Unfortunately, she was no closer to finding it now than when he'd walked out the door on her last night.

A movement on the cliffs far below caught her attention. She leaned forward, peering through the glass to identify the source. Frowning, she watched as someone walked out on a slim finger of rock and then stood on the very edge, staring down at the crashing waves while the wind whipped at his dark clothes.

Dylan.

Unreasonable panic mounted within her. What was he doing down there? Did he realize how dangerous his position was, especially given the growing intensity of the storm?

Perhaps he didn't care.

Misery was etched in every line of his body. Even from this distance, she could see how much he was hurting. Once again, she was struck with the certainty that he didn't really want to send her way, but somehow felt he must.

A sudden shiver ran down her spine. Had he been trying to protect her from himself? Did he want her to leave so she wouldn't be there when he hurt himself?

His mother had thrown herself off that very cliff…

Oh, God. She had to stop him.

Pushing away from the window, she lunged across the room and out the door. She rushed down the stairs and then hurried outside, pausing only for a second to catch her breath as the chill wind cut through the thin silk of her robe.

Ignoring the discomfort, she tore down the path toward the cliffs, scanning the horizon for any sign of him. *Please, God, don't let me be too late.*

At last, she saw him. He stood at the very edge of the cliff, his hands thrust deep within the pockets of his long overcoat, his dark hair whipping in the breeze. His head was tilted toward the sky, his eyes were closed, and he seemed to sway in the abyss of some terrible emotion.

Skidding to a stop a few yards away, Natalia fought to regain her breath as she pondered the best way to approach him. She wanted to scream his name and force him away from the edge. She wanted to shake him for his foolishness and make him swear he'd never even think of doing such a thing again. But she didn't want to startle him. She was far too close to losing him as it was.

"Dylan," she called. "What are you doing?"

He opened his eyes and turned his head toward the sound of her voice. Those blue-gray depths were filled with despair, but she saw no sign of desperation.

"Natalia," he said, with a weary sigh. "Must we have this conversation again?"

She clutched her robe more tightly around her waist and took a few hesitant steps forward, stopping an arm's length away. Was she close enough now to stop him from doing something horrible?

"That's not why I'm here. I saw you from my window… I just wanted to make sure you were all right."

He flicked a quick glance at the keep, then back, a frown pulling at the corners of his mouth as he took in her dishabille. "You ran out here in your robe? What were you thinking? You'll catch your death of cold." As he spoke, he shrugged out of his coat, closed the distance between them, and wrapped it around her shoulders.

The coat held his warmth, and by putting it on her, he'd stepped away from the precipice. Overwhelmed with relief, she flung herself into his arms.

"Oh, Dylan," she whispered, clinging to him with all her strength. "I was so afraid."

He tensed beneath her unexpected onslaught. For a moment, she thought he might pull away. Then his arms came around her, and his lips brushed her temple. "Why were you afraid?"

She tilted her head, blinking back her tears so she could look into his eyes. "I thought you were going to jump off the cliff. I thought you were going to kill yourself."

"Kill myself?" He gave an incredulous laugh and released her. "Why would you think such a thing?"

She shook her head, suddenly embarrassed. As usual, she'd jumped to the wrong conclusion. How foolish she must appear, running after him this way, throwing herself into his arms after he'd told her in no uncertain terms he didn't want her.

His gaze narrowed, and his frown returned. "You've heard about my mother, haven't you?" He turned his back on her once again, staring out to sea.

"Yes," she admitted. "Your... Mrs. Macpherson told me about it. I'm so sorry, Dylan."

She'd almost called the old woman his grandmother. What a slip to make, especially at a time like this.

A time like this...

She let her gaze rest on his broad shoulders. They were so tense he looked as though he carried the weight of the entire world upon them. Perhaps what he needed most was someone to help him carry the load.

Since he'd already decided it couldn't be her, perhaps she could at least leave him with a parting gift—a father and grandmother who obviously loved him.

He made an impatient gesture with his hand. "Well, even if you're worried that suicide is hereditary, you needn't be afraid I'll jump." He glanced at her over his shoulder. "My mother didn't kill herself, you see. I was there the night Warren pushed her to her death."

Natalia caught her breath, stunned by what he'd just revealed. The Earl of Warren had killed Fiona? This was what had been troubling him last night. He must've found out that truth while he'd been in the village yesterday. This was why he'd tried to push her away. The poor man believed his father had murdered his mother.

Gathering all her courage, Natalia stepped forward and wrapped her hand around his. "I can't even imagine how hard this has been for you." She circled him until her own back faced the edge of the cliff and the crashing sea, forcing him to meet her gaze. "But there's something I think you should know. Something that might make all of this just a little easier to bear."

He caught his breath, and then stared down at her, a strange, watchful look on his face. "What are you talking about, love?"

Love. Her heart thrilled at the casual endearment. Perhaps there was still hope.

She reached for his other hand and squeezed them both reassuringly. "I know this will come as a great shock to you, Dylan. But yesterday I discovered the Earl of Warren is not your father."

* * *

She knows about Patrick.

Dylan stared at his wife in open-mouthed astonishment. He couldn't imagine how she had found out, but the news of his humble beginnings didn't seem to bother her in the least.

She made love to me after she knew the truth.

"Your mother was having an affair," she continued, her cheeks pinkening. "She was in love with Patrick Macpherson. He is your real father."

He bowed his head and pressed his face against her hair, so she couldn't see the maelstrom of emotions her words had provoked. Dear God, she knew. She knew, and it didn't matter.

What a fool he'd been. He'd said terrible things to hurt her—he'd nearly succeeded in driving her away.

All this in a selfish attempt to keep her from breaking his heart.

But even now, after everything he'd done, she still cared enough about him to run outside in the bitter cold clad in nothing but her robe and nightgown. Hell, he was half convinced that if he were to step toward the edge of the cliff right now, she'd hold onto his ankle like a bulldog and refuse to let go.

Because she loves me. How could he have been so blind?

His body began to shake with suppressed laughter.

"It's all right," she whispered, cupping his head in her hands. "Cry if you need to. There's no shame in it."

"I'm not crying." Laughing openly, he picked her up in his arms and headed away from the cliffs.

"You're laughing." She stared up at him, utterly confused. "Why are you laughing?"

"Because I love you," he admitted. "I love you so much."

"You love me?" Natalia frowned and shook her head. "Are you listening? I just told you the Earl of Warren isn't your father."

"I already knew that." Dylan cradled her tighter in his arms, leaving the cliffs and the crashing fury of the waves far behind them. "Those things I said… God, can you ever forgive me? I thought you wouldn't want me if you found out my father was a mere groom."

Her exotic eyes flooded with tears. "Of course, I forgive you. I love you, Dylan. I've always loved you."

She loves me. God, how he'd needed to hear her say the words. It made all the difference in the world, gave him the strength to face anything.

Grinning, he bent down to kiss her, but she stopped him, bracing her hands against his chest. "I love you, and I forgive you, but I'm still furious."

They'd reached the outer courtyard of the keep, and he reluctantly put her down. "You have every right to be furious." He let her slide slowly down his body, keeping her pressed against him when she'd regained her feet. "I acted like an utter jack ass."

"You're an idiot," she agreed, shoving away from him and staring up at him with wide, wounded eyes. "I don't care whether your father is a chimney sweep or the Prince of Wales. How could you even think such a thing would matter to me?"

He sighed and speared his hand through his damp hair. "Let's go inside, love. We still have a lot to talk about."

"Yes, we certainly do." Turning, she strode toward the front door, which she'd left wide open in her battle to save him.

He followed, sealing the howling wind and cutting chill outside where they belonged. The great hall was warm and welcoming, both fireplaces crackling to keep the gloom and dampness away. Taking Natalia's hand, he tugged her toward the large comfortable chair where she'd fallen asleep waiting for him last night.

"Come here." He coaxed her to sit in his lap, cocooning them both in the warm folds of his overcoat. "You can yell at me all you like. Just give me a moment to enjoy having you in my arms again."

She laughed and relaxed against him. "Oh, Dylan. I don't want to yell at you. I just wish you would have believed in me a little bit more."

"Well, I think we both had a hard time believing," he told her diplomatically. "But I'm going to try harder, Natalia. Just don't give up on me."

"I won't," she promised, pulling his head down for a scorching kiss. For a long moment, he let himself get lost in her sweetness. It seemed as though it had been years, not mere hours, since he'd kissed her.

At last, he forced himself to pull away, brutally reining in the impulse to carry her up the stairs and spend the rest of the day making love. There were still many things they needed to talk about, including the debt of gratitude that had driven him out onto the cliffs that morning.

He'd gone outside hoping the bitter cold would clear his mind, because he'd been undone by her thoughtful gesture.

"Last night, after I left you, I went back to my room and found my mother's paintings." He cupped her face tenderly, staring into her eyes as he tried to convey just how much it meant to him. "No one has ever done anything like that for me before."

She smiled. "There are more of them. Dozens more. Patrick has kept them in his room all these years so the last thing he'd see before he fell asleep was your face."

That explained how Natalia had found out Patrick was his father. "I'd like to see them all. Perhaps you can show them to me later." He hugged his wife, melancholy with the wish that Fiona Blake could've known her.

His anger toward Warren rekindled, hot and bright. Someone had to make him pay for what he'd done.

Seeming to sense his sudden change of mood, Natalia touched his face, urging him to meet her gaze. "Warren was the man in your dream, wasn't he?"

Dylan nodded, trying to bring his anger under control. Anger had no place here, not today. "Your questions made me realize it wasn't just a dream. I was reliving the nightmare of the past."

"What will you do? Will you try and make Warren pay for his crimes?"

"I don't know what I want," he admitted. "My first impulse was to go back to London and kill him. God, Natalia. You can't imagine how much I hate him."

Natalia shifted in his lap, so she was straddling his hips, and he had to tilt his face to meet her serious gaze. "I know you want to hurt him. He deserves to die for what he's done. But you can't take the matter in your own hands without destroying yourself." She leaned down and kissed him. "I won't let you throw away what we've found for the sake of revenge. Let the magistrates punish him for his crimes."

Dylan closed his eyes, struggling to let go of the past, knowing Natalia was right. His love for her had changed him; he no longer had any interest in retribution. All he wanted was to live in Scotland with his wife and try to forget Warren even existed.

Another sobering thought occurred to him, something he hadn't even considered until now. "Michael will be devastated when I tell him. He idolizes the earl."

He opened his eyes and met Natalia's sympathetic gaze. "Warren's downfall will destroy him socially. He'll lose everything if he doesn't marry Miss Marks."

"Don't worry about Michael," Natalia told him. "I think he'd be the first to want justice done."

"Perhaps you're right." Utterly drained, Dylan let his head fall back against the chair. "I don't suppose I need to decide anything this very moment."

"You're absolutely right. Any decision about Warren and your brother can wait." Natalia pressed her lips to his forehead, her relief palpable. "For now, why don't you let me tell you about a decision *I've* made?"

He stared at her, praying whatever she had to say wouldn't eviscerate his emotions once again. "What decision have you made, love?"

Natalia gave him a sultry smile. "Remember when you asked me if I wanted children?"

He nodded, all thoughts of the earl vanishing from his mind. He slid his hands beneath her robe, cupping the luscious warmth of her breasts, knowing that one day soon he'd have to share them with his child.

"I do want them," she whispered, leaning down to brush his mouth with the sweetness of hers. "I want dozens of them."

He hugged her tight, overwhelmed with gratitude and a sense of rightness. His gamble on the duke's daughter had paid off in ways he never could have imagined.

The End

Other Books by Diana Bold
ONCE A PIRATE
A KNIGHT IN ATLANTIS
FORTUNE'S GAMBLE

UNMASKING PROMETHEUS SERIES
MASKED PROMISES
MASKED INTENTIONS

BRIDES OF SCANDAL SERIES
GAMBLING ON THE DUKE'S
DAUGHTER
MARRYING THE AMERICAN
HEIRESS
FINDING THE BLACK ORCHID

HISTORICAL WESTERN ROMANCE
ONCE A GUNSLINGER
ONCE AN OUTLAW
ONCE A BANDIT

Excerpt from BRIDES OF SCANDAL BOOK 2

MARRYING THE AMERICAN HEIRESS

Prologue

London – June 1867

"Lord Sherbourne? The Duke of Clayton has arrived. He wishes a moment of your time."

Michael Blake, Viscount Sherbourne, glanced up from the thick stack of ledgers piled atop the polished surface of his desk. "It's all right, Wadsworth." He met his butler's impassive gaze and struggled to hide his inner turmoil. "Show him to the drawing room. I'll be with him shortly."

"Very good, sir."

After Wadsworth exited the room, Michael sagged in his chair. *Bloody hell.*

He wasn't in the mood to deal with this. Not today, when so many columns of negative numbers swam through his brain. Not now, while he struggled to recover from the shock of betrayal.

Last night, Clayton's only daughter—the lovely Lady Natalia—had been caught in a compromising position with Michael's younger brother, Dylan. Michael had seen the passionate embrace with his own eyes.

His brother… and his future bride.

Though it was barely daybreak, Michael had been expecting the duke's call. In fact, he had just concluded a very uncomfortable interview with his own father, the Earl of Warren, about the matter.

With a weary sigh, Michael closed the ledger and pressed his fingertips to his throbbing temples. He'd wrestled with his family's dire financial situation all night, but if there was a way to save himself without the influx of Natalia's dowry, he couldn't find it. If he didn't marry Lady Natalia, the earldom would be bankrupt before the end of the year.

Pushing away from his desk, Michael strode from his office and up the stairs that led to the drawing room. His footsteps echoed loudly on the marble, shattering the stillness of the great slumbering house on St. James Square. Portraits of his illustrious ancestors lined the stairwell, glaring their disapproval at the unseemly racket.

Fear of these portraits had ruled his childhood. His father had dragged him bodily into this hall almost every day of his youth to remind him of his place in the world and his responsibility to his family.

Unfortunately, the portraits retained some of their power. He still felt as though he were on trial, as though he could never be good enough to earn his place among them.

This latest fiasco seemed to prove them right.

Michael paused outside the drawing room and tried to marshal his famed icy demeanor. He would listen to what the duke had to say and bear in mind his father's earlier threats and recriminations. But in the end, the decision must be his.

Taking a deep breath, he opened the massive oak doors.

The Gold Drawing Room, with its white satin, gold leaf, marble floors, and sparkling floor-to-ceiling windows, was meant to impress. The Duke of Clayton, however, did not impress easily. He waited in a gilt chair near the ornate fireplace, impatience resonating from him in waves.

"Your Grace. What a pleasant surprise." Somehow, Michael kept the irony out of his voice as he shut the double doors behind him.

"Sherbourne." Clayton rose and nodded as Michael crossed the room. "Forgive me for dropping by so unexpectedly, but I have a pressing matter to discuss with you."

Tall and broad-shouldered, the duke wore the weight and dignity of his position like a shield. Though his dark hair had grayed at the temples, he still looked far younger than his years. Michael didn't know the man well, but they moved in the same circles. He'd always admired the duke's conservative politics, which mirrored his own.

"Think nothing of it." Michael motioned toward the chair the duke had vacated. "Please, sit down. Can I get you anything? A drink, perhaps?"

He wasn't sure whether it was too late for alcohol, or too early, but given the circumstances, liquid fortification seemed to be in order.

Clayton resumed his seat with regal dignity. "I'll have a brandy, if you don't mind."

Michael moved to the sideboard, which was lined with crystal goblets and expensive liquor. As he poured them both a drink, the duke shifted restlessly and drummed his fingers against the side of the chair.

Michael understood the older man's need to settle things quickly and avert any hint of a scandal. They were a lot alike, he and the duke.

Handing Clayton his brandy, Michael took the chair across from him. "What can I do for you, Your Grace?"

Clayton met his gaze with startling directness. "It's about my daughter, Sherbourne. I've come to urge you to announce your engagement as soon as possible."

The duke's sheer bravado surprised Michael. Apparently, the duke believed he was above apologies or explanations. How dare the man sit there as though nothing had happened, as though his daughter's disastrous indiscretion held no bearing?

Michael took a bracing sip of brandy and reminded himself of all the reasons why he must do exactly as the duke and his father wanted. He needed to marry for money, and he needed to do it quickly.

It wasn't—as his brother Dylan had so angrily accused during one of their many arguments—to score points with their father. The earl's expensive tastes, excessive gambling, and blatant mismanagement had gotten them into this mess.

Far more lay at stake than his family's fortunes. If Michael couldn't find a way to stem these losses, his failure would hurt countless others who lived on his father's land.

"Does Lady Natalia still wish to marry me?" Michael ran his fingertip around the rim of his goblet and tried to sound disinterested. If he'd tried a little harder, courted the girl in earnest instead of merely going through the motions, perhaps he might not find himself in his current dilemma.

"Of course, Natalia wishes to marry you." The duke didn't bother to hide his irritation. "She's made a terrible mistake, but she realizes that now. She's more than willing to do her duty."

Duty. He wondered if Lady Natalia hated the word as much as he did. What an unhappy pair they would make, trapped together by duty.

With crystal clarity, he imagined living with this woman until the day he died, while she dreamed of his brother, and he grew more bitter and lonely with each passing year.

Michael cleared his throat. The consequences of refusing the duke were clear. He'd be forced to wed the only other great heiress on the market—Miss Emma Marks, an American adventuress who'd come to London shopping for a title. Hardly the sort of woman he'd imagined for his bride, but at the moment, even a low-born wife seemed preferable to the hell he was sure to find with Lady Natalia.

"I'm sorry, Your Grace. I can't marry your daughter." The words were remarkably freeing. Just saying them loosed something deep inside him, the part that had followed Society's rules and his father's unceasing demands for far too long.

The duke leaned forward, bristling with the haughtiness of his position. "I've already spoken with your father, you insolent whelp. He agrees that this marriage would be in the best interest of everyone involved."

Yes, everyone would be happy except Natalia, Dylan, and Michael. What a pair of self-serving old bastards Clayton and Warren had become. How easily they were willing to surrender their children's futures for the sake of their own fortunes and reputations.

"I'm well aware of my father's feelings," Michael assured his guest. "But he isn't the one who has to live with my decision."

"Don't be a fool." The duke got to his feet, his fury evident. "Natalia is a lovely girl, and she's certainly learned her lesson. She won't do anything else to embarrass you."

Michael stood as well, refusing to let the duke gain an advantage. Clayton's size probably intimidated most men, but Michael easily matched him in height, if not in girth.

"Your daughter loves my brother. Do you think I could ever trust her, having seen the way she looks at him?" Michael gave the duke a hard look. "You might want to think about that. Ask her what she truly wants. At this point, I think the best solution would be an alliance between the guilty parties."

Dylan might as well have Lady Natalia's heart *and* her fortune. Of course, Dylan would never contribute a farthing to their family's cause, but who could blame him, given the abuse he'd suffered at their father's hand?

Clayton shook his head wordlessly and downed the last of his brandy, placing the empty glass on a nearby table. "If you choose to refuse me, that's your business. But how dare you presume to give me advice!" Turning, the duke stomped from the room and slammed the door behind him with all his strength.

As the echo faded away, Michael allowed himself a brief smile. Very few men had ever crossed Clayton and lived to tell the tale. Unfortunately, his fleeting victory had sealed his fate.

Returning to the sideboard, he refilled an empty glass and lifted it in an imaginary salute.

To Emma Marks. My future bride.

Chapter One

Three weeks later...

Emma Marks peered intently over the rail of her luxurious, private theater box, scanning the crowd below with a deep sense of satisfaction. After three months in London, she still found it hard to believe she actually belonged here, among the glittering *ton.* No one would have disputed it, not when the Prince of Wales himself had declared her the most beautiful, wittiest woman to grace the city in a decade.

No small accomplishment for a girl who'd been repeatedly cut and shunned back in New York.

Her father's money was far too new for American Society. Nothing she'd done had ever been good enough to gain entry to Mrs. Astor's charmed circle.

But the English were different. They seemed more than willing to accept her, as long as her father's pockets remained deep, and she had a trunk full of beautiful Worth gowns for every occasion.

Emma's aristocratic companion, Lady Jane Bennett, leaned forward as well, her lovely face alight with sudden intensity. "He's here, Emma. Viscount Sherbourne. Look straight ahead, in the box directly across from ours."

Viscount Sherbourne.

Instantly intrigued, Emma lifted her jeweled opera glasses for a better look. Jane had been singing the elusive viscount's praises for quite some time, but Emma had never had the opportunity to evaluate him for herself.

"Straight across," Jane whispered impatiently. "You're looking too far to the right."

Emma redirected her glasses, but in truth, she wasn't expecting much. She and Jane had very different ideas about what sort of man would make a good husband. A title was extremely important—she wasn't hypocrite enough to pretend otherwise—but she also longed for a man to fall in love with. One who appealed to her on a wildly romantic level.

For instance, she'd much prefer a handsome young baron to an elderly potbellied duke.

Jane, however, thought elderly dukes the better choice. After all, she was bound to outlive them. Smiling to herself at this rather pessimistic attitude, Emma finally found the box Jane had indicated. To her surprise, neither of the two occupants appeared ready to drop dead of old age.

Both men were uncommonly attractive. The first reminded her of a warrior angel, stern and golden, while the second was as wickedly dark and handsome as Lucifer.

Captivated, Emma's gaze settled on the dazzling blond man. Awareness swept over her, startling her with its intensity. Something about this aloof brooding stranger touched a chord deep inside her and resonated through her very soul.

"Which one is Lord Sherbourne?" Emma asked, trying to contain her escalating excitement. *Finally. At last, I've found someone worth pursuing.*

"That handsome blond gentleman." A strange wistful note crept into Jane's voice as she, too, stared across the theater through her opera glasses. "The dark one is the Earl of Basingstoke."

"An earl?" Emma reluctantly dropped her gaze away from Sherbourne and gave the dark-haired man another look. She could certainly do worse than returning to New York a countess. "Perhaps I should set my cap for him then."

"No," Jane said sharply. "Basingstoke is a terrible rogue. No one will ever tame him."

Emma gave Jane a long considering look. To her amusement, Jane blushed and looked away.

Very interesting.

"I don't know," Emma mused teasingly. "Sherbourne is a mere viscount."

Jane frowned, oblivious to Emma's gentle taunt. "Sherbourne will be the Earl of Warren, eventually. Believe me, you couldn't possibly do any better."

Emma fought a smile as she met Jane's annoyed blue gaze. Despite their burgeoning friendship, Jane must rue the circumstances that forced her to sponsor an American upstart like Emma.

Jane's father had been a marquess, but he'd gambled away the family fortune and died without a male heir. He'd left Jane nothing but an elegant London townhouse and a mountain of debts.

Considered firmly on the shelf at the grand old age of twenty-five, Jane had agreed to sponsor Emma this season. The hefty fee she'd charged would help her save her home.

"I'm certain Sherbourne is every bit as wonderful as you say." Emma wondered at her willingness to drop all thoughts of pursuing the earl. Usually, she liked her men dark and dangerous, but something about Sherbourne repeatedly drew her gaze. "But I don't know. Look at him. Perhaps he's too perfect."

"Too perfect?" Jane laughed softly and shook her coifed blond head. "I fail to see why you consider that a bad thing."

As Emma continued to contemplate the beautiful viscount, Jane leaned forward and lowered her voice conspiratorially. "I have it on good authority that Sherbourne has no choice but to make a financially advantageous marriage. With Lady Natalia off the market, you're the only one with a dowry large enough to suit his needs. He must offer for you. It's merely a matter of time."

Emma winced at Jane's matter of fact announcement but couldn't fault her since her father had hired Jane specifically for this sort of knowledge. Emma's family had an immense fortune but no title. It was expected that the man she married would have a title but no fortune.

Lifting her opera glasses once more, she risked another quick glance in Sherbourne's direction. This time, to her chagrin, she found him staring back at her.

Her first impulse was to keep scanning the crowd as though she had no idea who he was, but something in his expression gave her pause. His finely chiseled features were set in grim resignation, as though the mere sight of her sent him into a deep dark depression.

While hardly flattering, his strange reaction intrigued her even more. Perhaps Jane was right. Perhaps this paragon of English decency really was desperate enough to ask for her hand.

She set her glasses aside and gave Jane an expectant look. "Tell me everything you know."

Jane smiled, completely in her element. "His father is the tenth Earl of Warren. The family holdings are extensive. The earl gives an absolutely smashing ball every year at the beginning of the season. Very exclusive guest list."

Emma shook her head in frustration. "I don't care about any of that. I want to know about Sherbourne. Has he ever been involved in a scandal? Does he have a mistress? Has he ever gambled too much on horses or made a fool of himself with brandy?"

Jane looked affronted at the very idea. "Of course not. He's a fine young man. He is—"

"I know. I know. He's a paragon." Emma held up one gloved hand in protest. "Please, Jane. Think. There must be something."

The music swelled in a final crescendo, signaling intermission. They'd whispered and plotted through the entire first act of the mediocre play. Not that it mattered. Socializing seemed to be the main entertainment on Drury Lane.

Jane looked around, as though to double check that no one was close enough to hear. "Did you know Sherbourne offered for Lady Natalia? It's not common knowledge, and I'm certain he doesn't want anyone to know. Especially given the fact that his brother stole her away."

"Viscount Sherbourne and Captain Dylan Blake are brothers?" Now *that* was an interesting little tidbit of information. Emma knew Captain Blake, though not as well as she would've liked.

"Captain Blake escorted me to dinner," she reminded Jane. "At the Duke of Clayton's party."

There'd been quite a scandal when Lady Natalia had been caught in a compromising situation with Captain Blake in her father's garden. Emma hadn't seen what had happened, but she'd heard all the gossip.

Jane raised a knowing brow. "Oh, yes. I remember. You were quite put out when you couldn't capture the captain's attention."

"He only had eyes for Lady Natalia." Emma shrugged, as though Dylan Blake's inattention had meant nothing to her. In truth, she had been extremely jealous, because Dylan Blake—while hardly the sort of man she'd consider marrying—was exactly the sort of man she could imagine herself falling in love with. Witty and darkly handsome, he was a decorated war hero and had traveled extensively.

"The whole thing was terribly romantic." Jane's eyes lit with pleasure. "I'm so glad the duke allowed Natalia to marry her dashing captain."

"Very romantic," Emma agreed. The star-crossed lovers had married just last week—a hasty private ceremony, followed by a lengthy wedding trip to Scotland—where they apparently hoped to wait out the scandal.

Emma wondered if Sherburne had loved Lady Natalia. Had his intended bride's betrayal hurt him?

Low male voices interrupted Emma's thoughts. Someone conferred with their footman on the other side of the brocade curtain that gave their box the illusion of privacy.

"Who could that be?" Jane rose gracefully, pleased as always by the prospect of visitors. The fact that suitors had actually begun to seek Emma out, despite her lack of pedigree, was a testament to Jane's social clout.

Jane swept back the curtain and her face went comically blank when she saw who stood on the other side. "Lord Basingstoke."

"Good evening, Lady Jane. I've come to arrange an introduction between my friend and your lovely companion Miss Marks."

Emma turned to see the dark half of the pair she'd spied on earlier. A hint of mischief lurked behind Lord Basingstoke's smile as he stepped aside to allow another man to enter the box.

Viscount Sherbourne. As though her interest had summoned him, he stood before her in all his golden glory, a sinfully beautiful man with the face of an angel.

Jane recovered quickly from her surprise and graced both men with a gentle smile. "Lord Basingstoke, Lord Sherbourne, may I present Miss Emma Marks of New York City?"

"It's a pleasure to meet you, my lords." Emma rose and extended her hand. She tried to exude as much grace and dignity as possible. Her father had spent a fortune to ensure her manners and bearing were fit for a queen, but she always worried that those who'd come from generations of wealth and privilege would see through her facade.

Sherbourne stepped forward. He cut an elegant figure in his finely tailored black evening wear. "The pleasure is mine," he murmured, his voice clipped, deep, and oh-so British. Taking her gloved hand, he brought it briefly to the lush heat of his finely drawn lips.

Such an extravagant mouth, on such a harsh and chiseled face.

As he lifted his head, their gazes caught and held. For a moment, she lost track of time and place. Intelligence and loneliness radiated from the rain-washed depths of his deep blue eyes and convinced her there was far more to this man than even Jane knew.

As she reluctantly withdrew her hand from Sherbourne's light grasp, Basingstoke offered her a charming smile. "Are you enjoying your visit, Miss Marks?"

"I'm enjoying London very much," she responded truthfully. Unlike New York society, English aristocrats had the ability to appreciate eccentricity, even celebrate it on occasion. Hence their easy acceptance of an American heiress who dressed outrageously and wasn't afraid to speak her mind.

"I hear you're quite the traveler," Basingstoke continued. "Tell us about your journeys. Have you been anywhere fascinating and exotic?"

"I've traveled extensively on the Continent during the past two years." Emma warmed immediately to the subject and wondered if Basingstoke might be the more interesting of the two after all. "I must admit, however, to being a bit of a history enthusiast, the older and dustier the better. I'd love to visit Egypt, but I haven't yet had the chance."

"What a coincidence." Again, Basingstoke seemed secretly amused. "Sherbourne is an amateur archaeologist. He's fascinated by all things Egyptian.

In fact, he's sponsored several expeditions and has an amazing collection of artifacts."

She let her gaze drift back to Basingstoke's friend, unable to contain her sudden excitement. "Have you been to Egypt, Lord Sherbourne? Have you seen the great pyramids and the Sphinx?"

Something hot and bright flickered in the depths of Sherbourne's cool eyes, but it disappeared so quickly she wondered if she'd imagined it. "I've never left England," he admitted remotely. "My responsibilities don't allow for frivolities such as travel."

Frivolities? She would have been incensed at his judgmental tone, if not for the fact that Basingstoke had mentioned the viscount's interest in history and artifacts.

For some reason, Sherbourne seemed embarrassed by what his friend had revealed. As if his pursuit of such things undermined the plain boring demeanor he obviously worked so hard to cultivate.

What other interesting things lurked beneath that cool perfect exterior?

As though she hadn't understood he'd meant to rebuke her, Emma smiled. "Well, no wonder you collect Egyptian artifacts. Everyone needs a little something exotic in their lives. I'd love to see your collection."

Jane gasped audibly at Emma's forward behavior, but Lord Basingstoke merely chuckled and gave her a covert wink. As for Sherburne, he looked slightly stunned. He obviously had no idea what to make of her.

"I keep my artifacts in the country, at Sherbourne Hall, but perhaps something can be arranged." Sherbourne took a deep breath, as though girding himself for something unpleasant. "In the meantime, would you allow me to call on you? At your earliest convenience?"

Emma shared a quick surprised look with Jane. Oh, the poor man. He must need her dowry even more desperately than Jane had implied.

"Of course, you may call upon me," Emma replied graciously. "I'd be delighted."

"Excellent. You may expect me tomorrow morning." Bowing stiffly, Sherbourne turned and left their box.

Basingstoke smiled and shrugged. "What can I say, Miss Marks? He's an acquired taste." He started to take his own leave, then seemed to think better of it. Turning, he extended his hand toward Jane. "It was a pleasure to see you again, Lady Jane. You've been absent from Society for far too long."

Jane stared at his hand, flustered for no apparent reason.

Basingstoke laughed and produced a single red rose with a quick flick of his wrist.

Emma had been watching him, but she had no idea how he had accomplished the magical feat.

"Oh, Julian." Jane accepted the rose with her heart in her eyes. "It's beautiful."

Julian? Emma couldn't contain an amused smile when her very proper companion used Lord Basingstoke's first name. Apparently, the earl's bad behavior was only one reason Jane wanted Emma to stay away from him.

As for herself, Emma couldn't wait for the chance to speak privately with Lord Sherbourne. She knew just the thing to rattle his icy reserve and reveal what lay beneath.